A Prophecy to Fulfill

Sara Kohan

Dedications

To those who feel like they have no choice

and want to take back control of their life.

Magia
Ashenridge
Bantius Mountains

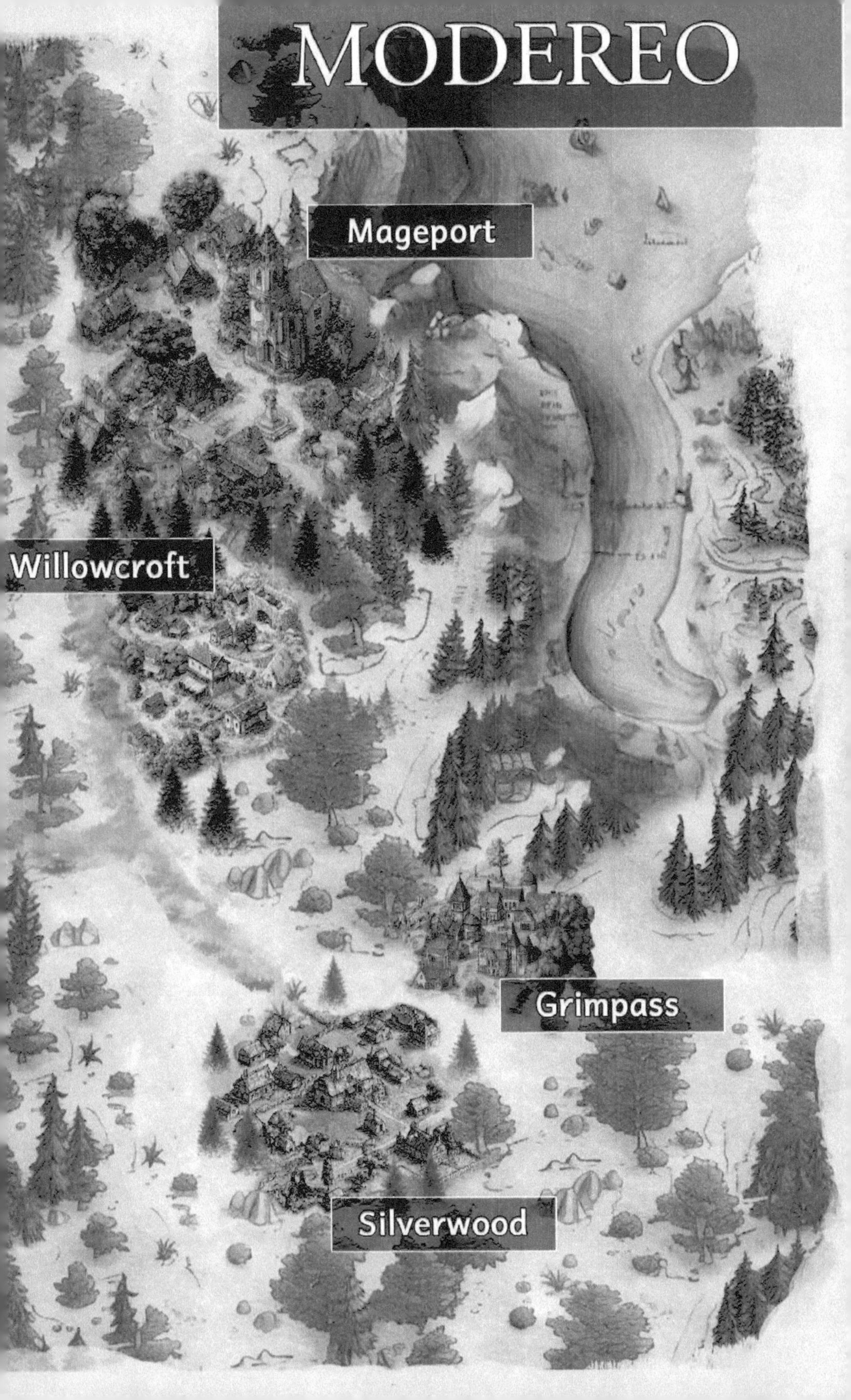

MODEREO
Mageport
Willowcroft
Grimpass
Silverwood

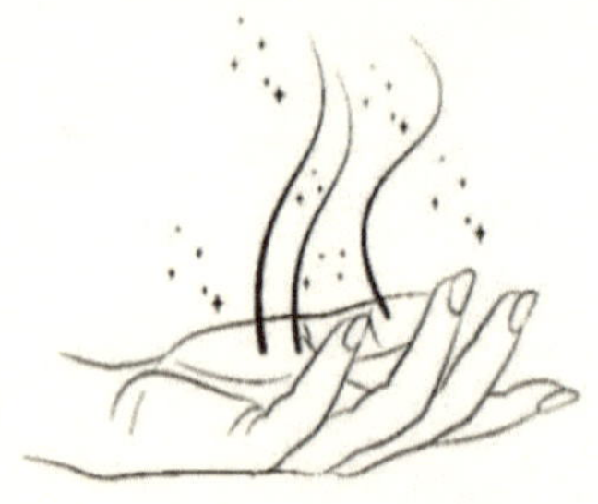

Chapter 1

Adira

*H*ow *many times do I have to escape prison cells? Shouldn't the prophesied one get some luck?* I half-plead skyward, as if the higher beings are listening. Scoffing at the thought, I direct my attention back to my cell. Sighing to myself, I recount the plan in my head.

Leaning against the coolness of the stones, I let the sharp sting clear my head. *Why did I come back to Modereo?* The jumbled mess of emotions from Soren's betrayal caused me to lose all sense of logic, I automatically came to a familiar place, home.

The metallic tang of the wards draws me back to the present. *And look how* home *is treating me.*

A bitter laugh escapes me. The echo of boots sounds closer. A guard slaps a baton against the bars.

"Shut it, traitor." He growls, venom in his eyes. Taking him in, I realize he's vaguely familiar. *We must have trained together.*

He strides away, shooting me one last glare. *Oh, how different our lives turned out to be.*

The air around me grows colder as night falls. The torchlight in front of my cell flickers. I watch the shadows from the flames dance across the concrete wall as the castle goes to sleep. The guards thin slowly until only one is left covering the cells.

Time to put my plan into action.

I rise to my feet, shaking out my stiff limbs. Taking advantage of my strengthened magic, gifted to me by the goddesses, I close my eyes in concentration.

Reaching for my power, it drags up through my reserve, fighting through the energy of the wards. The tingling sensation shifts to a piercing throb while it breaks apart the wall of eather. Sweat beads my forehead as I squeeze my eyes shut, envisioning what I want to happen. Simultaneously, I command a rock to form in a cell farther down the hall. A dull thunk sounds in the distance, heavy boots moving to check out the commotion. My head pounds lightly as I release the hold on my magic.

Opening my eyes, I peer down at my hands, startled by the amount of energy I still have. My heart beats faster, but the display barely dipped into my reserves. *Why was that so easy?*

Before I can ponder that, a sound echoes further down the dark hallway. I use it to my advantage, manipulating the stone around the cell's metal bars. It distorts and crumbles, making a brief rumbling sound. Dust flies up into the air.

Waving a hand in front of my face, I suppress a cough, cringing at the volume. *Well, there's no way nobody heard that. I better get moving.*

I hear a guard yell in shock. Jumping over the pile of stones, I quickly move down the hallway, in the opposite direction of my jailer. The air grows fresher as I head toward freedom, passing different paths leading deeper into the castle along the way. I hear the guard's cursing start again when he reaches my cell. I put up a thin ward in the hallway to buy some extra time.

Heading toward the wooden door that aided in my last escape, I grin to myself. *It's almost too easy.*

I push the door, but it doesn't budge. A grunt escaping me from the effort. I push against it again with my magic, but it still doesn't move. Pausing to examine the door, I sense a strong ward on it.

Fuck. Of course they would block the door you already escaped from. Think, Adira. What other doors do you remember from your guarding days?

The sound of footsteps gets louder. *No time.* I swiftly retreat, moving up the stairs and stepping into the wide, clean, castle corridors. Closing my eyes, I call upon my magic, imagining the guard that was watching me. I recreate his dark eyes, pale skin, and blue uniform with the kingdom's crest on it. Energy prickles my body, a sense of vastness present within me. My muscles throb, the ache spreading through me. The wind stirs with eather. My jaw clenches against the pressure of stealing someone else's identity, magic always resists it. I take a breath in, the air mixing with the excess energy. My brain spikes with oxygen.

When I open my eyes again, I glance at myself in a mirror, seeing a familiar middle-aged man staring back at me.

I start walking down the hall unhurriedly with my chin up, channeling a typical male demeanor. I'm just reaching the front of the castle when I hear yelling behind me.

I curse to myself. *Shoot, I should have strengthened the ward to last longer.*

The guards at the front come through the door, spotting me. I don't recognize either of them. The shorter one stares at me with confusion, trying to work out why I'm up there. The air shifts slightly, as if he is calling upon his magic. Before I can panic and retaliate, the taller one starts speaking. His dark eyes filled with authority.

"Jeffers, you check out the commotion," he commands.

At his name, the power subsides. He stares at me a moment longer with suspicion in his eyes. I keep my expression neutral, giving away nothing. He mutters a curse, stalking off the way I just came.

I try to hide the relief at his departure.

"And Curt." He points to me, his intense glower demanding compliance.

Ah, Curt. The name faintly rings a bell.

I obediently shift my gaze to his, straightening my shoulders.

"Guard the front while I secure the wards."

Before I can respond, he's already walking away. *Well, that was lucky,* I think to myself, giving the goddesses a short thanks for my fortune.

I let out a breath I didn't know I was holding. My steps are light as I make my way forward. Glancing up at the clock on the wall, I recall the frequency of guards.

I can't help but snicker at King Elijah's lack of nightly security. His ego will be the downfall of him. My lips drop, guilt fills me from that thought. *He may make a lot of mistakes, but I did swear my allegiance to him and this kingdom.*

The hard slap of boots on the tiled floor draws my head around.

Jeffers.

The suspicious guard from before is striding toward me with purpose. Dread grows in my stomach.

Shit.

Another guard turns a corner, coming face to face with Jeffers. He stops for a moment to say something to the other guard. I don't wait around to see what he says.

I rush out the front, blasting up a light ward on the door, giving me an additional minute, I keep hold of the energy, ready to strengthen the shield if need be. I vault down the slick steps, stopping at the edge of the grounds.

My eyes take in the suspended stones. Every time I see them, I'm still in awe of their beauty and the dangerous power they hold. Pushing images of them dropping from my head, I bound over them, moving faster than I ever have before. A pound rattles my skull, the ward I placed on the door shakes, but doesn't break. I reach the last stone spryly, leaping onto solid ground.

Splitting pain races through my head. I inhale sharply against the pressure. An alarm sounds through the palace.

The ward behind me shatters. I gasp at the rip of magic. Angry yells fill the air. I don't look behind me, I just race toward the treeline. I have less than a minute before the tall guard finishes securing the wards, never mind the fact that the growing mob of guards may catch up to me.

Sadness latches onto me. *I probably know some of them. I probably called some of them my friends.*

My emotions bubble up, but I shove them back down. *Not now, Adira.*

I sense the charge of magic in the air and subtly push mine out to delay the process. Sweat breaks out along my back as the hairs on my arms rise at the increased charge. The energy flows through me more easily and I can't help but wonder if the goddesses gave my powers an extra boost. I manipulate the ward magic to mix with mine while I burst through the barrier that was already surrounding the floating castle. I swiftly melt into the trees.

The shattered energy from the ward blasts through the air. A wave of magic washes over me, my disguise disappearing. My long dark hair falls onto my back.

Keeping my focus ahead, I delve deeper into the forest, changing paths every so often to ensure I stay hidden.

My breathing turns shallow and my legs turn to jelly. *Time to stop.*

Placing my hands on my knees, I lean forward. Taking deep gulps of air. Once my breathing is under control, I straighten. The shadowy forest seems to mirror my emotions: lonely and sullen.

Now what?

I close my eyes, taking the first deep breath I've had since leaving Enelon, the non-magic realm. My hand flies to my pendant, the strange energy it consistently expels shocking me out of my misery.

My mind drifts to the prophecy.

The child born from two realms, must bond back the creatures that fell.

I think about how secretive my mother constantly was. *Maybe she always knew?*

I let out a long exhale.

I'm so fucked.

Chapter 2

Soren

I slam my empty glass down on the table with a loud thud. I notice people's weary gazes turn my way at the sound. A waitress rushes over with a refill. Whispers cut through the off-key singing.

That's the King's assassin.

Why is he here?

Is he drunk?

I bet we can take him.

I listen more closely to the last comment. Looking toward the two brazen guards, the two guards I was sent to interrogate. I watch their tall figures snickering to themselves. They clink their glasses of ale together, the sound getting drowned out by the hum of conversation.

This will be fun, I remark, my anticipation surging. *I've been itching for a fight since Adira left.* My body tries to flinch at the thought of her, I instead pick up my fresh drink, letting the sharp tang of the alcohol drown out my guilt. *Because that always works.* I think bitterly.

A flash of dark hair swishes to my right. My chest aches as I twist toward the woman. She turns sideways, giving me a view of an unfamiliar face.

I let out a low curse. *Of course she's not here.*

A drunken man stumbles across the floor, spilling his sticky drink as he moves. The yeasty scent of ale engulfing the room.

Enough of this.

I stand up, loudly scraping my chair back when I do. I nod at the bartender, exiting through the back. I step onto the wet cobblestones of the alley, letting the door fall shut behind me, the music turns muffled. The door opens, causing a blast of the unpleasant music to follow me out into the quiet night. My lips twitch up in amusement.

"Hey," one of them shouts.

I turn around to face them.

"What do we have here?" the other one sneers. "The infamous Soren Banrs."

"What can I help you gentlemen with?" I say casually, unable to hide my snarky tone when I call them *gentlemen.*

"We think we ought to teach you a lesson. Knock you off the gold pedestal the King seems to keep you on," he says with a grin.

I shake my head lightly. *Ah, jealousy at its finest.*

"What do you say, Oren?" he asks his friend.

"I think we have to, Tommy," Oren replies with a vicious grin.

They both turn toward me, their eyes filled with violence.

Tommy starts forward first. I shift out of the way, but Oren is already there. His fist connects with my side. I huff out a quick breath, bouncing back. I snap my fist forward, driving it into Tommy's nose. The crunch of bone echoes through the darkened alley. He cries out and clutches it, blood pouring through his fingers. An uncertain look fills his face when he realizes I'm not as drunk as I led on.

I catch Oren sneaking up behind me and twist around him. I wrap my arm around his neck so he can't move. My nose wrinkles at the pungent smell of sweat and beer.

"So, boys, tell me—who are you working with?" I ask while Oren struggles to get out of my hold.

"No one, asshole," Oren spits out.

"Now, now. That's not very nice. We both know that you're working with the Enid rebels. Is this not true?" I demand, my intense gaze scrutinizing them. I've already investigated the group. They are a surprisingly secretive bunch, I'm still uncertain of their overall plans. Every rebel I question seems to have a slightly different answer.

Reaching into Tommy's head, I let my eather overwhelm him. He whimpers on the ground, realizing they've walked right into a trap.

I reach for my sheath, the cold weight of the dagger balancing in my palm. I press it against Oren's throat. A line of blood swells at the pressure.

"We won't talk," Oren insists. "You're going to kill us anyway."

I lock eyes with Tommy over Oren's shoulder. He appears to be the weaker one. I let my power slide through his mind dangerously. His panicked face pales further.

"There are things worse than death," I state coldly.

Tommy's eyes widen slightly before he opens his mouth.

"Don't even think about it, Tommy," Oren threatens his friend. I let my power squeeze him in warning. This would be easier if I would just slip into his mind myself, but sometimes the rebels' memories push me out. It's happened a few times, as if they have magic blocking their thoughts. *Another mystery to solve.*

"Bu-but he's -" He taps his mind, unable to voice it.

Oren looks confused for a moment, then his expression hardens. "I don't care what you are trying to say, but don't you dare talk, Tommy."

Huh, maybe not that close of friends after all.

Tommy ignores him, fear shining in his eyes.

"We are working with Enid. They have a camp about thirty miles northeast of here. The entrance is hidden on the side of an overgrown path," he confesses shakily.

I keep my expression flat, filing the information away for later.

"What are their plans with Linnea?" I ask.

Oren hisses at Tommy, and I push the knife further into his neck. He shuts up immediately, his throat bobbing with tension.

Tommy casts frightened eyes to Oren but lets out a resigned sigh.

"They're trying to stop the prophecy from being fulfilled. They have an easy way into Modereo."

My body tenses.

Shit! Adira.

My brows furrow. *Why don't they want the prophecy to come true?*

Tommy groans, the sound pulling me from my thoughts. I decide to ruminate over it later. The inevitable dread rising in me for what I have to do. What I *always* have to do for that monster that calls himself a King.

I push Oren away from my body while drawing my sword. Before he can recover, I quickly swipe forward, decapitating him. I swing toward Tommy, hesitating for a moment. *Striking down a man who's on the ground seems wrong.*

The pause costs me. Tommy produces a small blade, slicing it across my thigh.

"Fuck." I curse, swinging the same leg toward him. I connect with his wrist, sending his measly blade flying across the filthy road. My breath hitches when my injury pulls. I shift my weight forward, drawing my dripping blade.

Tommy starts to cry out, but the sound is cut off by the thump of his head on the ground.

I try not to let myself feel guilty. The night turns silent once more, the muggy air pressing into me. I expertly wrap the shallow cut on my thigh.

You had to bring their heads to the King, I tell myself. King Dahak still has to believe you work for him while you devise a plan to kill him.

I ignore Adira's voice in my head, asking me how I chose whose life was more important. I especially don't dwell on thoughts of her calling me a monster. The guilt sits heavy on my shoulders, but then, it always has, the feeling has never gone away.

I toss the evidence into a brown sack before burning the bodies. I watch them fade away, the fire taking the remnants of their lives into the forest beyond. *Did they have families? Do they believe they are fighting for the greater good? Do I?*

The area smells of sharp copper and burning flesh. The remorse and smell are too much. My stomach rolls violently. I turn away from the odor, striding back to the alleyway. Grabbing a bucket of water, I toss it on the burned area. The flames die down, leaving charred remains behind.

I heave a deep sigh, rolling out my neck.

Slinging the sack over my shoulder, I make my way back to the castle, keeping to the shadows. *Now I need to plan what I'm going to say to the King so I can go find Adira.*

Chapter 3

Adira

After running for an hour, I let myself sink to the ground. Finally, the distant voices having faded completely. The thick, humid air presses in on me. I fan myself with my hand, trying to cool myself down. The sound of my ragged, uneven breath filters through the forest.

While I catch my breath, I think of a plan.

To bond back the creatures that fell. This must mean the Teràstios.

I heave out a sigh. *They've been dead for twenty-five years, just before I was born. How am I meant to bond back creatures that are dead? Perhaps I need to go to their birthing grounds and perform some kind of ritual?*

I wince to myself. *It feels like a stretch, but it's the only idea I have.*

I need to ask someone for help.

The thought saddens me while I mull over the lack of people I can count on.

Don't think about him. Don't think about him. Don't think about him.

You would think that telling myself this repeatedly would get the point across, but my mind still drifts to him.

My chest squeezes painfully. I press my hand into the hard soil. Sharp sticks dig into my palm, grounding me.

Goddess, I can't even say his name to myself.

Shaking my head, I consider my options. *I have no one to trust in my own realm; in Modereo; to ask for help. I can't go to the library at the castle anymore... it was a stretch to begin with.*

I glance at my surroundings, realizing I'm close to a hidden portal to Enelon. I count myself lucky that my mother had so much knowledge about the hidden portals. The one uncomfortable part of knowing was that she made me swear not to tell anyone. Not even the King I had sworn to serve. To say I had felt guilty would have been an understatement, but as I uncovered the appalling things the kingdom has done, it made it easier to cope.

At least there is one person I can always count on.

I smile to myself.

Fortunately, I'm near a portal that is not known to King Elijah. I stand up, walking through the thick bushes. Leaves and branches catch on me as I push through. The covered remains become visible. As I get closer, I spot faint carvings along the stone wall and trace them with my eyes. At the end of the carvings, there's a moss-covered section of stone. I peer over the wall, a flicker of light catching my attention.

I breathe in deeply. The magic of the natural portals predictably making my stomach flip.

So, I walk fast toward the mossy stone, closing my eyes as I step into it. The air around me feels heavy as the world bends, colors swirl together into a dizzying tunnel. My body twists, an ache settling into my bones. Forcing my feet forward, I step through the other side, the magic clinging to me while I fall onto the ground. I blink to reorient myself, the taste of copper lingering in my mouth.

I notice that I landed just outside of Linnea's stone walls. Close to where I need to go.

The downside to using natural portals is they can drop you anywhere in the realm. The entrances stay put but the way out moves around, the unpredictability due to the unattended ancient magic.

The air feels wet. Drops of water cling to leaves. A shudder rolls through me from the abrupt change of weather. The ache in my body fades.

I scan the area with my magic, ensuring no surprises are near. I push aside the sharp pain I feel when I think about how close I am to Soren.

I shove those emotions down, repressing them deep within me.

Because bottling up your feelings always works, right?

Standing up, I head toward the little brick cottage. Excitement runs through me with each step I take toward my old friend.

****

Smoke curves up into the open sky before the cottage comes into view. My lips curl up into a smile at the sight of the familiar home. I walk eagerly up the worn path, approaching the door. I knock twice, pause a beat, then knock two more times. I wait with bated breath, uncertain whether the goddesses were truthful about his return.

I hear footsteps rushing to the door. A second later, it swings open to reveal my older friend. My smile widens at the sight of his friendly face. His hair has darkened, his deep gray eyes flashing with relief.

"Claude!" I exclaim excitedly. He pulls me into a tight hug, resting his chin on the top of my head. My throat thickens from the warm gesture. I breathe in his earthy scent, letting some tension out of my shoulders.

"Adira." He breathes out, pulling back to glance at my face. "Are you okay? What's happened?"

I wince, recalling the past month. "A lot has happened. I'll tell you about it over a drink."

He steps aside, ushering me in. The pungent scent of rosemary tickles my nose. I wander over to the warm fire, plopping down in a plush, brown chair. I sink in with a sigh, running my hands over the soft texture. A weight I didn't realize I've been carrying since the meeting with the goddesses lifts off my shoulders. I've always felt most at home here. *Why couldn't I have created a portal here?* I curse my stupidity. *I could have avoided being put back in jail, if only I didn't let emotion blind me.*

My chest tugs, the truth rising in me. *Or perhaps I wanted a realm between me and Soren.*

Claude comes around the corner with his gray hair pulled back out of his face. He walks over with two glasses of copper liquid, wordlessly handing one to me. I take a sip, welcoming the burn that it gives me. Relief spreads through me at seeing him alive and well.

"How are you?" I ask Claude. "I was so worried when we came back from the castle, and you were taken."

My mind flashes back to the magic stamp of Claude being attacked and dragged out of his home by the King's guards. My gaze flicks down in shame.

A large hand covers mine. I look up, meeting Claude's patient stare.

"I'm great now," he says with a crooked grin. "Two days after you and Soren left, guards were pounding at my door. I didn't tell them anything, but they still took me to the dungeons in Morvan."

I gasp at the name. Morvan is a place where the most dangerous criminals are kept. It's to the west of the Linnea Kingdom and is on a desolate island. No one's ever escaped before.

"I was just as shocked as you. Not sure why they thought I was such a threat. But anyway, I was there for about a month, and when I woke up in the morning on my twenty-ninth day, I was back here. I was about to go into hiding, when a soft female voice told me I was safe. She said her name was Tatsuya. I almost didn't believe it, but I sensed an old magic, so I didn't doubt that it was true. Even though I believed it, I stayed inside, alert for days after, waiting for the guards to reappear, but they never came back."

Tears burn my eyes.

"I'm glad Tatsuya was able to do that. We made sure the goddesses got you home safely. But I am so sorry that we couldn't look for you sooner," I say guiltily, trying not to think about what he's had to endure for an entire month in that place.

He pats my hand gently.

"Oh honey, it's okay. I understand why you couldn't. So, tell me everything that's happened. Where is Soren?"

I flinch at his name. Claude notices.

"What is it, dear?"

"Soren betrayed us. Used me. Everything he said—it was all a lie." My voice cracks, heart squeezing painfully at the admission. Claude's eyebrows shoot up in disbelief.

"That boy? Are you certain?"

I almost scoff at his surprise.

Bitterness surges in, I spit out my response. "Soren betrayed us, Claude. Lied to my face. Used me as nothing more than a tool to reach the goddesses. All that talk of trust, all those promises... it was never real."

Claude's eyebrows draw together. Before he can comment, I push forward, needing to move on.

"Wilhema did give me my magic back, and it's stronger than before, but it's less of a gift and more of a weapon I'll need for my next task," I tell him ruefully.

"She told me of a prophecy that I must fulfill," I say while staring into the crackling fire. Taking a big sip of my drink, I close my eyes. "A prophecy that is about me."

The words of the prophecy float through my mind.

"The first part is—*The child born from two realms, must bond back the creatures that fell.*"

I open my eyes, glancing into Claude's stormy gray ones. His stare reflects his apparent concern.

"How do you know it's about you?" he delicately asks.

"My mother used to tell me that I was important. She said I was born in both realms. I never used to believe her because that's impossible and I was sure that every mother thought their child was destined for greatness. But the goddesses confirmed that it is about me," I say wearily, staring numbly into the chaotic flames. The orange flickers and sparks, as if dancing nimbly through the air surrounding it.

"I imagine the next part is about the Teràstios. But they went extinct shortly before I was born. You were the only person I thought to ask. I can't exactly look into the history books in my realm," I admit. "I'm – uh – kind of on the run."

Claude's eyes widen. "What did you do?"

I scoff. "*I* did nothing. I was framed for a murder."

A burst of laughter escapes him. I watch him in confusion.

"Adira, only you could bring me out of a dungeon and into a prophecy. You've always had a way of finding trouble." he remarks.

My lips twitch.

"I'm never bored, that's for sure."

Although at this point, I wouldn't mind a little boredom. I muse to myself, sighing.

He just shakes his head in amusement.

"Let me tell you what I know about the Teràstios." He settles deeper into his chair, taking a large sip of his drink.

"They were incredible creatures. We already know that King Dahak started killing them and instilled fear of them into his subjects. Once the realms split, the Teràstios in Modereo were still fearful. They were able to bond with Stregoni and humans, as they were almost at the same power level as gods and goddesses. Which meant they *chose* if they wanted to bond. When too many refused, people turned bitter. They thought if they couldn't have the power that the Teràstios' companionship offered, then no one could."

I clutch the arm of the chair, cold disbelief sweeping through me. "So they were punished for saying no?"

"Punished, hunted, slaughtered. The Teràstios were furious and attacked back." Claude lets out a long sigh. "King Tobias made a lot of mistakes in his reign. I believe this one to be the worst. Letting his subjects attack those other-worldly creatures was appalling."

I squeeze my eyes shut in disgust.

"I knew he was a weak ruler, but I can't believe that King Tobias allowed that to happen."

Claude scowls, the motion twisting his face to one of cruel hatred—something I'm not used to seeing on him.

"He was a fool. He didn't enact punishment on those who committed the appalling crime." Claude shivered, as if he couldn't even say the treacherous words again. "He was more worried about keeping control of the land than he was of protecting the ancient creatures. And now they are gone."

I close my eyes, shaking my head in revulsion. "That's what it always is with these rulers. They are all greedy for more power." My stomach roils at the thought of the horrors the world has gone through to satiate a power-hungry ruler.

Claude nods in agreement. "The Teràstios used to reside in the Bantius Mountains. It's difficult to get to where the bonding ceremonies took place. A strange magic lingers. Many have died on the mountain."

"Of course it wouldn't be easy," I grumble, thinking of the massive mountains in Modereo.

Claude chuckles. "If anyone can do it, dear, you can."

I reach over, squeezing his hand.

"Thanks, Claude. I'm glad you're okay."

He gives me a smile, squeezing it back.

"Now, tell me the rest of this prophecy."

I gulp audibly. "Right."

I take a healthy sip of the liquor, rolling out my shoulders.

"To find out the truth, you must venture back to when divinities were youth. To rebalance what was torn apart, you must forfeit the life of which you hold closest to your heart."

Claude stays silent while he processes this. The fire crackles loudly through the room. A log breaks in half, the flames eating through the center. I watch it crumble to ash.

Claude shifts in his chair, drawing my attention.

"First of all, it sounds like you will need to research the past and the creation of the world. That would be easy, if the gods hadn't hidden away the early traces of themselves."

He grimaces as he comes to his own conclusion.

I shrug, letting the alcohol numb me. Fatigue pulls at me as I finish my glass.

"The next part..."

I cut him off. "I don't want to talk about the next part. It doesn't mean anything good and that's all I need to know right now."

I stare intently at the flames, ignoring his pitying look.

"Of course, dear. We can talk more tomorrow."

I shift my gaze to his, giving him a nod of appreciation.

"You should get some rest. You have a tough road ahead of you," Claude says while standing up.

The weight of the prophecy threatens to knock me down. I try to shake it off while I follow Claude out of the room.

"Goodnight, Claude. I can't thank you enough for all the help."

Claude smiles. "Goodnight, dear."

I walk upstairs, pausing on the landing. As I look down the dim hallway, I can't help but think of Soren. He seemed so genuine.

How could I have fallen for that? Stupid.

I reprimand myself, stepping into the guest room and closing the door. *Out of sight, out of mind. I have more important things to worry about.* My chest tightens with pressure, *like rebalancing the realms.*

Chapter 4

Soren

The large doors to the throne room open, I stride through, surveying the scene in front of me. King Dahak sits on his throne with a woman on his lap; she's in a dress so small she may as well be naked. Another scantily dressed woman to his right holds a goblet of wine and a bowl of grapes, ready to serve his every need.

I hide my sneer of disgust at the scene. At the blatant show of power.

Stopping ten feet in front of him, I toss the bag in front of me. It hits the tile floor with a thud, and the heads roll out. The woman on his lap gasps, jerking back. Wine spills on the pristine marble. The other one shrieks out loudly, stumbling away from the severed heads. They hastily rush from the room. The courtiers pale at the sight, one looks like he might vomit. I shake away the uncomfortable observation that I don't show the same level of revulsion as them.

The King sits as unaffected as me. His dark eyes latch onto my face, trying to read whether I'm having a moment of disobedience.

I internally roll my eyes, staying silent.

After a moment, his eyes go back to the ground. My lips twitch up at the contrast of the bloody heads on the shining white tile.

"So, it appears you found our traitors," the King's voice reverberates through the now half-empty room. His jewels glint in the torchlight whilst he addresses those remaining.

"They told me that the rebels will be stopping the prophecy, Your Majesty." I report with a bored tone.

A deep chuckle bursts out of King Dahak. "They can certainly try. But I doubt they will be able to accomplish much with their men being picked off like fleas."

His courtiers laugh along, similar to trained dogs.

The cloying smell of incense expands through the room. My gaze does a quick pass over the space, finding a quiet servant extinguishing a match. The courtiers visibly relax as the metallic tang of blood is overpowered by the new aroma.

"Have you heard the prophecy, Soren?" King Dahak asks, staring down at me. His tone mocks, gearing up to further make a fool of the rebellion.

"No, Your Majesty." I say smoothly, bowing my head. "I leave prophecy to poets. My duty is your enemies' blood."

I keep my expression flat while he eyes me before turning his attention back to his true audience, his ignorant underlings.

"Would you all like to be privy to a prophecy foretold by the gods themselves?"

Many cheer, some have astonished looks on their faces.

The King grins as they give him the reaction he was hoping for.

"Jorn!" he summons.

An older man with short gray hair ambles up to the throne. He stops in front of it and bows.

"You summoned me, Your Majesty," he crows out. His voice rolls down my spine like nails on chalkboard.

"Repeat the prophecy to me and my loyal followers." Dahak commands with a falsely sweet smile.

"As you wish, Your Majesty," he rasps back, rising to his feet.

"In darkness lies dominion. The heart is the prize. But beware... those who know will kill to keep it from you."

Shock whips through me as I eye the seer. I subtly slip into his mind. I immediately feel trapped in his dark thoughts. Hate surrounds me. I reel back in surprise. The darkness clings on, not letting me go. Mystified, I pull back my eather, but I slam into a wall of energy.

Hello, Soren. You aren't where you should be.

I freeze in place. *What's happening?*

What's happening is you think that you can just slip into people's minds with no consequences. Naughty, naughty boy. The world has much to teach you yet.

I don't answer. Because I didn't think much about others that had this gift, I thought I was the only one in this realm.

Now get out before the King notices, you little shit. And if I find you snooping again, I'll shatter your mind.

Before I can answer, the wall gives out, my eather slams back into my body. I stumble slightly, hiding it with a cough. The King glares at the interruption before turning back to the courtiers.

My eyes find the seer. His stare stays glued to the King, no sign of our earlier conversation. I shake off the lingering press of magic, ignoring the pit in my stomach from finding out that I'm no longer as powerful as I thought.

On the bright side, I think with an internal chuckle, *he's giving the King a false prophecy.*

The King dismisses the seer with a wave of his hand, the man bows and walks out. He doesn't look back once, just stumbles across the tiles, his steps being drowned out by the court's whisperings.

Dahak claps his hands once. Silence descends on the group.

"The rebels chatter like insects, but the prophecy is mine. I will choke their defiance before the first spark turns to fire."

"I will be the ruler of both realms," he finishes smugly, no hint of doubt in his tone.

The court claps eagerly, the sound bouncing off the painted walls. Dahak turns his attention back to me.

"Do what you must and end this foolish rebellion," he commands darkly.

"Understood. I will leave right away, Your Majesty."

I bow low, forcing the grin tugging at my mouth back into a mask of obedience.

"Assassin." Dahak stops me with the word; I flit my gaze up to his shrewd look. "I trust that you will get the job done, but just remember, that someone is always watching."

I mentally flip him off as I dip my head in understanding. The tone of his words at odds with the apparent *trust* he has in me.

"Of course, Your Majesty."

I turn, striding towards the large doors. Doubt works its way into my head. *How is he always watching me? It can't be true or else he would know I'm no longer under oath.*

My footsteps echo loudly against the tiled floor. I push my panicked thoughts to the back of my mind.

Now.

Time to find Adira.

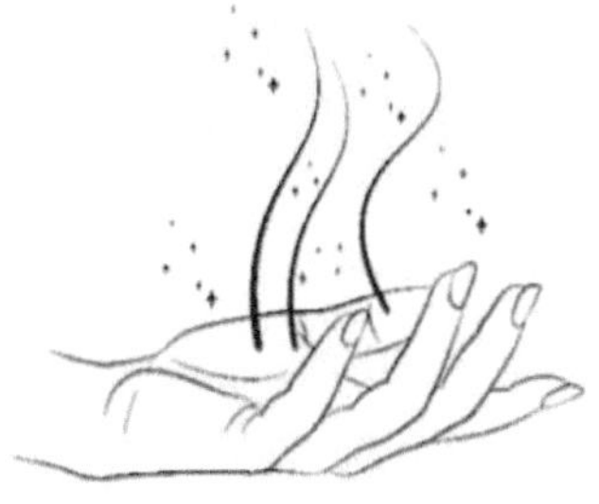

Chapter 5

Adira

A chill slithers across my neck seconds before blackened hands clamp down, their grip bruising, suffocating. I gasp, flailing as I try to pull in air. The skin on the hands melts away, leaving white bone. My eyes flare in horror. I follow the hands back up to the face, and a hollow skull fills my vision. I shriek, pushing it off.

It clatters to the ground, falling apart easily. Shadows lengthen around the room, taunting me. A cold sweat trails down my back.

You are nothing. Only a tool to be used. You will die and no one will care.

The shadows morph into the shape of a body. It floats down beside me on the bed, drifting closer with each taunt. It shifts, becoming more opaque.

Anguish and anger flow through me. I latch onto the anger.

I shove at the figure, it thumps to the ground. I peek over the edge, but the ground is empty, the last of the shadows dissipating as the whispers trail off.

My heart beats erratically. I gulp down my breaths, staring around the room. In the corner, the shadows appear darker. I stare intently at the spot. The darkness moves, gliding forward. It shifts into a figure.

I tense in preparation.

The figure steps forward into the gleam of the moonlight. I gasp at the sight.

It's me.

I step towards myself in shock. The shadow me shoots forward, wrapping a hand tightly around my throat. Their nails break skin, the smell of iron tickling my nose.

I gasp for breath, staring up at myself with wide eyes. The shadow me smiles wickedly.

"Did you think you were invincible? All those that you have killed want revenge. Why did your life matter more than theirs?"

Blackness creeps into my vision. Shadows start frantically bounding around the room.

"Look at how many lives you've taken. Think about the poor choices you've made."

My mind flashes to the trust I easily dole out.

"Watch your back." The hand on my throat squeezes impossibly tight. The darkness overtakes me, and I black out.

My eyes flutter open, the dream forcing me upright. My hand flies to my throat, finding unmarred skin. A pounding ache beats through my head. Looking down, I realize why. Sweat clings to my body, soaking the sheets. I take in my surroundings, remembering I'm at Claude's. The low light through the small window tells me that it's still early.

I run a trembling hand through my hair, slowing my breathing down. Frazzled energy fills the tiny space.

In through the nose, out through the mouth. I follow my instructions for a minute before I finally feel more like myself. The scent of herbs drying wafts up through the floorboards, grounding me further.

I slip from the bed on unsteady legs, heading to the bathroom to wash off the nightmare. Remnants of it clings on to me while I get ready. A sick feeling intensifying as I reflect on what I saw. *It's never a good thing when the dream version of you attacks yourself.* I shove it from my thoughts, refusing to think of it like the dark omen it appears to be.

I change into my black cotton pants and tug a slim fitting shirt on. Once I finish tying my black boots, I pack up all my belongings.

Slinging my bag over my shoulder, I head downstairs. The steps creak under my weight.

Claude is placing some toast and eggs onto two plates. Two full mugs of coffee wait on the table. My stomach growls at the sight.

He looks up at the sound and smiles. "Someone's hungry."

"I guess I am," I say sheepishly.

"Well, sit down, dear!" Claude commands, while ushering me to take a seat. A soft creak groans under my weight as I settle onto the bench. He turns, grabbing the plates and sitting across from me. I dig in and finish fast.

I sit back, content. Not realizing I'd been so hungry.

"Thank you, Claude."

He waves me off.

"You don't have to thank me. I enjoy having you visit. No matter the circumstances."

"No, I really need to thank you. I feel safer and more at home here than any other place... in both realms. And it's because of you."

His eyes shine. "I'm just glad I have someone to share all the liquor with."

A chuckle escapes me before we fall silent once more. He watches me for a moment with his stormy gray eyes.

"Do you want to talk about Soren?" he asks gently.

I flinch inwardly, trying to keep my expression neutral. I stare down at a twisted knot of dark wood as if it's the most interesting thing in the room.

"There's nothing to talk about," I force out. "He lied and betrayed me, and now I will never see him again." I ignore the pain saying that brings me.

I sense Claude's gaze on me, when I look up his face is filled with sympathy. "There is a lot of unknown in this world. As much as I don't condone lying, he may not have had a choice."

I open my mouth to argue, but he holds up his hand to silence me. "It's tough when a person you know and have come to care for betrays you," he says knowingly, patting my hand.

He pauses a moment, softening his expression. "But I think your paths are still yet to cross."

"Alright, wise old sage. Tell me how betrayal is supposed to be instructive." I reply sarcastically, refusing to consider that. He just gives me a soft smile back, knowing I don't like talking about my feelings.

"Do you want to talk more about the prophecy?"

"I appreciate the change in subject." I tell him bluntly. "But I'm okay right now. I'm just going to focus on one part at a time. I have a few ideas for the remainder of it anyway."

"If you're certain." He responds.

I huff out a laugh. "I doubt the Arae would let me fail without interfering. So, I'm just going to focus on each step because..."

I clear my throat. "I can't think about that last part right now."

Understanding takes over his expression. "Okay, dear. Once you conquer the first part, which you will, because you are the strongest person I know, you can always come back to me for help. I'll be here."

My vision hazes. I blink back the tears. "Thank you, Claude. I won't disappoint you."

"You could never."

I turn away from the emotion in his eyes. We both finish our coffee in comfortable silence.

"Well, I suppose it's time I head out," I say grudgingly, wishing I could stay and visit longer. But the threat of the prophecy bears down on me, making me feel as though I am carrying a two-hundred-pound man on my shoulders.

"Okay, dear, let me get you some food to take with you," Claude says while heading into the kitchen.

I watch him walk from the room, sadness taking hold. I don't get to see him often, but he's like a father to me. My mother never talked about my birth father. Whenever I asked, she would scoff and say that I'm better off not knowing him. She wouldn't even tell me if he was alive or not. When I was younger, I used to imagine him strolling into town and saving me from my mother's lessons.

I gave up on that thought a long time ago, and a hard realization came with it. *No one saves me but myself.* A low ache strikes my chest. I grip my pendant, frowning. *Was that my body or my necklace?*

Claude returns, drawing my thoughts away. I pack away the food he brought for me. He holds out his other hand, the flash of silver metal drawing my attention.

"Take this, Adira. You never know when it'll come in handy."

I grab the object, realizing it's an accendino. My hands tighten around the device that will allow me to easily wield the fire element.

"You remembered I lost my other one." I state, already knowing the response.

"As I recall, you can't seem to keep hold of them."

I chuckle slightly at the truth. Even if I don't need to touch the element to wield it, it makes it easier to summon when I'm low on energy.

Walking over to him, I give him a hug. A lump fills my throat as he squeezes me tight. His embrace feels more like home than anything ever has.

"Be safe, my dear. You know where to find me if you need anything."

I clear my throat of emotion. "Thank you, Claude," I say softly.

He eyes me for a moment.

"And I know that trust will break you at times but just remember. To trust isn't a weakness. It has the potential to be the greatest strength you can possess."

I nod weakly, knowing it's easier said than done.

I walk out the door, glimpsing back at the small cottage to see Claude looking out at me with misty eyes. I lift my hand up to wave, and he returns the gesture.

As I say goodbye, I can't help but think of Poderosa. *Two of the most important people in my life would never meet. My chosen family.*

Refusing to bear that sad thought, I steel my shoulders and focus on the soft, cool breeze of the forest.

I inhale deeply, giving myself a pep talk. *You got this, Adira. You can do anything.*

Chapter 6

Soren

Once I'm outside of the castle walls, I head east through the thick trees. I spot smoke billowing up into the sky before the familiar cottage comes into view.

I rub the back of my neck, my heart rate kicking up at the prospect of seeing Claude again. *What does he remember? Has he seen Adira yet? If so, will he hate me too?*

Before I lose my nerve, I stride up to the door and knock. The sound of footsteps gets louder before the door swings open.

Claude's eyes widen in surprise at me. I tense, waiting for a verbal lashing.

"Soren. What a surprise," he sputters out, his face filled with shock instead of anger. *I'll take it.*

"I need to talk to you. Can I come in?" I ask hopefully.

He steps to the side. "Of course."

I step in, immediately feeling the warmth of the fire, not realizing how cold the weather had turned outside. Slipping off my coat, I follow him to the seats near the fireplace. He pours two glasses of whiskey before he sits. I take one and watch him out of the corner of my eye, trying to get a read on him.

You could read his mind, I remind myself.

No, I scold myself after a minute, *I shouldn't do that for people I trust. Especially ones that have helped me.*

I clear my throat, refusing to entertain the thought further.

"So, how are you? Last time we were here, you were taken," I ask. My eyes scour the tidy space, no evidence of the prior struggle.

"I'm fine. Nothing I can't handle," he replies easily.

I tilt my head at that, gathering that there is more to the story. Sensing he doesn't want to talk about it, I let him change the subject.

"But it seems you have a lot to fill me in on," he states with a raised eyebrow.

My chest aches at his words. "Adira has been here already?"

"She has," he confirms, eyeing me with a serious expression. "She left four days ago."

A gnawing restlessness fills me when I realize our paths had almost crossed. *If only I'd come a few days before.*

"You have to know that I didn't want to lie. I had no choice," I plead.

He sits silently, mulling over my words. I wait in suspense, wondering if he will choose to believe me or not.

After a moment of silence, I can't wait. I have to ask, "How is she?"

His eyes flick up to mine, and he must read the desperation on my face because his lips curl up into a small, knowing smile.

"She's overwhelmed, but she's strong. She can do this," he states with a hint of pride in his voice.

"I know she can," I agree. Squeezing my eyes shut, I imagine the pressure and loneliness she must be feeling. *I shouldn't have let her go*, I think to myself bitterly.

"But," Claude continues, "you have a lot of work to do before you earn her trust back."

"I understand there are many elements to higher power and beings. I tried to tell her to keep an open mind. But in this case, all she can see is someone who she was close to and trusted, betrayed her."

My head dips, shame rolling through me.

"I gathered as much," I say quietly.

I glance up, locking eyes with understanding gray ones. "You should hate me, Claude. Maybe you do. But you still let me in. That's more grace than I deserve."

"You've made mistakes, kid. But I've seen enough of you to know— you're not beyond redemption." he says playfully with a wink.

I huff out a bitter laugh.

"Well, good, because I came here to help Adira. Do you know where she went?" I ask.

"She went to the Bantius Mountains to find more information about the Teràstios. You won't be far behind. But tonight, you should get some rest."

Although I itch to close the distance between me and Adira, I don't argue with him, the mental exhaustion of the past week hitting me hard.

"Okay. Thank you, Claude. I really appreciate it."

He stands up, taking our empty glasses to the kitchen.

I head up to the room and settle onto the bed. Closing my eyes, I let my mind wander back to when Adira and I were here. The image of running into her in the hall fills my head. The desire in her eyes when she looked at me.

That was the first time I wanted to kiss her, I recall in surprise. *This is where it started.*

Just before sleep pulls me under, the distant crunch of boots reaches my ears. I sit up, listening intently.

A loud crash sounds from below. I leap out of bed, my body moving before I can process it. Crossing the room in three quick strides, I slide my sword out in one swift movement. I fling open the door, racing down the stairs.

My eyes widen in shock at the scene. There are four Enid soldiers, the sewn yellow axe flashing in the dim light. One is holding Claude's arms behind his back while another points his sword at his heart. The other two are standing watch near the wooden door.

I act quickly. Springing forward, I attack the two guarding the door. Surprise flickers on their faces. I use that to my advantage and disarm the one closest to me. My boots scrape against the floor as I turn with the sword and slash across guard number two's chest. He drops his sword in pain, clutching the wound. The scent of copper chokes the air.

I kick his weapon away, whipping around. The other two guards are tense and shouting at me to 'drop my weapon or the old man gets it.'

I pause in panic, slowly dropping the sword. My mind races for a solution.

My mind...

I keep my movements slow as an idea comes to me. They keep their eyes locked on me, tension racking their frames.

I look at the guard with the sword pointing at Claude's heart and slip into his mind. *I've never tried to control someone's thoughts before, but if there was ever a time to try, it would be now.*

I sense his intention to kill Claude at the front of his mind. I hesitate only for a moment, my moral compass from earlier going off. Feeling the guard's anger behind his thoughts, I know I can't let him go through with killing Claude. He's innocent.

Decision made, I concentrate, noticing a hazy cord beside the thought. *Woah, I've never seen that before.* I can't help the surprise that overtakes me. *Maybe it's because I've never tried this?*

I shake my thoughts from my head, focusing on the string of eather. I will myself to pull it, and the thought jerks to the side, slipping out of his head.

The guard blinks in confusion, the hand holding the sword lowering slightly. A wave of dizziness washes over me. I steady myself, then lunge forward, tackling him to the ground. He grunts, fighting back. I slam my elbow down onto his right hand, the sword clattering onto the floor.

Reaching out, I wrap my hand around his throat and cut off his airway. It only takes a minute before he falls limp under me.

I turn, noticing the guard holding Claude has pulled his sword out and is holding it close to his throat. His hand is trembling slightly, the motion causing a bead of blood to swell up. I slowly rise to my feet.

"Easy there," I say with my hands up.

"Stay back," he stammers out. His eyes darting back and forth between his friend and me, probably wondering what just happened.

I just stare at him, keeping my expression as innocent as I can. Focusing on his thoughts, I pull at the cord. He jerks with the intrusion, his sword slicing into Claude's neck. A rasp escapes him as the blade cuts deep.

"NO!" I shout. My vision blurs. I fight to keep upright. I blink a few times, focusing on my breathing.

My sight clears just in time to see the guard rushing forward. Reaching down, I scoop my sword off the ground in one quick motion.

Extending my weapon out, I stab the guard through the chest. He falls immediately. Panic drowns out the remorse as I fall to my knees beside Claude, checking the wound.

Shit, it's deep. Too deep.

Claude opens his mouth to speak. Blood streams out of his wound and forms a puddle around us, dripping through the wooden boards. Fear latches onto my chest. I grasp his hand tightly, offering him the only support I can as the light fades from his eyes.

"They want her, Soren. Protect her...," he sputters out, blood spilling from his mouth.

"I will." I promise him.

The promise fills the air, changing the pungent smell of blood to a sweet scent. But I'm not sure if he hears me, because when I look into his eyes, they are lifeless.

He's gone.

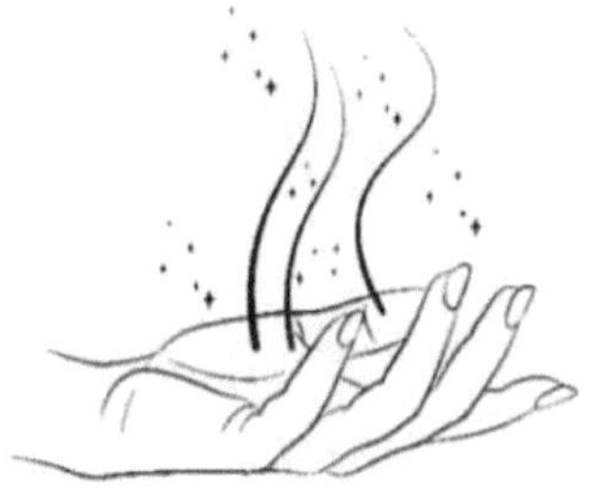

Chapter 7

Adira

After striding through the forest, I come up to the side of the cliff. A sense of déjà vu washes over me as I take the familiar path down to the cave. Fortunately, the tide is low right now, so I easily navigate around the cave and along the rocky edge of the water.

I balance on two rocks, staring at the side of the cliff. *Where was it again?*

I slowly scour the air in front of me. A few feet to my left, the air distorts into itself. It occupies the space above the water.

Ugh, it couldn't be over a rock or in a cave. I groan to myself.

Looking down at the stones, I plan my path. I nimbly leap over each rock. The waves crash against them, spraying me with salty water. I focus on my steps, bracing myself with each jump.

Landing on the last rock, I take a quick moment to observe the tumultuous waves. Their harsh movements slam into the terrain, as if they want to be one. I shake my head, a strange sadness encompassing me from that thought—that the ocean will forever be set apart due to its intense nature.

Turning back toward the shimmering air, I bend my legs and jump through. The world distorts, spiraling around. A hint of nausea creeps in. The heavy air weighs me down, causing me to land with a jarring thud onto the grass below me. I spit out the taste of copper before pushing to a stand. Breathing in the invigorating air of Modereo, I let it rejuvenate me.

Night begins to fall as I look at my surroundings, seeing the looming Bantius mountains in the distance. I close my eyes and summon Charcoal, my horse.

While I wait for Charcoal, I start a fire, settling down beside it. I eat some of the bread and meat Claude gave me. As I sit in silence, my mind starts to play tricks on me. Every rustle of leaves has me tensing. Preparing for the worst. Eventually, I force myself to relax and with the heat of the fire, I drift off to sleep.

****

I'm woken up by something nudging my face. My hand reaches for my dagger as my eyes fly open. I breathe out a sigh of relief when I see two familiar large eyes staring back at me.

"Hello, sweetie," I coo to my horse, petting his black mane. Leaning into his neck, I give him a friendly squeeze. My throat thickens when I consider how close I came to never seeing him again.

"Thank you for coming so fast. We have a big adventure to go on now. Are you ready?" I ask Charcoal, trying to push enthusiasm into my voice.

He lifts his head, neighing in response.

I'll take that as a yes.

I notice that dawn is creeping up, so I pack up my supplies.

"Might as well leave now," I say out loud to both Charcoal and myself.

I swing onto his back with practiced ease.

"I've missed you, boy," I tell him softly.

My mind flashes back to when I first got him. Mother had taken me to the market. She told me it was time to get a horse for myself. I was so excited. A man had an enclosure of five horses. I saw the sleek black horse and couldn't look away. He noticed me walking toward him and met me halfway. He pushed his nose into my outstretched hand, and I grinned.

I turned back to my mother to tell her I wanted this horse. At first, she dismissed my choice and told me that we don't choose a horse with our feelings— we choose a horse that's strong. Lucky for me, the breeder told her that he was a sturdy horse for his age, and she agreed. When we got home, she lectured me on how feelings can be a weakness. I nodded my head in agreement, but I knew that I had a new friend.

"Let's go, Charcoal," I command while clicking my heels into his side.

He starts off with a trot, then picks up speed. I smile as the wind whips my hair back. I grasp onto the feeling of freedom as we soar through the field, knowing that for me, that feeling is only an illusion.

****

The time passes quickly. We only stop for a few hours a day to refuel and rest. Before I know it, it's already been five days.

The land blurs by us, to the far right I regard the darkened aftermath of the Vormr. I let the now brittle lands urge me on. At the pace we're going, we will make it to the mountains tomorrow. My back aches from the constant jostling. I ignore the pain, letting it drown out my nervous thoughts.

Charcoal slows down, navigating through a thick area of trees. I relax into him, enjoying the slower speed.

Then, a roar reverberates through the air. The sound increasing rapidly, telling me this thing is practically upon us.

Shit.

Somehow knowing we won't outrun it, I leap off Charcoal, unsheathing my sword as I dismount.

"Go hide," I tell my horse. Charcoal twists, galloping in the opposite direction.

The trees in front of me are knocked down, slamming to the ground with force. In the newly made clearing stands a beast I've never seen or heard of. Its fur is barely hanging onto its skin, and its green, sunken eyes have a crazed look, as if it only has one goal and will stop at nothing to complete it. The sight of it tickles something in my brain.

Have I read about this creature before?

It leaps forward.

No time.

I lunge to the side, narrowly avoiding it.

Calling upon my magic, I summon vines to trap the beast. The rush of power makes me dizzy with oxygen. The beast screeches when I immobilize it. I swipe with my sword, managing a cut across its right side. Black blood oozes out, the density an unnatural thickness. I leap back to avoid the vile substance.

It roars in anger, breaking free of its earthly bindings. The beast swats me away. Flying through the air, I try to get my bearings as the ground rushes up toward me. I crash into the hard terrain, the air whooshing out of me.

"Yep, that's going to bruise," I rasp out to myself.

Pressing up, I ignore the sting of pain and focus on the beast. Dampness draws my attention. I look down at my hand, noting the water droplets that cling to it. I reach back down, placing my palm on the earth.

The ground is thick with moisture, so I imagine a watery sword. It forms in the clearing. I will it to turn to ice. I watch in awe as it shifts from clear to frosted. *I've never made something so beautiful.*

I snap forward, wrapping my hand around the cold handle, instantly shoving it toward the creature. The jab lands where its heart should have been, but the thing doesn't die. More black blood gushes out, sticking to the surface of the earth.

Dammit. What is this thing?

While it's getting up, I rush over to it and swipe at its legs. It crashes forward, unable to hold its weight up. An idea forms in my head. I ignore the exhaustion that's starting to tug at me, my internal reminder that I'm using too much magic, too fast. My power rushes up through me, swirling down my blade and extending it. It now stands about seventy-nine inches long, with the end made of sharp, solid ice.

I teeter a bit at the shift in weight before adjusting myself. Before the beast can retaliate, I swing the blade toward its neck, pushing a punch of eather behind the motion. My arms shake from the effort. The adrenaline wiping away my fatigue. The sword begins to slice through its thick neck, stopping halfway. I groan in frustration.

Ugh, I hate when this happens.

Pulling the sword back, the beast sways, its cries shaking the forest. I'm panting as I arc the sword smoothly through the air. It latches onto its broad shoulder, its shrieks reaching my ear at an unearthly pitch.

"Enough. You're not walking away from me." I grunt out when it gets stuck.

A spray of its unusual blood lands on my bare hand. It starts burning, like the stuff is made of fire. I screech and grab a large leaf off the ground, wiping it off my hand. My blood sizzles, the skin bubbling up like I have a second-degree burn, my heartbeat pulsing from the new wound.

I swing again, *and you know what they say, third time's a charm.* It slides true, severing its head. The body falls to the ground, twitching, while the head rolls off into some bushes.

I slump to the ground, the adrenaline wearing off. My back screams at me. Hearing a faint galloping sound, I turn toward the left. A neigh echoes through the trees. I smile in relief.

Charcoal comes into view, stopping beside me.

"Thanks for not going too far." I rub his snout.

My vision swims as I push myself up, the use of magic and getting thrown around catching up to me.

"Let's move away from the disgusting body and find someplace to rest," I tell Charcoal, weariness evident in my voice.

I stare down at my burned arm. Fear filters through me at the danger of having a beast's blood attack you. The horror of what that could do makes me shiver.

We walk until the smell of the pine trees drowns out the foul stench of the beast. I plop down against a tree, not bothering to roll out my bedding. With the last of my energy sapped, I let sleep drag me under.

****

A sharp sting pulls me from my slumber. I blink open my eyes, groaning against the blinding light.

Something sharp stabs at my arm again. I hastily look down, noticing a bird pecking at me. Raising my hand, it startles, flying away.

Stupid bird. I think, peering down at my red arm.

I lean forward, my bruised body protesting the movement. Gritting my teeth, I slowly press to a stand, the feeling akin to getting trampled by a horse.

As if summoned, Charcoal trots into view. I hold my hand up, and he walks over happily. I smooth down his soft mane.

"Ready, buddy?"

I get a neigh in response.

"Yeah, me either." I mumble. The short rest not replenishing my reserves enough to risk using my magic on my wounds.

Reaching into my bag, I grab two apples. Holding one out to Charcoal, he chomps it down. I eat half of mine before giving the rest to him.

"You need your strength more than I do, buddy." I coo, adjusting the bag he's saddled with.

Flinging my body over messily, we start off toward the pointed peaks. A low hum of energy pulls at my power from the distance. The Vormr. The drain so minimal, I wouldn't have caught it without the silence surrounding me.

The rest of the day passes uneventfully. *Thank the goddesses.*

The sun dips lower as we reach the base of the Bantius Mountains. Fatigue pulls heavily at my body. I blink away my exhaustion, concentrating on the task at hand. I call upon my magic and use it to scour the foot of the mountain for any paths. After thirty minutes of searching, I find something.

I jump down from Charcoal. My legs shake unsteadily when I hit the ground—my body's way of telling me I need to take a break. Wincing in guilt, I turn toward an equally tired-looking horse and give him another apple.

"Good boy," I tell him. "I'm sorry I pushed you so hard."

Charcoal neighs softly, nuzzling into me. His hair tickles my burnt arm. A slight hiss escapes me. He neighs again, as if apologizing. I give him a small smile, running a hand over his mane.

A low buzzing sound faintly fills the air. Tensing, I turn to the forest, searching for the sound.

Suddenly, an arrow flies through the air. I bolt sideways on instinct to avoid it. It sinks into Charcoal's side, and he lets out a pained whinny.

"NO!" I shout.

I pull up a barrier just as another arrow hits it. I turn left toward the source, spotting two men in a tree. I let my anger flow through me and release it at the men. The ground shakes, and they lose their grip, falling out of the tree.

As soon as they hit the ground, I push a crack across the soil. They fall into it screaming. I stumble over the thrumming terrain. My magic flows out of me and closes up the hole, swallowing their screams.

I fall to my knees, breathing heavily. My head pounds vigorously. *Everything happened so fast.* I blink away the unease from my effortless slaughter. I look down at my trembling hands, surprised I was capable of such power and ruthlessness. Especially being near the bottom of my reserves.

"Charcoal," I breathe out.

I stand shakily, rushing toward my fallen horse. The arrow is sticking out from his side, and blood is already pooling under his large body.

Okay, don't panic, I tell myself. *I just need to remove the arrow, then I can heal him.*

I pull the arrow out, and black steam hisses up.

Shit. I curse, disbelief seizing me. Having learned about all types of weapons when I was training in Magia, I know what this means.

The arrow's been poisoned with magic.

He won't make it.

I choke on a sob with the realization. He whinnies weakly. Tears stream down my face as I stroke his back, trying to keep him calm. I call my magic up anyway, needing to try. Sending it out toward the injury, the black steam repels my spell. My power jerks back into my body.

A crack aches through my chest. *I just got him back.*

"I'm so sorry, boy. This is my fault," I whisper to him, tears spilling down my cheeks. As I'm stroking him, he stops moving.

He's gone.

I let my hand fall away from his body and curl into myself. Sobs wrack me. My power thumps erratically inside me. I press my hand to my chest, willing myself to calm down.

I let my emotions numb me while I build a pyre by hand. I maneuver the logs and branches to resemble a large dais. Gently wrapping my power around his body, I lift him up. Gliding him through the air, I place him on the dais. I stumble a bit, exhausted from the use of magic. Sweat drips down my back. I thumb the accendino Claude gave me, flicking it open, needing the additional help.

I open my hand, calling upon a flame.

Goodbye, old friend.

I turn my hand to the pyre and shoot out the flame. The branches catch first, then the fire roars to life. Within minutes, Charcoal's engulfed in flames.

My chest beats with sadness while the sky fills with smoke. I pull on my air magic to extinguish the dark fumes before I alert others of my location.

Anger takes control as my mind wanders back to the men. The men wearing green uniforms. The men from Enid.

Chapter 8

Soren

I toss the shovel to the side, wiping the sweat from my brow. I peer down into the hole, swallowing audibly. *It's big enough.*

I pick up Claude's body, the soft blanket I wrapped him in falling open to reveal his face. *Fuck. He didn't deserve this. He was like a father to Adira. He was the only person in this realm who didn't judge me for my past.*

Lowering him gently into the ground, I re-cover his face with careful hands. A mix of sadness and guilt chokes me as I refill the ground with dirt. *Adira's going to blame me,* I think bitterly. *And why shouldn't she? I couldn't save him.*

Poderosa's gone. Esper's gone. Claude's gone. All she has left is me, and I already let her down. I don't deserve to be forgiven... but I'm selfish enough to hope she still does forgive me.

I gather up my supplies, wallowing in my remorse as I move. I take in a deep breath, reluctant to leave.

My eyes track back to the grave. "I hope wherever you are, Claude. You are at peace."

I swing my pack over my shoulder and head out, walking northeast toward the rebel camp. As the trees grow denser, the tension leaks out of me. The calmness I always feel when I'm surrounded by nature soothing my frayed nerves.

A few hours later, I hear voices. I shift my somber thoughts from my head, focusing my attention. Pausing, I crouch down behind a tree.

Two men arrive from the west, walking toward a dense part of the forest. Long strings of ivy hang down to the ground on all the trees. They don't pause as they walk through the middle of it.

My lips twitch up. *That was too easy.*

Once they pass through, I check the area to make sure no one else is near and come out from around the tree. I silently creep forward, parting the ivy. I blink as my eyes adjust, a long cavern emerging. Fortunately, no one is in the cave, so I quickly stalk forward. My nose wrinkles from the scent of damp stone. *Ugh, it smells like wet dog.*

The cave opens up into a small, stony room that branches off to four smaller tunnels. I sense a presence behind me just in time.

I dart sideways as a whoosh goes through the air. Turning, I spot a guard gearing up to attack again. I reach forward, grasping the pommel of his sword, wrestling it from him. I back him into a wall, slamming his head into the stone. He falters but doesn't go down. I slam it once more, hoping the sound doesn't carry. This time he crumples to the ground.

Chest heaving, I drag his limp body back where I came from. I hide him in the vines, praying that the darkness of the cave will obscure him. I slink back to the stony room. Voices echo from the path to my left, so I move to the right.

A low buzz fills the air as I walk ahead. The hair on my arms begins to stand up. A light appears, and I slow down as I reach the end of the tunnel. More voices carry over to me.

"What do you think, Felix?" a man asks.

"I think we need to find the bitch and put an end to this prophecy," Felix spits back.

I tense at the topic. *They can't know about Adira, can they?*

I peek out from behind a large stone, seeing two guards in front of a shimmering wall. I gape at the sight.

That's why they chose this damp cave, I deduce. *They found a natural portal.*

"Hopefully Enzo and Brutus found her. We only have a few of those poison arrows," the first guard says.

Poison arrows? Shit.

"Those things are the only time I will voluntarily use magic," he spits out in disgust.

"They do come in handy," Felix agrees easily.

The disgusted guard inspects his companion. "Careful," he warns.

"It almost sounds like you enjoy using magic. You know the Divinità won't appreciate that."

"You think I like dipping my hands in that filth? Magic's a curse, not a gift." Felix defends.

The name stirs in my memory.

The elusive Divinità doesn't want his people using magic, yet he uses it to his advantage. I wonder who the hypocrite is.

I store that information away for later.

"Not to mention I'm fucking exhausted. The captain is spreading us too thin. He won't listen when I tell him we need to recruit more soldiers."

"I know, I haven't had a pub night in over a week." A laugh sounds, bouncing off the walls and through the tunnel behind me.

The sound of dripping water shields the scrape of my sword being drawn. I pick up a loose stone, tossing it to the left of the guards. They both turn their heads toward the noise. I pounce forward, ramming the pommel of my sword on Felix's head. He collapses to the ground with a light thud. The other guard turns in surprise and opens his mouth to shout, but I wrap my hand around his neck, cutting off his air. He starts to thrash with fear. I keep a tight hold, willing him to pass out. His eyes are wide and panicky. *Can't you see I'm trying to save you?* I want to shout at him, but I stay silent. His eyes roll back and he falls with a thud, I cringe at the sound.

Before others can come, I quickly turn to the portal. A flicker of nerves swirls in my gut.

Here goes nothing, I think, stepping through.

The air thickens, the taste of copper filling my mouth. The world turns. I squeeze my eyes shut. Pressure pushes against my body, charging me with frazzled energy. I sway slightly with the foreign feeling, falling to the soft grass.

My head spins, the ground a whirl of green. Quelling down my nausea, I stand up and shake off my dizziness.

Looking around at the lush landscape, I let myself smile.

I made it to Modereo.

****

I don't know much about this realm, other than what Adira has told me and the little that I've read, but it's much more abundant than I realized. Trees and bushes full of berries and fruit span out over a large field. My gaze greedily drinks up the greenery. I twist around and freeze.

Farther to the left, a dark patch of dead trees sits. The area bleak and rotted. A waft of air travels toward me, the scent putrid. I shift away from the acrid smell, straightening with the reminder of the prophecy.

I take a deep breath, remembering what Adira said about the air. I focus on it and notice a charge—almost like energy is floating all around.

I stop gawking and move away from the portal.

Okay, the prophecy. I need to go to the Bantius Mountains.

I survey the land, noticing the odd shape of the mountains I've only read about. *Thank gods for its distinct features. It makes coming to a new realm easier.*

I start walking west toward the pointed mountains. I swallow down the fear of seeing Adira. A bubble of excitement worms its way in, but I squash it, remembering Claude's lifeless eyes and Adira's anguished expression.

I'll make her understand my side. I have to.

Chapter 9

Adira

The tears dry on my face as I start up the path I found earlier. The rocky terrain is steep, and soon my breathing becomes labored. I focus on the ground, letting the physical exertion clear the fogginess of loss from my head.

Halfway up, a foreign sensation presses in on me. I stop on the path, blinking in confusion. The ground looks flimsy, like it's made of rubber. I take a step forward, swaying as my body tries to right itself.

What's going on?

The world swirls uncontrollably. I try to stay steady, but I can't discern which way is up or down. A thought floats loosely through my scrambled mind.

This must be what Claude warned me about.

I delve into my power and blindly toss it out, hoping to eradicate whatever is happening to me. Sweat beads my brow as my power keeps flowing. Dizziness grabs onto me from the ever-moving world.

Then, it stops.

My magic recedes, and I take a breath of air, grounding myself. I look down, noticing that I was unknowingly teetering toward the edge of the cliff. Loose gravel slides down the side when I stumble back.

I gulp at my almost fate.

That was close.

My feet start moving along the path, faster than before, the urgency in my magic telling me it will be harder to stop an attack like that a second time. I focus on the earth below my feet, willing the terrain to stay solid. My breathing becomes shallower as the air grows thin. I slow my steps, hoping to limit my oxygen intake.

I force myself to stop when I start wheezing. Placing my hands on my hips, I glimpse out into the sky, noticing dusk fall. *Damn, when was the last time I was this taken out by exercise.* My head pounds, chest tightening from the lack of air.

Pressing my hand to my ribs, I tell myself not to panic. *You have enough air. Don't freak out.*

I find some large stones off the path and settle against them. My head calms when I stop my movement. My thoughts drift back to my lost companion. Staring off into the forest below, I don't even flinch as the sound of a tree cracking reverberates through the air. I watch it fall. As if it couldn't bear to hold itself upright anymore. I stare at it long after it crashes to the earth, wondering if I would become it.

I call upon my magic to warm the ground around me, not wanting to risk a fire in case more Enid rebels are nearby. My head spins from the simple spell. The taste of bitterness fills my mouth as I think of them.

They died too fast. They deserved to suffer.

I shake the dark thought away, letting sleep pull me under.

****

I'm up before the sun, barely having slept at all. I eat some stale bread and cheese, my tired eyes scanning the still rocky pass as I eat. I stand and stretch, my muscles groaning from yesterday's steep hike. Dew clings onto every available surface, turning the rocks slippery. *Great, something else to worry about.*

A flash of a shadow flits through my peripheral. I tense, twisting toward it. The area is silent. My heart beats fast as my mind trails back to the ghosts that haunted my dreams.

I shiver, shaking off the remnants of the nightmare. Dragging a hand over my exhausted face, a feeling of hopelessness latches onto me.

Will I ever be able to sleep again without nightmares plaguing me?

I shrug to myself, already getting used to my frazzled state. My hand moves to my pendant, clasping the warm stone. Despite my mixed emotions about my mother, I would still welcome her company. At least then I wouldn't be alone.

I swallow hard, my gaze tracking over the quiet mountain.

Very alone. All the time.

I sigh, knowing I can't do anything about that. Hoisting my bag over my shoulder, I walk back to the worn path. My foot slips once before I fix my steps.

I hear a stone drop in the distance, the scraping of stone on stone letting out a low screech. My mouth tightens at the sound. I don't know if my mind is just so fragile right now that I'm imagining it, but the noise almost sounds like a horse whinnying.

I glance up at the cloudless sky.

I'm so sorry, Charcoal. You deserved better.

Melancholy washes over me, filling the air with a despondent atmosphere. Keeping my focus on the path, I take step by step. Every so often, I peek upward, relieved when I notice the peak looming closer and closer. I keep my breathing under control, not letting anxiety in.

Halfway through the day, I stop for a quick break, needing to replenish myself. I promptly start back on the climb, the sweat on my back drying as the sun dips lower. When the sun is almost gone, I finally reach the top.

Confused, I look around. The wide base is mostly flat except for large rocks littering the area. I notice a shallow cave to my left, so shallow that I don't need to step into it to see the end. A few sparse tree trunks scatter the ground.

There's nothing here.

I run a hand frustratingly through my tangled hair, wandering around the jagged rocks and searching the entire area. Near the shallow cave the air seems to vibrate. I press my hand to the wall. The stones hum faintly.

"I must be close." I say to myself excitedly. My eyes pass over the area slowly. A lighter spot catches my eye. Squinting at it, I lean in closer. It's a pair of broad wings with a heart connecting them.

The mark of the bond between the Teràstios and its rider, I tell myself, recognizing the mark. My heart pounds faster. I bring my finger to it, pressing into the faded symbol.

Nothing happens. It doesn't move.

Looking near the mark, I try to spot any hidden levers but have no luck.

I plop down on the ground, sighing. *I feel like I'm missing something. What was the saying that was said between bonded pairs?*

I close my eyes in frustration and mentally go through all the lessons I had in school. After what feels like an hour, I finally remember.

"*Alterum dimidium*," I say out loud. It means *my other half* in the old language.

For a moment, nothing happens. Then, the ground starts to shake and the back of the cave crumbles, revealing a narrow tunnel. I stumble to my feet, staring into the newly formed hole. A hint of nerves flutter up inside of me.

Like always, I ignore the fear and trudge forward.

Well, here goes nothing.

I step over the loose rocks, walking down into the darkness. The air is thick with dust. I cough, waving a hand in front of me to clear it. Eventually, I come to an opening and see a large area that drops down so far that I can't perceive the bottom.

I gasp to myself.

I'm in the mountain.

I notice a pulsing orange light to my left and turn toward it. Before I can take another step, a sword at my throat stops me. The gleam of the blade shines in the dim light.

I freeze in place.

"Who are you?" a deep voice demands.

I hesitate a moment, the shock from finding someone inside the mountain causing me to falter.

"Adira," I reply slowly, not wanting to alarm them. "I'm here to learn about the Teràstios."

"Why? So you can learn new ways to hunt them down?" he accuses roughly.

"Of course not. Aren't they extinct?" I ask with confusion.

He stays silent.

"They aren't, are they?" I whisper excitedly, coming to my own conclusion.

"I'm here to fulfill the prophecy," I confess.

He scoffs, his judgmental stare locked on me.

"You're the one?"

The skepticism in his voice grates on me.

Who does this guy think he is?

"Yes. Really. You know nothing about what I've lost—or what I've survived." My voice cracks. I clear my throat, hoping he didn't notice.

"Now. Are you going to let me go, or are you going to slide the sword across my throat? Hurry up and choose," I say with a bored tone.

He holds it there a second longer, as if deciding. Then, he draws the sword back to himself. I turn to face him.

My mouth parts open in shock before I snap it shut.

Holy goddess, this man is attractive. Of course it's always the ones that want to harm me. I think, taking in his short black hair and muscular legs.

"Who are you?" I demand.

His face twists. "Why would I tell you?"

I sigh at the stalemate.

"Come with me," he demands.

"Where?"

"Walk. Every moment you hesitate tests my patience." He snaps, his boots thundering as he paces away. I roll my eyes. *And they say women are more dramatic.*

I sigh, following behind him.

Well, this is better than the alternative. Whatever this 'test' may be.

As we walk, I appreciate his tall form. The shadows dance over his features, making his brown eyes brighten. We turn down another tunnel and the path opens up to a cramped area. My nose wrinkles from the rusty scent of dried blood. *That's never a good sign.*

In the center is a large stone slab with a bejeweled dagger resting on top. His presence feels heavy in the confined atmosphere. I immediately slow at the sight, my eyebrow raising as I shoot him a glance.

"If you're going to kill me, it doesn't need to be so elaborate."

He looks over at me, and I swear I see his lip twitch up.

"I'm not going to kill you," he states. Then, under his breath, I hear, "Yet."

"You have to drop some of your blood onto the stone. If you pass, it will open for you, and all the knowledge you were looking for will come forth."

"That's it! A little blood?" I ask, though a sliver of doubt works its way into me.

What if this is all a mistake? What if I'm the wrong person?

"And if the stone doesn't open?" I inquire, peering at his long sword.

He doesn't say anything but lifts his eyes up to the ceiling. I follow them up there and notice another large stone slab, hanging precariously by a thin chain. Dried blood is splattered across the cream-colored rock.

Well shit. There would be no outrunning that.

I move toward the stone and climb up the two small steps. I grab the dagger and focus on the cold handle, willing my heartbeat to slow.

Taking a deep breath, I lift the dagger up. I don't react as I slice it through my hand. The blood drips onto the stone and a gust of wind flies at me, blowing my hair back.

I hear stone grinding together, and I tense, waiting for the slab to fall on me. To my relief, the stone shifts and opens. A blast of warm air rushes around the area. I'm giddy as I peek inside.

And see... nothing.

I whip around to the man.

"Empty? You said this stone held answers. Don't tell me I bled wrong." I end off with bitter sarcasm.

He appears shell-shocked for a moment, then grimaces. As if he expected the giant slab of stone to fall onto me.

"You are the one who will carry out the will of the Arae," he says to himself in disbelief.

"I'm to be your guide," he states ominously.

"Guide for what?"

"You'll see."

Chapter 10

Kalon

I *can't believe that small girl is the one the stories prophesied.*

I ignore her smooth skin and shiny hair, focusing on the responsibility that's been ingrained in me since childhood.

Kalon, you must guard the stronghold. Over the years many will come looking for it. If they are clever enough to enter, you must test them. Only one will pass the test, the prophesied one. They will be the one to complete the Arae's will. You must aid them by teaching them the ways of the Teràstios.

My father's voice fills my head. I had endless questions for him, with most of the answers being *the Arae willed it.* I knew enough to know that nobody crossed the Arae, that would be a death sentence.

"Follow me," I tell her, turning and walking through the tunnel to the right. A path I'd taken a million times before. In fact, I could walk this whole mountain with my eyes closed and not get lost. I hear her footsteps following a few paces behind.

"Now will you tell me who you are?" she asks warily.

"The name's Kalon. I'm here to help you learn about the Teràstios," I tell her.

"Why?"

"My bloodline has guarded the Teràstios longer than your realm has told its bedtime stories. Duty is all I've ever known."

I resist the urge to ask her about the outside world—the world I've been wanting to explore since I was a child. Doing so would only torture myself, it always does. Temptation is the weakness of duty. *Or so my father repeatedly said.*

"So they really aren't extinct?" she asks excitedly.

"Impatience belongs to the untested. Your questions will matter only if you prove worthy of the answers." I toss back in response, ignoring her confused sound of frustration.

A second later we enter the pit. She gasps at the sight.

I try to view it through her eyes. The rocky terrain drops to a deep pit. There are wood bridges and ladders to move to different floors. The top stretches out as high as the cracked rock at the highest peak of the mountain, a place unreachable by humans. My ancestors did a good job building it, although the legends say they had help from higher beings. *I'm not sure how much I believe the Arae cared enough to help build this.*

The air whips at us, and Adira takes a few steps back in alarm.

Azurith, my beast, lands beside me with a loud thud. He tucks in his large wings and cranes his neck down to me. I reach up, stroking his fur.

Azurith means unexplored skies. I named him because he was born in the mountain and has yet to taste true freedom.

He notices Adira and growls in defense, taking a step toward her. She hisses, drawing out her dagger.

I turn a glare on her. "Put that away. He won't harm you."

I place a hand on his head. "It's okay, Azurith. She won't hurt you." He senses my calmness and stops growling.

Azurith lets out a booming roar, and all the other Teràstios start flying around. They are intelligent creatures and were hiding until they could assess the threat. That's been their whole life, hiding in this mountain. *Maybe that's why I feel so connected with them. We've lived the same life.*

I guess Azurith isn't too concerned with her.

I glance at her from the corner of my eye. *I'm not so sure though.*

Her eyes are wide as she takes in all the creatures flying rapidly through the large space.

"This is amazing," she whispers to herself. Then, as if remembering her own duty, she straightens and turns to me.

"So, what must I do?" Adira asks me. I stare at her a moment, noting her gloomy expression has mixed with an agitating eagerness.

"You have to bond with one of them."

Her head whips toward me, eyes swirling with an indescribable emotion. "Bond? After everything I've done... how can I be what they need?"

I was thinking the same thing.

"Like I said before. Your questions will be answered if you prove yourself worthy." I remind her with a pointed look. "For now, I'll show you to your room and we can get started tomorrow."

"How can I prove myself worthy? Isn't being the one chosen to fulfill the prophecy enough?" A bite of anger laces her words.

"Just sleep on it, you will know come morning." I can't help the mystery that clouds the words, so I don't bother to wait for a reply. Turning on my heel, I walk to the left.

Reaching a short ladder that hangs from the open entrance above, I climb up. I pause a moment, waiting for her to catch up and lead her to the corridor with rooms. I place her in the room across from mine.

Just in case she gets any ideas, I tell myself. Sure. That's why. It's not like everything that comes from the outside world isn't a temptation, especially one so attractive.

I open the door, waving her in.

She takes in the rounded cave ceiling and the double bed sitting on a wiry frame. A large wooden wardrobe sits in the corner beside an empty desk. It connects to a small bathroom, just big enough for a tub and toilet.

It looks more like a prison cell than a proper room.

I clear my throat. "This is all that duty affords. Comfort is not a priority here."

"It's no problem," she says back easily.

"I've slept in worse situations," Adira admits with a side smile.

Frowning at that, I step back toward the hall.

"Get some sleep," I tell her before shutting the door.

I hear a quiet "thank you" after it closes.

This is going to be harder than I thought.

Chapter 11

Soren

I've only been walking a day when I come across a small village. The bustle of voices reaches my ears before I spot the buzzing crowd. I take in the colorful buildings and streets lined with vendors. The sharp tang of spices flows through the air. My gaze sizes the town up, evaluating any potential threats.

To my left, I notice someone selling stones that have been runed to execute one spell. Beside them, a rotting booth with amulets sits on a blue velvet cloth. The deep stones almost lure people passing by to lean in closer. One patron holds one up, examining it. It spins slowly, the blue stone catching the fading sun, causing it to shine brilliantly. My eyes glaze at the sight, my surroundings fading to background noise. The sound of my thumping heart is all I can hear. A child's shout breaks through the deafening silence. I snap out of it, shaking off the abnormal feeling.

My skin tingles as the remnants of magic leave my senses. I rub my chest. *That will take some getting used to,* I admit to myself warily, glancing around at all the people who can use magic.

Turning my attention back to the road, I almost run into a group of children. They are laughing while they pull a string attached to a small fire dragon. The fire dragon moves back and forth as the children move, like its motion is that of its owner. I watch the faint flicker of magic that accompanies the scene. Awe floods me at the blatant show of power. The shock from the two realms differences diverting my focus. I shake myself out of it, forcing my eyes to scan the location more logically. I take note of all the exits, ready in case things go awry.

Up ahead, I see a large group of people gathered. *I wonder what that's about.*

I get to the group, pushing toward the middle. Spotting a man with light green eyes standing before everyone. He's up on a wooden bench to be seen. A plaque with the name of the town rests behind him. Willowcroft.

"Stregoni," he bellows out. "Listen to me now. King Elijah feasts while the Vormr rots our land. We starve, while he prays for miracles that never come. If you want change—real change—you'll stand with me." He finishes off loudly. A lot of the crowd cheers noisily while others clap with more reserve.

I blink once. *It seems like all kingdoms have their own problems and rebellions.*

Stepping through the dispersing crowd, I find an inn at the end of the road. I approach the dark blue building and step through the door. As soon as I step over the threshold, my eyes fly up to the impossibly tall ceiling. *The building wasn't this tall when I saw it from the outside, I* think with confusion, backing out into the street. When I assess the building anew, it only shows a short blue structure. I walk back in, watching the walls intently. Once I cross through the doorway, the same scene meets my eyes.

Adira was right, they really do use magic for everything here.

A draw of a harp catches my attention, and my gaze wanders to the corner of the main area. I gape as the harp plays itself.

Someone clears their throat behind me, and I turn, realizing I'm standing in front of a sanded wooden counter.

"Do you need a room?" a petite woman asks in a bored tone.

"Yes," I reply, "please."

"That'll be five Ellyr," she says, holding out her hand. I breathe out in relief at the similar currency. Pulling the coins out of my pocket, I hand them over to her. She grabs them and whips around to slip a key off the shelf behind her.

Holding them out to me, she nods to the left. "Here. Go up the stairs and to the right. You'll be the second door on the left."

"Thanks," I mutter, turning toward the stairwell. The chatter from the tavern fades as I climb the steps.

Following her instructions, I get to the room and unlock the door. I step in, taking a cursory glance around the space for any threats. The room looks to have cavern walls with a standard bed in the middle. *The*

Stregoni's powers must be replenished when they stay here, I realize, remembering the power of caves. *Smart.*

I place my pack down on the bed, walking over to the window. I push the shutters open and am met with a wide view of a valley. Plants and flowers bloom everywhere, and I see creatures of different sizes leaping around in the fields. The sight differing from Enelon's dried lands that I usually witness.

I peer down, noticing a bunch of youths standing around in a circle. In the middle sits a bowl of water, a small fire, and a pile of loose terrain. They laugh, each bending down to an element, touching it and creating shapes and creatures with their magic. I watch in amazement as the energy flows from the material element into their will. A hint of wariness accompanies the wonder. *Any of those kids could best me easily with the use of magic.*

I shrug off the discomfort of not being on top of the food chain. *Fear. That's what I'm feeling.*

I head back down the stairs to the tavern and take a seat at a table in the corner, with my back to the wall. The noise from the crowd amping up my unease. My finger taps steadily, the only sign of my nerves. I make myself stop when a server with a sultry expression on her face sways over to me.

"What'll it be?" she asks, her tone too sweet to be casual.

I lean away from her, giving her a tight-lipped smile.

"Some stew and an ale," I state, keeping my tone flat.

She straightens and nods, noting my tone. With a longing look, she turns and walks back to the kitchen.

I breathe out and release the tension I didn't know I was holding. I keep my eyes moving casually over the patrons, wondering what their powers are.

A few moments later, the server saunters back to me with my food and drink. She places them down in front of me and pauses.

"If you change your mind, you know where to find me," she says, pinning me with a sensual look.

"No. I... already belong to someone." Even I hear the yearning in my voice when I say this.

She huffs out her disappointment and leaves my table, sauntering over to a pair of men to try her luck. I settle in while I eat, paying attention to the conversations around me.

"Did you hear what Amod was talking about in the square?" someone whispers to another.

"It's bold of him to talk so openly about dethroning the King," a small voice agrees.

"King Elijah doesn't bother dealing with small villages like ours anyway."

"Still, he's going to bring trouble to the village," the small voice says like they are haunted by a bad omen.

I focus in on another table as the word *'prophecy'* drifts toward me.

"Who do you suppose it's about?" a woman with dark hair whispers to her companion. Other voices drown out the response. All I can hear is 'spreading' and 'weakening their magic'.

The responding gasp echoes over the noisy chatter.

"Oh no. If it reaches the port city, many more villages won't receive food. Is there anything we can do?" she desperately whispers to him.

I lean in closer, catching the man's defeated response.

"The only thing we can do is pray to the goddesses and hope they can fix this."

I lean back in my chair, a sense of despair hanging around like a dark cloud as I hear their words. *Little do they know, the goddesses can't do anything.*

I wince at the pressure Adira must be feeling.

It all falls to her.

Chapter 12

Adira

I'm walking down a dark hallway. The torches flickering against the walls as I move. The space opens up into a forest. I frown in confusion before realizing I must be dreaming.

A fox sits between the trees, staring at me. A strange swirled pattern is shaved onto its back.

I warily gaze back. It looks docile, but the size of it is almost as large as an Umbrai. I look around, confused as to what I'm supposed to do. A dagger lays on the ground next to me. I crouch down to grab it. Once I pick it up, a growl echoes over the terrain. My eyes flick up to the now rabid looking fox.

What happened to it?

It starts rushing me. I panic, not wanting to kill the animal. My hands fly up instinctively, dropping the dagger in the process. I summon up my magic, enforcing a cage around the fox. It slams into the bars, whimpering. I wince at the sound.

"*I'm sorry.*" *I tell it.* With a wave of my hand, I will food into existence. It appears in the makeshift cage. The fox gobbles it up happily.

I sigh peacefully, relieved I didn't have to kill an innocent animal. Even if it was trying to attack me. I settle against a tree while the fox eats, my eyes drifting shut.

I wake, disoriented. Glancing around, everything starts coming back to me.

The Teràstios, they're alive, I think excitedly. My mind swivels back to the dream about the fox. *Strange. It felt so real.*

Swinging my legs over the bed, I grab my leather boots. Just as I finish lacing them up, someone pounds on the door. The stiff frame groans when I shift. Standing, I head over to it.

"Wake up. It's time to start," a deep voice growls.

I fling it open, and Kalon pauses in surprise, like he didn't think I'd be ready to go.

Smirking up at him, I reply, "Lead the way."

He scowls, turning on his heel.

I guess he's not a morning person, I think back to last night when I arrived. *Or... an evening person.*

I stifle a giggle, and he turns a questioning look on me.

I clear my throat and raise my eyebrow in challenge, waiting for him to ask me why I was laughing.

He doesn't say anything as he turns left and passes under a small archway. I step through, glancing around the room. The roof is made of jagged stone that runs down the walls. I almost slip on the slick rock below my feet. I take note of the books on the shelf and the large rectangular wooden table in the center of the room. Long benches line each side of it, spanning nearly the entire length of the space. Toward the back of the room, there are two more archways that lead into dark passages.

Damn, I wonder how big this place is. I open my mouth to ask, but he cuts me off.

"Have a seat," he says gruffly, sliding smoothly onto a large bench. I tentatively take a seat across from him, sinking down onto the chilled wood.

He stares at me a moment then grunts. "You passed the first test, you've proven you can handle the knowledge."

I gape at him. "How do you know that? What was the test?"

His lips twitch. "Did you dream of a fox?"

My eyes widen slightly before I neutralize my expression. "I did. How did you know that?"

He ignores the question, again. "Good. You must've handled the situation correctly."

I run a hand through my hair. "Gods, do you ever speak clearly?"

He shrugs, pulling out a book and dropping it down onto the table with a light thud. I look up at him, meeting brown eyes.

"Do you know the history of the Teràstios?" he interrogates.

"Not much of a morning person, are you?" I mutter to myself.

His eyes narrow, and he leans forward.

"What?" he snaps out.

"Nothing," I reply louder.

He eyes me, waiting for the answer to his question.

I sigh and begin telling him what I know.

"The Teràstios are terrifyingly stunning creatures. They are able to bond with any Stregona, Stregone, or human if they choose to. King Dahak killed most of them a quarter-century ago, before the realms split. Once they were split, both realms still tried to execute them. King Tobias let his subjects hunt them when they would refuse to bond," I relay with a wince. "The realms know them to be extinct."

He nods. "That's right. The Teràstios didn't want to live in constant fear, so they alluded to being dead and went into hiding. Over the last twenty-five years, they have been building back their kind in these mountains. Some have tried to search for the bonding spot but have given up. Some have made it into the cave and perished when faced with the test," he states grimly, his face twisting as if remembering all the bodies being crushed.

Yikes, I would not enjoy cleaning that up, I say to myself, thinking of the dark stone slab.

"And some have heard of the prophecy and thought themselves to be the one it refers too."

I tamp down the guilt that threatens to rise. *It's not my fault they chose to test themselves.*

Kalon's sharp voice interrupts my thoughts.

"Do you know anything about the bonding process?"

"No. King Elijah keeps all the books about traditions locked away in his personal library."

"Typical tyrannical King," Kalon mutters.

I choke on a laugh, covering it up with a cough.

He glances up at me. "Does that offend you?"

I throw my hands up jokingly in defense.

"Hey, I'm with you on this one," I admit.

His brown eyes pierce me, deciding whether I'm lying or not.

A second later, he turns his attention to the book in front of me.

"Read it," he demands. "It will tell you all you need to know about the bonding process."

I arch a brow at his tone but wordlessly take the book. I read a few chapters, feeling his eyes on me while I do. Huffing out a breath, I glance up.

"Are you just going to watch me read?"

"You're taking a long time," he replies. I fight the urge to roll my eyes.

I hold the thick book up. "Look how big this is."

He rolls his eyes, taking the book from me.

"Fine, I'll just tell you what it says."

"That was an option?" I ask him incredulously.

He ignores me and settles onto the bench.

"Bonding begins only when power is whole. For Stregoni, that comes with age. For humans..." he starts.

I interrupt before he can get any further.

"They don't have any powers. How do they bond?"

He shoots me an annoyed look at the interruption.

"That's true. But that means that they are already at their 'full powers.' This makes it easier and harder for them. Easier to be able to bond, but harder to pass the trial to complete the bond."

"Trial. I didn't know there was a trial."

He takes a deep breath in, the frustration evident in the sound.

"Did you think they would just walk up to you and bond?"

I look away, heat flaring in my cheeks.

"Well, maybe." I mumbled, not having thought about it too much.

"Anyway." He begins again with exasperation. "When you enter the bonding trial, you are given no instruction. You must figure out how to pass on your own. Once you are able to, you will be transported back to the bonding ground where the Teràstios will be waiting for you. They watch the entire trial, their decisions coming from what they see. Afterward, one of them may come forward, showing that they choose the bond."

"That sounds easy enough," I answer, though my gut tells me it won't be.

"There have been many that have died in the trial, so no, it's not easy."

I grasp my necklace, Kalon's gaze following my nervous gesture. *Did I really think it would be easy?*

My spine straightens. "You're bonded."

"Your point?" he replies dryly.

"You've been through this. What did you see? What can I expect?" I ask hopefully.

"It is forbidden to share details of the trials. You will learn nothing more from me."

I take a deep breath in, rolling my shoulders. *Naturally, his helpfulness has limitations.*

"Okay, then let's do this."

"You want to do it right now?" Kalon asks speculatively.

"Yes. No time like the present," I respond, pushing up from the bench. *Sitting around isn't going to do anything.*

He shrugs his shoulders and stands from the other side.

"Okay, follow me."

He leads me through one of the doors in the back of the room and down a narrow hall. We climb up two ladders and pass through three rooms before we come to a cavern. A faint scent tickles my nose, the smell of musty terrain. I duck to walk into the new space, noticing its emptiness. I open my mouth to ask, but then I see the mark of the bonded carved into the floor. I step toward it, but he puts out his hand to stop me.

"Once you step on that mark you will be transported into your trial. Unless you complete it, you will be trapped or die. Are you ready?" Kalon asks intently.

"I'm ready," I state, mustering courage into my voice.

"I wish you good luck." He says formally.

I give him a quick nod of thanks.

Walking forward, I take a deep, calming breath. I don't hesitate as I step onto the mark.

Nothing happens.

I turn back to ask Kalon, a confused frown on his face. I move around a bit, walking the entire area of the mark.

Still nothing.

"What's happening? Why didn't it work?" I ask while walking back toward him. Defeat slinks into me. I can imagine my mother's disappointed face clear as day. Reaching up, I grasp my pendant, the only remainder of her.

"I'm not sure," he mutters to himself. The confusion doesn't leave his face as he regards the mark and me. Then, as if he has come to a conclusion, his eyes snap to mine. Incredulity in his expression.

"I know why it didn't work." His voice is full of surety.

"Your full powers aren't unlocked."

Chapter 13

Kalon

Adira's gasp echoes through the chamber.

"What? That's impossible," she insists, the disbelief evident on her face. I raise my eyebrows at her declaration.

"Clearly not."

"I – I would know if I hadn't. I can feel the bottom of my reserve," she replies with furrowed brows, her arms crossing in determination. "It's not true."

I just shake my head.

"It could be hidden within you. It's been known that gods and goddesses have blocked one's powers as a precaution."

"A precaution?" Adira echoes back, her suspicious gaze widening.

"If they came into too much power, or if they were part of a prophecy and needed protection," I tell her with a pointed look.

"That seems too obvious." She mumbles to herself. Then louder, "I've never heard of that, why would I believe you?"

"Just think, if you had your full powers when you were younger, the King would have captured you and possibly killed you."

She swallows noticeably, but I notice her doubt lessen at the logic.

She starts pacing, her expression clearly revealing her exasperation. I let her work through her own thoughts.

Her head snaps toward me.

"How do you know all this?"

I hesitate, wondering how much I want to tell her. Her wide eyes seem to pull the truth from me.

"Before I was born, the Arae appeared for my father. They told him of his duty and of the prophecy that would come to pass. He's been ingraining the information into me that was given to him since I was a child."

"I've been preparing for your arrival since my father passed," I admit, rubbing the ache in my chest at the reminder of him. "I've never even explored the realm or been to a town of people."

I slam my mouth shut, not meaning to share that last bit. Her mouth drops open.

"You've never left the mountain?"

I draw in a ragged breath. "Once. When I was very young. My mother took us to a small village near here, but the Arae were not happy that we left. They appeared to us, angry for breaking their rules, and then snapped their fingers." The grim silence that followed the cold snap of the Arae's fingers still haunts me.

"Just one snap, and my mother disappeared. We never saw her again."

Adira's eyes grow impossibly wide. I cross my arms as if the motion will protect me from the rush of emotions.

"So yes, I've never left since then. I learned to grow my own food, and I've survived just fine here," I press out, not wanting her pity.

"Survived, not lived," she whispers.

I let out a grunt, not responding to that statement, because it's true. *I've never really lived. I've never even overindulged at a tavern, the most fundamental thing a man could do.*

Sure, I've been with women. But all of them were promptly killed by the 'test' that I must dole out. I wince to myself, thinking about that.

"I'm sorry."

My eyes snap up to her. Sympathy lines her face. I force a smile, hating that look.

"Thanks."

Silence stretches around us uncomfortably.

I rub the back of my neck. "As I was saying, I understand more about the prophecy than you may realize."

She gives a shallow nod, her eyes glazing over as if she is back to thinking about my earlier statement.

"I guess you're right, but it just seems unlikely," she argues weakly.

I clear my throat.

"I can help you unlock your full powers."

"You? How?" Adira asks skeptically.

I try not to roll my eyes at her doubtful tone.

"My magic."

"I didn't even know you had powers." She responds, the suspicion clear in her tone.

"The Arae left me with just enough to be able to handle any problems that arise with the Teràstios, which parallels with the prophecy." I take a deep breath, already knowing she'll hate the next part. "I have the ability to draw magic out of another."

She takes a step away. "Like take it from me?"

"Yes, I could," I say bluntly. "But I won't. I can trace your powers down to your reserve and find the block, releasing it."

"And how do I know you won't take my powers?"

"I would never do that, Adira," I tell her plainly. Doubt still covers her face, as if saying *I just met you, why would I believe you?*

She places a hand on her hip, determination etching her features. "What happened to all the people before me? Did they all take the test?"

I whirl back at her unexpected questions.

"Why does that matter right now?"

She cocks her head. "It matters because I won't willingly trust someone who has had a hand in killing a bunch of innocent people."

I swallow against the sting of her words, my head turning away. *Is she right? Am I to blame for all who perished?*

I harden my expression. "I didn't have a choice. My instructions came from the Arae themselves."

She rolls her eyes, but her gaze softens slightly. "Yes, it appears as if we never have a choice."

I note the hint of defeat in her own voice.

"So." She starts. "Are you going to answer the question?"

I clench my fist, letting my nails dig into my palm. I face her head on. "Not all have died during the test. Some have fallen from my sword."

Adira's expression stays perfectly neutral, not giving me any idea to her thoughts.

"And why is that?"

I run a hand through my hair. *Fuck. She's not making this easy for me.*

"Anyone who has entered the mountain knows the Teràstios still live. The Arae gave explicit instructions that no living soul shall leave with that secret. Save for the prophesied one." I gesture to her.

"I see."

I bristle at her flat tone.

"What did you expect? If I disobeyed, the Arae would waste no time in snapping me out of existence."

Her eyes glaze over, like she's stuck in a memory. "And what makes you think your life is better than theirs?"

I look down in shame. "It's not better than anyone else's. But it's also not my life. If it were, I would have chosen a different path, one that didn't result in so many dying. But I swear on Azurith that I won't take what's yours."

Locking eyes with her, I try to silently communicate my sincerity.

Her cheeks flush under my intense gaze. After a moment, she sighs, releasing her tense stance.

"And if you're lying? If this is a trick to strip me bare?" she directs with an apprehensive look.

I grab my dagger, flipping it around. I hand it over to her with the handle up. She takes it slowly.

"What's this for?"

"The process will weaken me, if you notice that I've taken your powers, you can stab me."

Her eyes widen. "What?"

I chuckle at her shock. "I'm not worried, because I'm not going to take your powers."

She nods gingerly, reluctantly agreeing.

"I need to be touching you," I tell her cautiously, while taking a step toward her.

She nods her consent, and I grab her cheeks. Her smooth skin makes my pulse jump, so I focus on her stunning eyes.

"Your eyes..." I clear my throat, shifting my thoughts. "Are steady. Good. Hold onto that."

Her eyes narrow with doubt before she utters a quick, "Thanks."

"This shouldn't hurt," I tell her, closing my eyes.

I pull from my reserve, letting my powers flow down my arms and into Adira. I hear her gasp at the intrusion, but I keep going. I push it down into her power, following the strings of magic to her reserve. I reach the bottom and prod it with my magic. It stiffens, trying to push back at me. I press harder, gritting my teeth at the effort. Our magic entwines while each one fights for the upper hand. They seem to have a mind of their own as they battle each other. While they do, memories are thrust into my mind at an alarming speed.

A woman with green eyes like Adira rushes across a snowy forest. I hear yelling behind her as footsteps crash through the trees. The woman grimaces and holds her hand to her stomach. I look down, seeing her hand pressed under her large, swollen belly. She races toward a cavern and runs through, navigating the pathways with ease. She comes up to a small room and pauses for a second, searching for something. She finds it and leaps through the shimmering air. The magic instantly pushes into her, and she falls in pain. Stuck between the two realms, she swears and turns over. Putting her head down, she whispers to her expanded middle, 'it's time for you to come into the world, my sweet Adira.' The vision fades to another as she starts screaming.

Adira, as a young child, she's on a boat with her mother. Her mother tells her to find her magic to save herself, pushing young Adira into the water. The rock tied to her follows her off the boat, dragging her down to the cold lake floor. Her fear rushes into me as she struggles to hold her breath. She tugs at the rope with no success. Closing her eyes, she looks to be concentrating. She screams out her frustration. Bubbles fly up to the surface. I hear her heartbeat start to slow. The water surrounding her vibrates and her eyes snap open. Water bends around her and pushes her up toward the surface. She breaches the top and guides the water to place her back onto the boat. Her mother smiles at her brightly, 'I knew you could do it.' Adira seethes beside her and doesn't say anything, but a dark thread of betrayal makes its way into her heart.

Adira, in her adolescent years, riding on a horse as black as night, racing through a field. She turns and I see her face filled with panic. A second later, a Neldara jumps through the treeline. Adira cringes at the large, hairless creature with glowing orange eyes. It opens its large mouth and roars, exposing its enormous teeth. She shivers at the sight, pushing her horse faster. It gains on her just as she reaches the shoreline. Her horse jumps into the water just as the Neldara slices its tail toward her, hacking into a tree with its spurred length. The tip of it catches Adira's side and she screams as she falls, landing with a splash in the water. She pushes herself up, holding a hand over the wound, and maneuvers herself painfully back onto the horse. Adira urges the horse deeper into the water, crossing the rough river. Once she's on the other side, she turns to the Neldara. The creature growls at her in anger, unable to pass through the water. Adira wheezes as she turns and leads her horse away from the creature, clutching her side in pain. The sound of galloping thunders in my head, pulling me back.

My mind jolts back into the present, and I notice a crack in her reserve. I force it open and a blast of magic slams into me. I skid backwards, crashing into the hard wall behind me. Pain radiates through my back. I blink my eyes open, and they widen at the sight. Adira hovers in the air with a blue and silvery glow around her. Magic is swirling throughout the small space, she follows it with shocked eyes. Pulses of eather crackle out from her, the air humming with raw energy. My magic strains away in response.

My own power darts into my mind, explaining the feeling that I'm having. *By the gods, she's a semidea.*

Her eyes snap up and lock onto mine. Subconsciously, my body bows down to her.

My action grounds her and she floats down to the floor. The eather recedes, leaving a coppery taste in my mouth.

"What are you doing?" Adira asks confusingly.

"Showing you respect," I admit, lifting my gaze to hers.

"You are no mere Stregona, Adira. You are a semidea—the blood of the gods runs in you."

Chapter 14

Soren

Sun filters through the shutters of the window, waking me. Breathing in the natural air, I push myself off the bed, feeling refreshed. The silence is stifling while I pack up my belongings.

Sighing to myself, I leave the room. *Soon enough I'll be back with Adira.*

The stairs creak as I descend into the main area. There are a few drunks passed out from the night before, but the tavern is otherwise silent. A few patrons watch me leave warily, whispering amongst themselves. I shift uncomfortably, worried the strangers know that I don't belong.

Just before I step through the door, I tip my head toward the lady who checked me in. She waves her hand dismissively without sparing me a glance.

A balmy warmth surrounds me the moment I step outside. My unease dissolves as I put more distance between myself and the Stregoni. The streets are quiet as the sun rises, leaving me alone with my thoughts.

It's not long before Adira's hurt expression flashes into my mind. Grimacing, I tell myself what I wanted to tell her. Imagining her forgiveness.

When I was a younger boy, four winters before my family was killed, I woke in the middle of the night. Something urged me from my room, beckoning me outside. I followed the eerie feeling to the lake near our house.

A pale figure drifted up from the water. I gasped, my blood freezing as I fell straight on my bottom. The being reassured me and a wave of calm energy surrounded me. The chill of the night bit through the new warmth. Smiling down at me, the being told me that there was a prophecy that will be occurring in the near future, and I will play a role in it. The hint of sorrow I saw in his expression was overshadowed by his daunting presence.

He told me his name was Cain Aamon and he was going to help me. The mist from the night swirled through his hazy outline, breaking through the calm that was soothing me.

He lifted his hand up toward me and a beam of light shot out, instilling magic into me. He told me I could now read minds and to be careful. Reciting the prophecy, he told me I mustn't speak to anyone about it.

His smile was mournful, as if he already knew the curse he'd bound me to. He insisted that I could not let this prophecy come true or the cost would be dire. Before he dissipated into the chilly night, Cain placed a spell on me to ensure I couldn't speak any of this.

I breathe out deeply, *if only I could have told Adira all of that.*

Focusing on the treeline ahead, a wet drop hits my arm. The dark clouds above have decided to open. Rain pours down, soaking me in seconds. Lightning strikes in the distance, the sound of thunder rolling closer.

Really? I ask the sky. Shaking my head at my luck, I quicken my pace. Hoping to reach the dense area of the forest faster. My boots suck into the mud, sinking my mood with it.

I stop short, a small creature bounding out in front of me. *What is that? It looks like a giant ball of fur.* It sits on my path, staring up at me with large eyes.

"Well, aren't you a cute thing," I coo warily. Not knowing much about it, I decide it's best to go around.

I start pulling out my sword and its mouth opens, showing sharp, jagged teeth. Freezing in place, I gape at this contradicting creature. I slowly push my sword back into its sheath. The creature closes its mouth and turns docile again. *Well then.*

"I'm just going to go around you," I tell it. "I won't hurt you."

It watches me pass, staring the whole time. Once I walk ten feet forward, it bounces away. *Very strange.*

Turning back to the path, I start forward. *Just a few more days.*

* * * * * * * * * * * * *

The next day, I wake early to the sound of footsteps. My eyes snap open and I reach for my knife. Before I can grasp the handle, a boot steps onto my arm.

100

"Look what we have here, boys. We found a stray," a deep voice taunts. Laughter fills the area.

Lifting my head up, I spot three men. The largest one sneers at me as he presses down on my forearm.

"Shall we have some fun?" he asks his companions. They both nod eagerly in agreement.

He steps back from me, but before I can move, a stream of water appears from the ground. The liquid wraps around my arms, forming restraints. The bite of the cold water waking me fully. Tuning out their laughter, I struggle against the bonds. I look up at my captors, noticing one has a canteen of water hanging around his body, except it's choppily cut in half. One hand is shoved in the water, while the other lets out a stream of eather, binding me.

One of the other men steps forward with a sly grin. Lifting his hand up, a flame appears, dancing over his skin and through his fingers. I jerk back instinctively. Confused, I search for a fire pit but find nothing. Then, I notice a small square metal device in his hand. When he flicks it open, a flame appears.

"I think this one's going to be a fighter," he states excitedly.

"Let me go," I demand.

"Since you asked so nicely," the big one responds sarcastically. The others laugh.

"Why are you doing this?"

The big one shrugs. "Magic is disappearing, might as well have some fun with it while we can."

Horrified by the inhumanity, I shake my head at them, "So this is what you decide to do?"

Fire-hand stalks forward. "Yes. Now quit stalling." He brings the flame close to my face, it crackles loudly, the eather electrifying it. I jerk back and forth, trying to keep distance between us.

He growls in frustration and glances over his shoulder at the big man.

"Hold him still."

The big man grunts, flicking his arm up. The water holding me become solid. Glancing down, I see that ice cuts into my wrists, numbing my skin.

Disbelief courses through me as I figure out what to do. I've never had to face an opponent like this.

Okay, think. The best way to fight magic is with magic. Use your powers, I tell myself somewhat desperately as the flame licks my skin, leaving a trail of burning flesh in its wake.

Hissing at the pain, I close my eyes and focus on the threads around me. Sensing the three men, I pull at the strings with force. They snap toward me, and I hear thuds of their bodies hitting the ground.

Opening my eyes, I gape in horror at the scene in front of me. I didn't just take the intention out of their minds; I ripped out their minds. *By the gods. How could I do that? How did I do that?*

I stumble on my feet, falling to my knees. I notice that my arms aren't straining against the bonds anymore. Clenching my fists, I tear through the ice, shattering it around me.

I stare down at the men in disbelief, waiting for them to start getting up. But they lay strewn across the ground. Dead.

Eerie silence covers the area.

My head spins, my body feeling weaker than it ever has. I sit with my head in my hands, willing my head to stop spiraling the same way my powers are.

I clench my fist, frustrated at my own actions. *I'm no better than they were.*

Reaching into my bag, I shakily take a sip of water. *Gods, I can't tell anyone about this. People have been killed for less. Way less.*

My mind travels back to Adira and her powers. *This is a heavy secret to keep. No wonder she felt so alone.*

Forcing myself up, I push through the unsteadiness of my legs. I snap up my pack and stagger away, putting what just happened behind me.

I think back to Adira's words, once again hoping that she doesn't find me a monster.

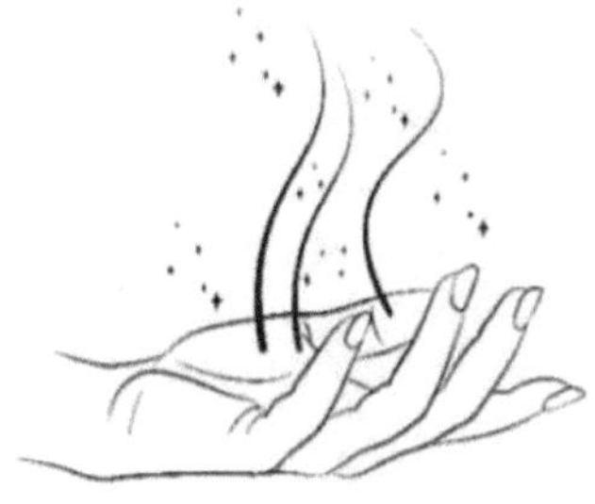

Chapter 15

Adira

I stare at Kalon in shock. *Did he just say what I think he said?*

Gaping at him, I shake my head to myself.

"Get up," I say, discomfort latching on as I look down at him. "I'm not a semidea."

Kalon slowly rises to his feet.

"You are," he states undoubtedly.

My pulse pounds rapidly, roaring in my ears.

"But how is this possible?" I wonder aloud.

Kalon takes a slow step closer, as if approaching a wild horse and not wanting to scare it.

"Who are your parents?" Kalon asks.

"My mother was a Stregona and I never knew my father," I admit.

Could my father have been that powerful?

"The only way a semidea can be born is when a god or goddess procreates with a Stregoni," he reminds me. My nose wrinkles when I think about the secrets my mother kept from me.

No. There's no way my father was a god. I panic to myself.

"Your father must have been or is a god," Kalon voices my internal thoughts.

"But who?"

"There were only three original gods, so it would have to be Conri or Tiamat, since Cain was killed so long ago."

I recoil into myself at the options. *They aren't exactly the best father figures.*

What did you do, mother? I ask upward. My pendant flares slightly, as if she is telling me that it's obvious.

Kalon stays quiet, giving me a moment.

Closing my eyes, I focus inward, delving deep to the bottom of my reserve. My breath hitches as I pass my usual depth, going further than I thought possible. *Holy goddess, this is a lot of power for one person.* I swallow down my unease. *Especially for someone who has killed as much as I have.*

Kalon's voice breaks my thoughts. "This must be why your mother pushed you so hard when you were a child. She knew you'd have immense powers and tried to teach you control early on."

Grabbing my pendant at the reminder of her, I grumble to myself. *First the prophecy and now this.*

Panic grips me, my mind spinning through everything. In hindsight, the signs were there. Having control over four elements. The ability to create portals. *I've always healed faster than most, I just thought it was due to my extra element.*

I sigh heavily, recalling my studies. There wasn't much information about semideas, as they are so rare. My hands shake as I stare down at them. Numbness spreading through me. *How is this possible? And how does Kalon know about my mother?*

Ragged, uneven breaths fill the air. I glance up, shocked to find it coming from me. Pressing a hand on my chest, I will myself to calm down, trying to physically push these overwhelming emotions back into my body.

Breathe in. Breathe out. My inner voice mixes with my mother's. Slowly, my heart returns back to a less frantic pace.

I shake my head. *This doesn't change anything. If anything, it will be easier to fulfill the prophecy.*

See? I tell myself. *I can still see the bright side of a situation.*

I shove the spiraling thoughts out of my head. Squaring my shoulders, I look to Kalon, his expression tentative.

"There is something else."

Dread rises in me, anticipating his next words.

"When our magic intertwined, some of your memories flew into my head."

Um. What?

"If my power is stronger, shouldn't I have seen *your* memories?"

He winces. "Ideally, yes. But your power was driving outward, so the memories must've been shoved to me."

"What memories?" I ask, though I can already guess based on his earlier comment.

"One of you training, one of you fighting a Neldara and the first was the day you were birthed. Your mother was running from something and got stuck between realms. That's when you were born."

I swallow hard. "What was she running from? Which realm was she in?"

"I couldn't tell. I'm sorry, Adira."

I give him a small smile. "It's okay."

So many secrets. She kept so many secrets.

Overwhelmed by everything, I close my eyes and imagine my lockbox of emotions. Shoving them in, I slam the box shut and lock it. *Don't want to panic about those.*

Turning to Kalon, I force a smile on my face, hoping my brain will catch onto my facial expression and calm down.

"Thank you for your help. Truly. Now I should be able to step into the trial." I push confidence into my voice, though the last thing I am eager to do is vault into a trial. My emotions still raw and messy, a feeling I'm unused to.

His brows jump up.

"You want to try again? Right now? You don't want to take some time to think about your newfound powers?"

"The Vormr is spreading. There's no time for me to come to terms with it," I inform, trusting my method of suppressing my feelings. The barren lands flash in my mind, followed by Saline and Atin. *I hope they are okay.* I pray upward, even as anger laces my concern at their lack of trust in me. Guilt quickly overtakes the feeling. Esper's piercing scream and Charcoal's pained whinny ringing through my mind. *I can't wait around for more lives to be lost.*

"Surely you can take a day," Kalon insists, incredulity in his tone.

"No. I want to do it now," I declare, shooting him a thin smile that says, *don't argue with me.*

He stares at me a moment longer, then lets out an exasperated sigh, nodding his head in defeat.

"Okay. Good luck," he tells me, flourishing his hand toward the marking.

Giving him a nod of acknowledgment, I step back toward the engraved ground.

I slowly walk onto the mark, preparing myself for the shift. Once I'm in the center, the chamber fills with a whirlwind of cold air. The ground cracks beneath me, opening.

I fall through.

I try not to scream as I'm dropped down the vertical tunnel of darkness. My stomach flips, gravity dragging me lower. Hearing a trickling sound below, I brace myself. Seconds later, I slam into a pool of water.

Holding my breath, I push upwards, trying to break the surface as my lungs burn. Adrenaline rushes through me at the weight of the water.

A light reflects from above, and I burst through, gasping for breath. With shaking arms, I pull myself onto the muddy edge. Flopping down onto my back, I take a moment to slow my heart rate.

My body tingles with its newfound powers, daring me to test them out. "Not now," I grit out, like my magic could answer me. The energy seems to understand, and my magic settles back into me, although now I feel fuller than I ever have.

Once I'm back in control, I stand, glancing at my surroundings.

I landed in a vast pit with a large shimmering pool of water in the center. Mud spans the ground and walls, making it appear darker than it is. I look up where I fell from, only seeing darkness. *Well, I'm not getting back out that way.*

Spotting a sizeable hole in the wall, I walk toward it. It opens to a straight, narrow tunnel, the walls turning from mud to stone. *Only one way to go.* I keep my senses sharp as I move forward, unsure of what kind of test this will be.

I walk for what feels like hours before I see a thin stream of light ahead. *Finally,* I think to myself, quickening my pace. The light expands when I get closer, revealing an opening shaped like a pentagon.

Stepping through, I pause at the sight. "Oh my goddess," I whisper, awestruck.

There's a narrow beam leading to an enormous silver pendulum. It hangs over a stone altar that has a single candle on it. The pendulum appears to act as a divide, the left side has an expanse of land that is dark and twisted. Thunderstorms roll through the sky as bursts of flames shoot up from the ground aimlessly. Whereas the right side has fields that hold a bright, sunny disposition with a haze of mysticism over it.

Focusing on the thin slab of wood beneath me, I carefully tread forward. My shoes grip the plank, and I make it to the other side without fault. I step onto the solid ground and make my way to the massive instrument. I notice that it's hanging more to the left side.

Favoring the nightmarish lands.

Glancing around, I don't spot anything else. *That must be what I need to do. I have to somehow balance it back.* I peer down at the altar, seeing a phrase carved next to the candle.

Let me guide your way, but be warned as when my heart stops beating, you will no longer be competing.

I ponder the phrase. *So, I light this candle, and I must complete the trial before it's done burning. Easy enough,* I think, staring warily at the short candle.

I summon my magic, and it flies to the surface of my skin easier than before. My body feels electric with energy. *Woah, that will take some getting used to.* I concentrate a flame to my finger. Aiming it toward the candle, I let the energy go. It surges out, blasting the candle. The wick flares to life.

A sense of urgency fills me, and I let out a controlled breath. Turning to my left, I step into the darkened land.

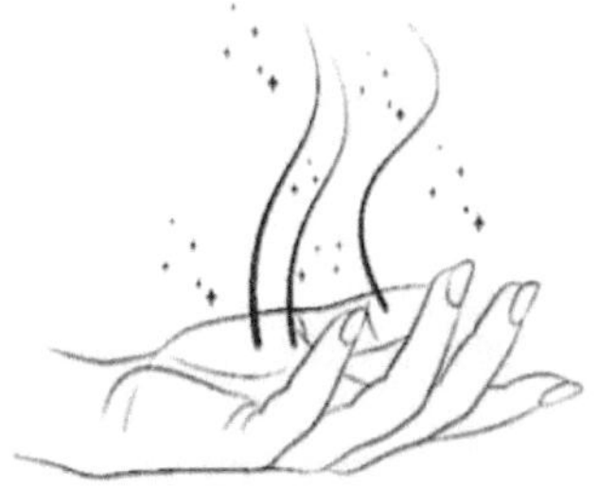

Chapter 16

Adira

Despair fills the air, shadows dancing around the darkened trees. I repress a shiver, hurrying down the rugged path. Gnarled tree branches reach out, obscuring the way. I duck and twist to avoid getting pierced with the pointed edges. Thick smoke curls the ground around my feet, the musty scent wrinkling my nose.

A rustling noise to the right causes me to pause. Damp leaves squish under my feet as I slow. The sound gets louder, like a creature is plowing through the bushes and trees. I unfreeze and run.

Sprinting down the path, I hear a deep growl that reverberates through the forest. The hair on my arms stands up. Its huffs of breath get louder and louder. My heart thrums frantically.

I'm not going to outrun this, I admit to myself. *Time to use that new magic.*

I stop in a clearing and turn around, spotting the beast immediately. Its gigantic body knocks crooked trees down as if they were paper. Deep red fur covers its lithe, muscular body. It moves closer, its bright yellow eyes holding an almost feline quality to them.

Closing my eyes, I summon up my power. It flares up quickly, threads appearing to me. I mentally poke at one, and it vibrates, showing me what I can do. I try a few others, the warm energy filling me up as I hastily explore. My eyes widen at all the possibilities, and I pull at one. The beast freezes twenty feet in front of me. The trees behind it snapping in half. I frown at the slip of control, used to having a stronger grip on my powers.

Focusing on the thread again, I will the beast to disappear. My magic pulses once, as if in warning.

The beast emits a low rumble, shaking against my restraints. I pull at the string, and the beast dissipates, a curl of smoke replacing where the creature just stood. I gape at the now empty clearing in front of me. My powers vibrate within me, a sharp pinching following the sensation. I clutch my stomach, unused to the feeling.

One pull, and it was gone. Too simple. Too dangerous. Horror replaces the pain in my gut.

I stare down at my hands, trying to comprehend the new power I possess. *What was it warning me about?* My mind curls in on itself, trying to discern the answers. But my magic doesn't respond to my question, just caresses me for my actions.

A sliver of fear trickles into me from the unknown of it. *This must be how Poderosa felt.* I close my eyes against the wave of emotion that accompanies her name. *I miss her so much.* I try not to dwell on those feelings because I know she is where she's meant to be. Even if I may never see her again.

Slowly, I keep moving down the hazy pathway. I push my spiraling thoughts out of my head when I think of the candle. I quicken my pace, letting the damp smell of the forest ground me. Once I reach the end of the path, a temple stands before me. The exterior looking to have stood for centuries with no care. The rocky walls crumble into themselves and green plants fill the cracks, growing out and falling toward the earth. *The beast didn't kill me, but a deteriorating building will,* I tell myself uneasily.

I carefully step inside and find that it looks pristine. As if an old magic has preserved the sanctuary. Pausing my steps, I faintly hear unsettling whispers in the stone. The noise accompanies a faint divine energy, I tense, hand flying to my dagger to calm my nerves. Spotting two doors at the back of the room, I choose the one on the right. I walk towards it, staying alert, in case any other foul creatures ventured in.

I step through the white marble archway, scanning the room. Rose-colored furniture fills the space. A few paintings adorn the pale cream walls. I do a quick walk-through to make sure I don't miss anything, but it is completely dull.

I retreat back to the main chamber to try the other door. The hair on my neck stands to attention, I'm unable to shake off the sensation of eyes watching me. Covering the distance to the second doorway, I step into the new room. My attention goes to the dark, ash-colored walls, deepening the glow of the room. A lone item sits in the middle of the space.

A large selenite crystal.

The only thing shining bright in the darkness. I cautiously walk toward the crystal. It hums as I get closer. I do a slow circle around it, trying to find any hint of what I am supposed to do. When I find nothing, the dread inside me increases, realizing there is only one plausible option to figuring it out. I take a deep breath, steeling my nerves.

Here goes nothing, I think, reaching out and touching it. It melts to the floor in a silvery heap, changing its matter to a honey texture. Before I have time to react, it traps my legs, hardening. It continues to climb up my body and I struggle in a panic. *What is going on? This is going to suffocate me.*

Alarm swells as it reaches my head. I take one more deep breath before the crystal covers me fully.

Feeling smothered, I notice that I can still breathe. *Strange.* I focus on slowing my heart rate down. Something taps against my mind's shield. I hesitate, lowering them slowly. An unknown power thrusts into my mind, delving deep into my memories. I fight the urge to struggle and try to submit to the trial.

Images flash through my mind, showing me at my worst moments. Showing me how many beings I've killed, and the lack of remorse or mercy shown. I wince, shame pulsing through me.

Then, my worst memory, my biggest regret starts to play back to me. I recoil on instinct, knowing what's coming. The feelings I felt that day rush back to me.

My initial upset and frustration toward my mother for putting me through yet another form of perverse teaching.

The sharp sting of the dagger cutting through me, made even sharper by my mother's hand.

My anger rising up, overtaking me in a way I'd never felt before.

Blood splattering against the leaves.

The shock on my mother's face when my powers unconsciously thrust those weapons back at her.

The thump of her body falling onto the autumn ground as blood pooled from her.

My hands, bloodied, trying to staunch the bleeding.

The light dimming in her eyes, blurred by my tears.

The numbness I felt as I used my magic, the magic that killed her, to aid in her burial.

Anguish threatens to drown me, but sanity leaks through. *What is the point of this? How will making me relive my awful memories balance back the pendulum from the darkness? It makes no sense.*

My mind is trapped on the image of younger me holding my mother's blood-soaked body. I resist, trying to close my eyes, but they remain wide open. *What am I supposed to see here?* I try to process it logically, glancing around the scene. Nausea is a constant friend as I stay trapped in the memory.

An idea enters my mind. *Maybe I need to clear these dark thoughts. These memories may be the same amount of twisted darkness that's causing the imbalance. But how do I do it?*

My mother's voice enters my head, *facing your problems is a one-way street, you have to venture down it to reach where you wish to go.*

I wince at the twisted irony of my mother being the one to help me move on from what I did to her.

Taking a deep breath, I force myself to relive all those memories again. The box of emotions I keep buried cracks open, remorse leaking through. I focus on what I was feeling at the time. Telling myself that, *it's not okay to kill, but I did what I thought had to be done. Forgive yourself,* I whisper. *The only thing you can do now is try and be better going forward. The dark parts of yourself are what got you here today.*

Willing myself to believe those words, a tension I didn't know I was carrying disappears. Promising myself and all the higher beings that I would be wiser and more rational. The box I carry feels lighter, no longer brimming with unresolved emotions.

I hear a distant crack, and the pressure of the crystal eases off. I crumble to the ground, surrendering to the shadows.

****

When I come to, the crystal is once again solid in front of me. Each breath I take is lighter. I pace away from it, exiting the dim room. My legs shake slightly from the whole ordeal. The whispers buzzing through the walls seem more calming now. The pounding in my chest lessens with each step I take further from the crystal. I look within myself, noting the shame is still present but greatly lessened. Gripping my necklace, I can almost imagine my mother whispering her words of forgiveness to me. My own mirrored back.

Remembering the candle, I rush back the way I came, running down the path while keeping my magic out and ready.

The twisted landscape blurs by me as I sprint down the same path. Shots of fire shoot up around the terrain, fortunately far enough away that I don't need to worry about getting blasted. I hang on to the lightness in my chest, unused to the sensation.

I see the pendulum ahead but can't tell if it's centered. Bolting forward, I halt in front of the altar. A breath of relief escapes me. *Thank goddess, it's centered.* Glancing down at the candle, I notice it's still burning, close to the stub, but still burning. *And thank goddess for that.*

Reaching out, I place my hand on the altar under the pendulum. I'm yanked forward, the world spinning as my body is thrust forward at the speed of light. My feet slam to solid ground, I swallow down bile, noting that I'd been transported back to the bonding grounds. Shaking off the dizziness, I lift my head up, seeing a circle of Teràstios staring back at me. Their sharp eyes holding an intense look. I freeze and lower toward the ground, granting them a clumsy curtsy. Fear that I failed the test and will fail the realms clings onto me. *What if they still don't find me worthy? Surely there are others more suited to bond, people that haven't taken as many lives as I have.*

A motion to my left causes my head to snap up. One of the creatures stalks forward. Its body smaller than the rest. Holding my breath, I wait to see what it will do.

I hold in my gasp as it lowers its head toward me, bending into a slight bow. It walks forward slowly, and I instinctively extend my hand. Its beaked face nuzzles my open palm. A sense of euphoria and relief fills me at the touch. I let out a laugh of astonishment, noticing a mark on my forearm. A pair of wings and a heart stare back at me. *I did it, this is the mark of the bond,* I wonder giddily.

The other Teràstios back away, breaking the circle. The pressure eases off as they turn their focus away from me. Kalon walks through, coming up to me.

"The mark has chosen you. Few survive. Fewer are worthy." he spouts off wisely. Then, his face twists into a grin. "Congratulations."

Grinning back, I respond happily, "Thanks."

"Now, we train."

Chapter 17

Kalon

Pausing, I glance back at Adira.

"Do you need a minute? After the trial?"

She nods her head sideways, her brown hair twisting with the motion. I watch her face for any signs of distress, but all I find is determination.

"Okay. Follow me," I tell her, turning toward one of the training grounds.

My mind flashes back to my trial and the horrors the crystal made me face. *That's something I do not want to relive.* Suppressing a shiver, I focus on my steps.

Taking a sharp right, I lead us up two sets of ladders. I walk through the muddy archway, and the room reveals a substantial area with a wide floor. One side of the space is open to the center of the mountain, making it easier for the Teràstios to fly up. The pungent moss assaults my senses, wafting in from the less used tunnels. The echo of wings gets louder as we reach the end of the path.

When we enter the area, the Teràstios that bonded with Adira flies up and lands on the ground with a light thud.

She breaks out into a wide smile, the sight distracting me momentarily. I clear my throat to rid myself of any reckless thoughts.

Adira turns at the sound.

"First step is opening your mind so that you are able to communicate with your bonded."

Excitement takes over her expression. "I'll be able to talk to her?"

My lips curl up at her enthusiasm.

"Yes. You will be able to."

"Can we start now?" she begs.

I smile fully at that. "Yes, we can."

"There is an area in your mind where your connection stems from. You will need to delve into your mind and find it. Then, you just open it," I explain.

My tone turns warning. "When you open the connection, there is a sharp ringing noise for a moment, but it doesn't last very long,"

Adira immediately closes her eyes, a concentrated look on her face. A few minutes pass, and she groans in frustration.

Her striking eyes snap open, latching onto mine.

"Where is it?" she half-demands.

I huff out an amused laugh.

"Did you think it would be that easy? It's in a different spot in each person, so I won't be able to help you."

"What do you mean?"

"Every bond begins as a hidden thread, buried in silence. You must listen, not search, until it answers you."

She grumbles something under her breath and plops down on the ground, closing her eyes once more. I slide down the wall, sitting on the floor across from her. Azurith flies up and lightly lands on the ground. The loose stones trembling from the motion. Walking toward me, he sits down, placing his head in my lap. I stroke his fur while we wait for Adira.

I watch her as she silently battles with herself. Her brows furrow in concentration. Her beauty brightens the cave. *Does it go deeper than that? Or am I just lonely and noticing how attractive she is?*

I sigh, telling myself to keep this new infatuation under wraps.

Around dinnertime, I go and grab two portions of stew. The aroma catches a light breeze, wafting toward Adira. Her eyes open, annoyed at the interruption. She reluctantly eats it before promptly getting back to work. The rest of the evening passes without change. Just before I'm going to call it a night, Adira's face scrunches up in pain before letting out a shout of joy.

"I did it!" she exclaims. Her energy flows around her in her excitement, lighting up the dim cave.

She stops her movements, looking around in shock.

"Did I do that?"

I nod. "With your newly found powers, you will need to learn control all over again."

She tucks a piece of hair behind her ear. "Of course."

My lips twitch up at her embarrassment. Her bonded shuffles its feet, drawing Adira's attention.

"Great job," I tell her earnestly. My thoughts jump to compare our differences. It took me two full days to find the connection with Azurith. I can't help but be impressed with her.

"Now what?" she asks eagerly.

I chuckle lightly at her.

"Now, we sleep," I voice.

She looks around the dim cavern, as if she can see through the walls into the approaching night. Cold air streams through the tunnels.

"Has it been a full day?" she asks, biting her lip. I sensed the change in the air as soon as the sun went down, but I have a bit more practice at discerning night and day, having been stuck in this mountain all my life.

My chest tugs at the bleak thought.

"Yes. Night has settled. Tomorrow, the skies will test you in ways the crystal never could."

She stares at me for a moment.

"What?" I shift uncomfortably.

"I can't get a read on you." She admits. "Some moments, you appear normal. Other times you slip into the use of strange phrasing."

My cheeks heat, I turn away to hide my embarrassment.

"I haven't had much contact with people. I only go off of what I have read and been told. Therefore, my words sometimes come out more elaborate than I realize."

"That makes sense." I sense the quiet pity in her tone.

I ignore her, saying goodbye to Azurith.

"What's her name?" I ask, nodding my head at the creature.

She presses a hand into the Teràstios' fur. "It's Lyra."

"Beautiful name."

"She was named by her elders. Lyra means 'lyre' which is a musical instrument that the goddesses were rumored to have used. Apparently, she was always crooning when she was young. The elders thought she was trying to sing."

A low chuckle escapes me. "I remember hearing a warbled sound coming through the walls when I was a child. I thought it was two stones rubbing together."

Lyra snaps her beak at me. Adira laughs.

She grows silent as she bids her beast goodnight.

We both head out the doors, silently walking to our respective rooms. Her long hair swishes behind her, swaying elegantly with each step. The gracefulness of her walk similar to how a princess would carry herself.

When we reach the hallway outside of our doors, I stop her with a light touch. The torch in the hall flickers over her face, highlighting her luminous eyes.

"You did good today," I declare with a gravelly voice. I cough to clear my throat.

Her cheeks redden slightly. "Thank you."

"Anytime, princess," I reply with a smirk. The nickname slipping out.

She freezes, and a flash of hurt crosses her face.

"Don't call me that," she tells me coldly.

Confusion fills me with the quick change of mood.

"I'm sorry," I say slowly.

She gives me a tight smile.

"It's fine," she says quietly, turning away.

"Night," she mutters.

"Goodnight, Adira," I reply, feeling somewhat dejected. *I wonder what that was about.*

Chapter 18

Soren

After a few more days on the road, I realize that this journey might not be too bad. *I shouldn't have said that.*

A group of ten men jump out of the bushes, landing on the path in front and behind me. Pulling out my sword, I turn in a slow circle to assess. *I'm not liking these odds*, I think bitterly. I notice their Enid emblem and can't help thinking that they are far from Enelon.

I start lifting my sword up when an arrow flies through the air, striking the ground beside me. *Make that eleven men.*

"Drop the sword. You're coming with us," one of them demands. I try to hide the surprise that fills me. *Why don't they want to kill me?*

Slowly, I lower my weapon, lifting my hands up in defeat. The men behind me snap forward, grabbing my wrists and tying them together with a worn rope. Gritting my teeth, I have to physically stop myself from retaliating, my body not used to submitting.

They lead me to the left, dragging me deeper into the bushes. We come upon a dense area of the forest, and they part some vines to reveal a ladder. My eyes snap up, and I see tons of wood slabs above me.

We climb the ladder. Well, I wiggle up the ladder, trying not to fall backwards. The smell of sap grows as we pass each rung.

Once we reach the top, my mouth gapes at the sight. I slam it shut and take in everything. *It's like a whole new world up here,* I contemplate with fascination.

The wood floor spans as far as the eye can see, making a new ground fifty feet above the earth's surface. My head spins slightly from the dizzying height. Houses disperse the area in a sporadic pattern. The part in front of me forms a long lane with a few vendors lining each side of the wide path.

Someone pushes me forward from behind. I turn my head at the last second, and my cheek slams into the ground. Laughter rings around me.

"Enough." A deep voice cuts through the laughter. "Take him to Sterling."

Rough hands jerk me to my feet, tugging me forward. Eyes follow us while we walk through the whispering crowd. Wood creaks below our feet as we travel over the thick boards. They take me to the end of the long street, stopping before a huge building. Without pause, they pull me in.

The smell of pine hits me first when we enter. Glancing around, I notice an oversized seat in the middle of the main area with two small statues resting at its feet. Three doorways are scattered around the room. Two long tables line the sides of the space, creating a narrow pathway to the chair. A man with deep red hair sits lazily on the makeshift throne, the seat made of gnarled wood. He smugly peers down at me. *This must be Sterling.*

"What do we have here?" he jeers.

I don't say anything. I just hold my head high in defiance. *Probably not my best idea,* I think as the pommel of a sword strikes me on the back of the neck. Hiding my wince, I don't break Sterling's stare. Sneering at my bravado, he turns away.

"Take him to the interrogation room," he demands.

Confusion flits through me. *What am I doing here?*

"Yes, sir," one of the men holding me replies, forcefully directing me to the exit on the right.

The door opens to a short hallway lined with multiple doorways. The guard moves to one of the doors on the left and swings it open. He roughly jerks me forward, and I stumble. Quickly righting myself, I look around the small room. A worn chair sits in the center with chains coming up from the floor, strewn against the rotting wooden ground. A dark substance stains the floor surrounding the chair, my gut churns at the sight. *It doesn't take a genius to figure out what that is.*

The guard shoves me onto the chair, his companion holding a sword to my neck as they strap me in with the cold chains. They wordlessly leave, and minutes turn to hours while I wait, my body stiffening in the hard chair. I shift to get some feeling back, the chains rattling when I move.

The sound of footsteps causes me to straighten. *It's about time*, I think sarcastically. The lock clicks open, the noise echoing through the room. A large man strolls in, carrying a bag. It clangs with each step.

"Hello, Soren."

Hiding my shock at my name, I respond with a flat tone, "Who are you?"

"The name's Erve. And we are going to have so much fun." His face stretches into a smug smile as he reaches into the bag, pulling out different devices.

I sigh at the display.

"And do I get to know why you are torturing me?"

He eyes me distrustfully. Holding his stare, I smirk slightly.

Scoffing, he says, "You have information we need."

"How am I to give you this information if you won't tell me what you need from me?"

"What do you know of the prophecy?"

My eyes widen before I swiftly school my features. Apparently not fast enough, as a manic grin takes over his expression.

"Good. This won't be a waste of time."

"I know nothing about a prophecy."

"You will," he tells me confidently. "A few days with me and you'll be singing the answers."

I just give him a bored look, conveying that I'm not worried.

He ignores the look and examines his devices, humming to himself as he picks up a sharp silver one, considering it. The muffled cries from other rooms adding to his twisted display.

"Perfect," Erve mutters to himself.

Turning to me, he walks forward, crouching down so he's eye level.

"Ready to talk, pretty boy?"

I spit in his direction. "Do your worst. Pain and I are old friends."

He smiles widely, almost like he wanted me to refuse.

Erve levels the device with my chest. Pulling it down sharply, he cuts my shirt open. Eyeing my exposed chest, he places the sharp end against my sternum. He presses down, slicing through my skin. An intense burning follows the motion. I grit my teeth, keeping silent. His eyes flicker with annoyance before he applies more pressure.

Blood trickles down my chest, soaking into my pants. I breathe heavily against the pain, refusing to black out. My gaze locks on the flickering torchlight, using it as a distraction. He sighs like he's disappointed and stands back up, swapping out the sharp tool for a different one.

The sound of dripping startles me. I look around for the source, realizing its dribbling steadily from a pool of blood on my chair.

This time he grasps my hand, placing the circle clamp device over my finger. I tense with apprehension. He smirks at the movement.

"How about a different question..." his eyes spark eagerly. "Where's the girl?"

Shock momentarily drowns out the noise of the room. My ears ring like they are full of cotton.

I look him in the eye and sneer, "You'll bleed me dry before I give you her name. And even then, you'll still know nothing."

How do they know all of this? I thought the prophecy was more protected than this.

Erve just shrugs at my response, pressing down on the clamp. My bone shatters, and a scream rips through me. A sick excitement flares in his eyes at the sound.

Dark edges creep into my vision as I breathe through the pain.

"How do you know so much anyway?" I ask Erve, knowing I won't get a response. He gets up, placing the tool back in his bag of torment. He slowly paces across the room, determining what to say. The motion makes my head spin. *Or the blood loss.*

He surprises me by answering.

"Every prophecy has cracks. And cracks have a way of talking." he cryptically says.

Who is feeding them information? Do they have a spy? Or are they working with someone powerful?

The thoughts are swirling around in my mind as the pain finally drags me to unconsciousness.

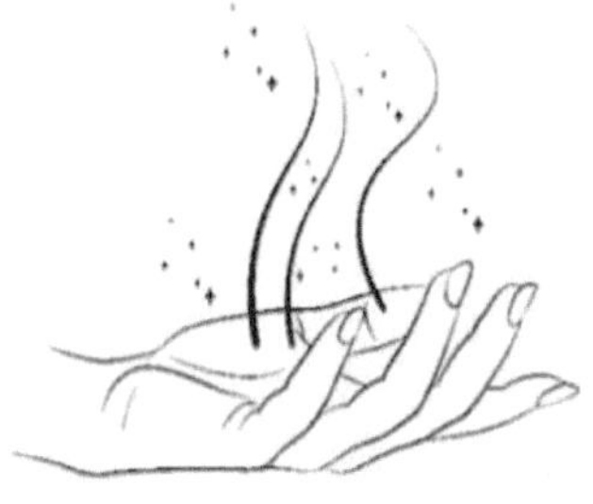

Chapter 19

Adira

I gasp awake, blinking away the skeletons that still plague me. My nights are now filled with a mixture of all the darkest times in my life.

I squeeze my eyes shut. *And there have been a lot.*

My mind swirls with every wretched thought that refuses to leave. *I have so many horrors replaying in my mind that my nightmare doesn't know which one to grasp.* I huff a bitter laugh at that depressing reflection.

Throwing the thin blanket aside, I swing my legs over the bed, sitting there for a moment. Peeling off my sweat-soaked clothes, I swap them for fresh ones.

A knock sounds on my door. I go to answer it, and Kalon stands there with an unsure smile on his face.

Thinking back to last night, I internally wince at my reaction when he called me *princess*. I just couldn't help but think of Soren when he said it. The feeling of betrayal came flooding back.

His voice rises unbidden. *You have to come back, Adira. Not for this mission-for me.*

I scoff to myself.

Lies. All lies. I wonder if he's starting his new life somewhere.

I rotate my neck, shaking off the lingering bitterness as much as I can.

At least today I can distract myself.

I give him a smile and say, "What's the plan for today?"

"Today, we fly," he tells me with a hint of excitement in his voice.

Nervousness and eagerness fill me at the prospect. I choose to focus on the latter.

"Great. Let's go then."

A small chuckle escapes him. "First, breakfast."

My stomach lets out a low rumble at the words. "Right, okay," I respond, turning toward the breakfast room.

****

As we eat in comfortable silence, an apology slips out of me.

"I'm sorry about yesterday," I blurt out.

He stiffens slightly at the reminder of it.

"No worries," Kalon says easily.

"I didn't mean to snap at you. But someone from my past, my recent past, who betrayed me... he used to call me that."

Understanding dawns on his face.

"I was just caught off guard when you said that," I explain further.

"Thanks for telling me," he says gruffly.

"This man..." he continues, "he's gone from your life?"

My chest tightens painfully when I reply.

"Yes. He's in Enelon."

"Well, he won't find you here," Kalon affirms.

"I'm not worried about that," I tell him bitterly, thinking about Soren's plan to kill King Dahak. "He won't be in Modereo or trying to find me anytime soon."

Before Kalon can ask why, I shoot to my feet.

"I'm ready. Let's go fly." I muster more enthusiasm into my voice, pushing Soren to the back of my mind.

He wordlessly stands up, and I go to follow him. Instead of going to the training ground, he goes the opposite way, and we end up on the outside of the other side of the mountain. Brisk air wraps around me as I stare out at the tips of the other surrounding mountains. A forest looms below, its lush greenery swaying with the breeze.

The beat of wings sounds in the distance, getting louder. Seconds later, the Teràstios fly upward, hurtling toward the sky. They fly in a large circle before two detach, gliding down to us.

"How do you keep them a secret if they fly out here?" I wonder aloud.

Kalon winces. "They don't get to do it often. If they see someone, they ensure that they don't leave with that knowledge."

I read between the lines. "They kill them?"

He nods in confirmation. "They have to. It's imperative that they remain a secret."

I turn away, staring down at the forest below. Wondering how many innocents have lost their lives just for walking by.

Lyra and Azurith gently land on the even ground. Lyra traipses over to me, and my hand stretches out instinctively. She nuzzles her large head against my palm. A sense of contentment and fullness surges up, my earlier worries dissipating. Her voice fills my head, *I've missed you, little one.*

I've missed you too, I respond back to her in my mind. The novelty of this form of communication thrilling to me.

Silence descends as I stroke her head. A happy sigh escapes me.

Kalon's voice shatters the silence.

"First thing I'm going to do is show you how to mount," he tells me.

I hide my scoff. *How hard could it be?*

Several attempts later, I land back on the hard ground with a thud. Rubbing my backside, I glare up at Kalon, who is trying to hide his laughter.

Ignoring him, I stand up and get back into my position. Standing at Lyra's side, she tells me that I can do it. I grasp my pendant, pushing down my mother's disapproving voice.

Easy for you to say. You just get to stand there. She snaps her mouth at me playfully.

I start bending my knees and launch upward, rounding my leg over her back as I'm in the air. Landing with a jarring thump, I squeeze my knees quickly, trying to keep my hold on her so I don't slide off... again.

Hold it. You can do it, little one.

I don't answer her, focusing instead on staying upright. Leaning forward, I grab her neck for extra support. Once I feel steady, I let myself celebrate. A smile spreads across my face.

"I actually did it... I'm really on her!"

Clapping comes from my left. I turn at the sound, finding Kalon smiling at me.

"Good job, Adira." His voice takes on a huskier tone, my cheeks heat. The reaction followed by the cutting pain of shame.

I turn my head out toward the view to hide my body's response.

"Now we can fly."

My stomach drops as I glance over the ledge. The hard ground suddenly doesn't seem so bad.

"What happens if I fall?" I ask aloud.

"The first rule of flight? Don't let go." he deadpans back.

"Great advice," I say weakly.

If you fall, I will catch you. The words float through my head, calming me slightly.

Thanks, Lyra. Let's do this then.

Lyra struts over to the edge, and I center my attention on my grip, ensuring I'm secure.

Ready? she asks, standing at the edge.

Ready, I confirm, even as unsteadiness fills me.

The world tilts when she leans forward. We nosedive down the cliff at a rapid pace.

A scream gets caught in the wind, my stomach flipping. My body is rigid as I tighten my hold on Lyra. In my mind, I shout to her.

We couldn't have started with an easier takeoff?

Her amused voice responds. *No. We don't have much time for you to learn slowly. Also, you're strong enough to handle this.*

Just before I respond, Lyra's wings snap open. We jerk into a gliding position. I fly out of my seat at the change of momentum.

A scream rips from my throat, getting lost in the wind. For a moment, I'm weightless. Then, gravity takes hold.

I start plummeting low, the trees rushing closer.

All I hear is Lyra's amused laugh.

Is she going to let me die? Was this some sick joke?

My body crashes into something. I reach out, grasping onto anything I can get my hands onto.

Don't you remember the first rule?

I choke out a disbelieving laugh. *I can't believe I'm alive.*

I told you I wouldn't let you fall. She huffs in annoyance.

I shift my position, getting back to a more secure place. *Yes, well, it's easier to say that and harder to live it.*

Breathing heavily, I look around, feeling steady enough to explore the environment around me. We fly above the treeline. Clouds surround us, dispersing like smoke as we pass through. The wind whips my hair back, and I feel lighter than I ever have. A giddy laugh flows from me at the sensation. The feeling of true freedom.

This is amazing, I tell Lyra. *Thank you for choosing me.*

I knew we were meant to bond the moment I saw you, Adira. We will do wonderful things together.

We loop back around, landing softly on the ground. My stiff thighs threaten to loosen, so I quickly turn to Kalon.

"How am I supposed to get off?"

"Twist your leg over her body and slide down the side of her. You need to do it in one quick motion or else you'll fall."

"I'm almost certain I will fall right now," I admit. "My legs are so stiff that I can barely feel them."

He walks closer to Lyra's side.

"I'll help you. Just try it first."

I painfully loosen my hold on Lyra's body. Twisting my hips, I swing my aching leg over her back. It cramps up just as it's half over, and I start to slide sideways at the imbalance. My pulse spikes, but firm hands slow my descent. My weak legs give out, and Kalon's arms wrap around my waist, holding me up.

Gulping, I glance up and meet his intense gaze.

"Thanks for catching me," I breathe out quietly.

"Anytime," he responds back in a low voice. The heat in his gaze pulls my thoughts to the prophecy. *Could he be the one closest to my heart?*

My legs feel steadier, so I draw away from him slowly. Guilt threatens to overtake me as new emotions flutter.

No, my heart screams at me. *That would be impossible when all of my thoughts are consumed by Soren.*

Ignoring the tension, I ask, "What's next?"

"Next you will need to learn to stay on Lyra in different conditions. In different weather and when she needs to fly sideways to avoid something. The next part will be tough."

I nod my head in understanding, having already lived some of it.

As if he can read my thoughts he gestures toward the open air. "You caught a glimpse of that with the gravitational shift. You'll have to learn to hang on in those instances."

"Right. I'm sure I'll do better with practice. I was just caught off guard." I protest, unused to being lousy at things.

He notes my defensive tone. "Don't worry. It's not something you can learn right away."

I dip my head in acquiescence.

"Let's go eat," Kalon says.

My stomach grumbles in response. Before we leave, I turn back to Lyra. *Thank you for today. I will see you tomorrow.*

Anytime, little one. Get some rest.

Her soothing voice stays with me the rest of the evening. I fall asleep with a strange feeling of hope in my chest.

Chapter 20

Soren

Iwake in pain. Blinking my eyes open, I scan the room, disoriented. A figure to my right rises at my movement.

"Look who's finally awake."

Erve. That's his name.

I smile sardonically at my torturer. "I was hoping my day would be ruined by your face."

His upper lip curls in disdain.

"Since you won't supply the information, I'm going to be more specific. Sterling wants some answers, so you are going to give them to me."

My lips curve up. "Oh no. Am I getting you in trouble with your leader?"

Pulling back a fist, he clocks me in the skull. My head whips to the side from the impact, the front legs of the chair lifting off the ground for a moment before slamming back down. A ringing fills my head. Breathing deeply, the tone fades.

"We'll start simple. Where is the girl?"

"I don't know." I lie.

"Hm. You don't know." He repeats back to me. "Then tell me, why are you in Modereo?"

"I am here under the service of King Dahak. I'm only given names to do my job."

"Sure you are," he states with a knowing wink. "Is the name... Adira?"

I blink once, shock flaring through me. He notices the look on my face.

"Ho-how..." I cut myself off at his eager expression.

A snort escapes him. "Don't insult me. Why else would Dahak's blade be here, bleeding in Modereo if not for the prophecy?"

Inside my mind is spinning, but outside, I give him nothing.

He scoffs walking over to the tools and choosing a jagged dagger. *This is going to hurt*, I remark, eyeing the uneven edge.

Erve brings the dagger to my thigh, dragging it across lightly as he asks me once again where Adira is. My flesh rises with awareness.

Knowing what's already coming, I spit at him. An angry expression overtakes his face as he presses the dagger into my leg. My skin rips painfully and a stream of blood follows it. The room spins, dizziness threatening to knock me down. I bite my tongue to hold in my scream, breathing as deep as I can through my nose. The scent of iron swells the room, the burning fading to an ache.

The day passes quickly; he tries every tool in his bag. The guttering torches my only way of discerning the time passed. I let myself fall numb with the pain and blood loss.

A growl of frustration rouses me from my oblivion. I painfully lift my head, watching Erve stuff his tools into his bag. I shift my hands, the sticky blood on the chains rubbing against my skin.

He sees me up and sneers, "You will wish you had broken with me, boy."

I ignore the warning tone, losing myself once again to the blackness of agony.

****

When I wake, I'm unable to breathe. My eyes flash open, seeing a slim woman standing in front of me, holding her hand out in my direction. Shock flares in me when I realize she is wielding the air. The torches flicker as the air thins with each pulse of eather.

Once she sees me conscious, the pressure around my throat is released. The flames sputter, but roar back to life.

"I'm so glad you didn't break with Erve. It's been far too long since we've had such an interesting visitor here." The woman smiles wickedly at me.

I glare at her and spit back, "An air wielder. How surprising for the rebellion that hates magic wielders."

She just tilts her head and smiles again, the look laced with dark promise.

"This is so much bigger than you know," she states with conviction.

I just sigh to myself, mentally preparing for more pain. *Of course there's more. Nothing is ever easy.*

"My name is Daleka, in case you were wondering. So impolite of you not to ask," she purrs to me, trailing closer, her dark hair swirling as if caught in a tunnel of wind.

"You have my deepest apologies," I reply sarcastically. "I don't usually make an effort to get to know my torturers."

Daleka clucks her tongue. Her amber eyes are steely.

"Torturers. Such an ugly word. I prefer *revealer.* Since I will be revealing everything I wish to know."

"*You* wish to know?"

She waves a hand dismissively.

"Me, the Divinità, we all have the same end goal."

"And that is?"

Her head turns sharply toward me. She leans forward, dragging a manicured nail under my chin.

"I know what you are doing. Fortunately for you, I was going to tell you all of this already. Think of it as... an incentive. I will tell you what I know and hopefully that will nudge you to inform me as well."

I fight the urge to scoff. *Doubtful.*

Her hand trails along my throat delicately, then she grasps it, cutting off some of my air.

"We never know how important air is until it's gone. Do we?" she hums to me. I focus on breathing through my nose, a thin string of air getting past her grip. She opens her mouth to speak, her hold loosening slightly with the motion.

"The girl walks the path too quickly. If the next gate opens, the Divinità loses everything. That, we cannot allow." My eyes widen. *The next gate... does she mean a portal? Has Adira already completed most of the prophecy? I shake myself out of those thoughts. No, impossible, it's only been a short time.*

"This will not happen of course. The Divinità will ensure that the end does not come to light."

My mind races as I think about who this person could be. Clearly someone with a higher plan. I think back to the cave of Orlo and the way Adira retreated into herself when she processed the information. *Maybe she learnt more about the deities. Perhaps she has already completed the second part of the prophecy.*

My eyes flash to hers, my mouth opening before I can stop it.

"The Arae chose her for a reason, she will succeed."

She tightens her hold on me, her eyes flashing dangerously. "She will *not*. We have plans upon plans to stop her."

Fear trickles in. Not for myself, but for Adira.

Daleka releases me abruptly.

"I tire of this. Tell me what I need to know."

My features harden.

"I will sooner die than aid you in hurting her, Daleka."

She gives me a thin smile. "So be it."

The air starts to get thinner as she backs out of the door. My lungs expand with pressure when I can't fill them.

Daleka stops at the door and says, "One night of this and you'll be begging me to stop. Willing to tell me anything I want. I can't wait," she finishes off excitedly, slamming the door shut.

Forcing myself to stay calm, I focus on my breathing. My chest tightens from the lack of oxygen, and my head feels light. Only minutes in and I would do anything to be able to take a full breath again.

Just before I'm about to fade off, my breathing changes automatically, startling me back awake. This happens at least three times. *Will I make it to the morning?* I consider bitterly.

The doorknob wiggles. My head snaps up from the sound. *Is it the morning already?*

It slowly creaks open, and someone dressed in all black slips in. My sword hangs from their grip. They turn to me, seeing me awake.

"Good. You're awake. That will make it easier."

"What easier?" I stammer out weakly. *Easier to kill me?*

He frowns, seeming to notice the air in the room. With a wave of his hand, it returns to normal.

Gasping, my body adjusts from the rush of air.

He stands there watching me struggle before saying, "Well, come on. We need to go."

He waves a hand again, and the chains snap open, noisily falling to the floor. My body freezes, waiting for shouting to follow the sound. When it stays silent, I turn my attention back to him, eyeing him warily.

"Why are you helping me?"

His dark eyebrows raise at that.

"Would you rather stay here?"

"No," I mutter.

"Okay then. Let us go," he says dramatically, motioning toward the door. Only a dim hall remains behind him, no sign of waiting guards.

It is better than staying here, I reason with myself. *Plus, it's easier to elude one person than it is hundreds.* The Enid houses flash into my mind.

I force myself to my feet, following him out the door. My head spins before the rush of adrenaline chases it away.

He stops every so often, listening for noise. I stumble along behind him, making my footsteps as silent as I can. My limbs are heavy with disuse, the remainder of pain lingering with each step. Blood drips down my leg, soaking my tattered clothes.

We reach a long hallway. As we come to the end, we race down the steps. A single door sits at the bottom. My mysterious savior pushes through the door, leading us deeper into the forest. My tired brain tries to logically think about what I'm blindly doing. *Is he just leading me to inflict more torture? Why am I following?*

My ragged breaths echo through the quiet forest. I ignore the sound, turning my focus on staying conscious. *First, stay conscious, second, worry about the peculiar man and his unknown plans with me.*

We walk for miles before he stops, slinking through an entrance in a broad tree. I heave a sigh of relief when we slow, finally making it to our destination.

I didn't even see that, I regard the tree with shock, pausing briefly to take it in.

Cautiously, I follow him through. The trunk is hollowed out to a large room. Small lights litter the walls of the space, illuminating a small bed and wooden table. Strange symbols mark the surrounding wood. A thin counter sits along one of the walls, lined with fruits and different jars housing an unearthly glow.

I notice him watching me, and I turn.

"Time to tell me who you are," I say gruffly. I try to push as much strength into my voice as I can, even though I can barely stay upright.

"I'm Eiran," he replies easily, handing me my sword, seeming unworried to be giving me a weapon.

For the first time, I take in his dusty brown hair and deep-set golden eyes. *I've never seen eyes that color before.*

Frustration fills me with his response. My grip tightens on my pommel.

"Okay, Eiran. Why did you help me?"

"For the sake of Adira," he states, his voice deep as though it holds an old wisdom.

My chest jumps at her name.

"You know Adira?" I ask somewhat desperately.

"Yes. I do. But she does not know me," Eiran tells me ominously.

"How?"

"This world is not mine, though hers is mine to watch. She walks blind, and I... I was sent to keep her alive long enough to see. I am her guardian."

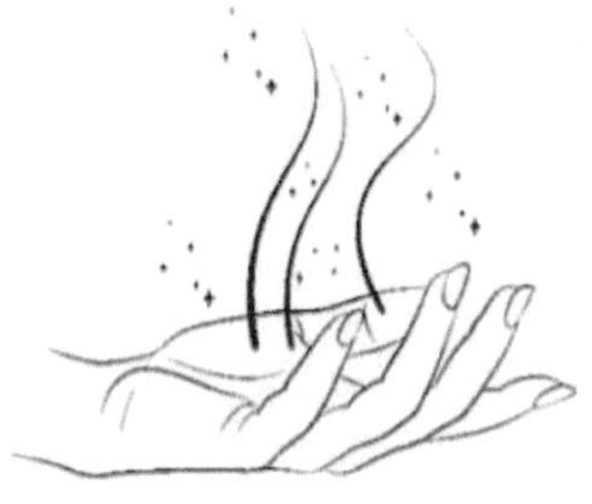

Chapter 21

Adira

I blink my eyes open, hopeful and sore. For once, my troubled dreams did not pull me from sleep. Swinging my legs over the bed, I wince against the stiffness. *Totally worth it.* I say to myself, reliving the freedom of flying through the air.

Heading toward the tiny bathroom, I get ready for the day. Yesterday, I wore a loose shirt, and it whipped in the wind. So today, I pull on my tight-fitting black clothes.

Striding to the door, I pull it open and pause in the hallway, wondering if Kalon is already up. *Oh well, I'll just meet him in the breakfast room.*

I stroll through the passageways, taking new twists and turns to explore the place. The rich scent of coffee reaches my nose. I breathe in happily, letting it sharpen my senses. When I get to the room, Kalon is already sitting down.

"Morning," he says.

"Good morning."

"How did you sleep?"

"I slept well, thanks."

Kalon tosses me a charming smile and my stomach flutters slightly. Guilt follows the sensation. *You have nothing to feel guilty for. Soren betrayed you. Leave him in the past.*

I give him a tentative smile back and his features soften. We hold each other's gaze for a moment before he breaks the silence.

"Are you ready for today?"

I steel my spine. "Absolutely."

We finish our breakfast before heading over to the training grounds. Lyra and Azurith wait for us. The fresh wind from the mountains caresses my skin. I breathe in the scent of pine, intent on today being a good day.

"Get on," Kalon instructs, mounting Azurith. He looks formidable on his Teràstios, the muscles in his legs flexing impressively.

My surprised gaze travels to his face.

"You're coming with us?"

"Someone has to show you how to do it. It would be a bit difficult on the ground," he states with a playful wink.

"I guess that's true," I answer with an amused tone.

I walk toward my Teràstios. "Do you patrol the area before flying? To try and avoid the unnecessary loss of life?" I try not to sound judgmental as I question his methods from yesterday. He looks sheepish before answering.

"There's a magical barrier to conceal the area. It's still dangerous though."

I peer down at the dark forest below, an incessant thrum of anxiety rolling over me. "How far does the barrier go?"

He winces, apologetic. "I don't know exactly. The Arae created it, so its magic is almost impossible to detect. This is so that Stregoni can't sense it and investigate, but that also means there's the danger of flying straight through it."

"That makes sense." I admit begrudgingly.

I scale Lyra, straddling her body. My muscles shake slightly, but I stay on with no problem. *Very good,* Lyra's voice praises.

Grinning to myself, I respond, *it's getting so much easier.*

Are you ready for some fun today?

Let's do it, I tell her excitedly.

We walk to the edge of the cliff and my eyes find Kalon's.

"I'll show you the first move and you can copy it," he says before pausing. "Well, you can try."

I roll my eyes. *Cocky male.* I give him a short nod of acknowledgment, and he takes off. I watch as they swiftly fly through the air, turning two times before looping back to us.

They land softly beside us.

"Try that first and we will move onto hard inclines and declines."

"Okay." We move forward to the edge, my stomach dips with nervous excitement. I recall the freedom of flying and my nerves dissipate, leaving behind only anticipation.

Hang on tight, little one.

I brace myself as she leaps from the cliff. Picking up speed, I try to focus on our surroundings. Wind whips past me, making my eyes water.

Now, Lyra's voice tells me.

The world tips, the force of the air pressure keeping me on her back. Gravity tugs at me, trying to force me in the opposite direction. I gasp in a breath, the pressure on my ribs overwhelming. My fingers are clenched tightly as we rotate again. The wind stings my face painfully, but I manage to hang on. We glide back toward the training ground and Kalon claps loudly. The pressure lessens then disappears when we soar down, gravity now satisfied with where I am.

"Great job, Adira!"

"Thanks." I beam at him.

"The next one is a bit harder," he tells me. "You'll dive straight down and shift, flying straight up. As you fly up, you'll feel like you're twice as heavy due to gravity working against you. I passed out the first time I tried this one and Azurith had to catch me."

"So, focus on not passing out. Got it." I sense Lyra's amusement and determination at my words.

I won't let you fall, little one.

Thanks, Lyra. I respond, more willing to believe her after yesterday.

Kalon leaps onto Azurith and they take off, dropping down toward the forest floor rapidly. Just before they run into the trees, they sharply level out before shifting upward. Zooming past us, they disappear into the clouds. Shielding my eyes from the sun, I scan the sky. I spot something dark move to the left and they come gliding out of the clouds.

Landing beside us, Kalon smoothly jumps off Azurith.

"Okay, that was pretty cool," I admit. He just smirks at me.

"Your turn."

Taking a deep breath, I push my nerves down. We slowly walk to the edge and peek over. The height is dizzying. Lyra lets herself fall forward without warning. Tucking her wings in, we shoot down toward the ground. My stomach flips in protest at the unnatural speed.

Holy goddess, this feels wild. Lyra's voice laughs in response.

The ground races toward us, my pulse beating faster in response. A sharp sting cuts across my cheek, the trickle of liquid announcing to me that the biting wind broke skin. Just before I'm about to question Lyra, her wings snap open, catching the wind. My body jerks at the change of trajectory when we switch directions. My grasp tense, fighting to hold on with everything I have.

Now we go upward, she reminds me. She shifts up, my butt slamming back down onto her back.

An intense sting hits me just as I'm about to respond.

Little one! Lyra shouts frantically.

Looking down in confusion, I find an arrow protruding from my side. Shouts come from below, I follow the noise seeing men in green holding crossbows. Anger rises swiftly. Lyra turns away quickly.

Hang on, she urges me.

Gritting my teeth against the pain, she shoots upward. She frantically lands back on the cliff and Kalon races over.

"Shit, what happened?" he asks.

"It's not too bad," I tell him, slowly sliding from Lyra. My legs threaten to give out on me when I hit the ground, but Kalon keeps me upright.

"Let's go," he says, leading me into the mountain. "Stay hidden," he tosses back to the Teràstios.

Don't die on me, little one.

I won't die, I tell her, internally rolling my eyes. *I've had worse wounds.*

There's poison in the arrow.

Cursing to myself, I turn to Kalon. "There's poison in the arrow." I think of Charcoal, the pain matching what he would've felt.

"Fuck," he mutters. Shock fills me.

"I've never heard you swear, and you've sworn twice in the past minute." I tease him weakly. "One might think you were worried." I can hear the rawness of my voice, revealing how vulnerable I feel.

"Of course I'm worried." He mutters, leading me through a small archway. Each step I take shifts the burning sensation to a cool numb.

That's not good. I tell myself, trying to look down at the wound, but my head lolls to the side. I let it hang there, too exhausted to drag it upright. My eyes scan the room we ended up in. The faint scent of herbs tickling my senses awake.

A rigid bed sits in the center, shelves surround the walls, lined with supplies. A wooden table sits off to the side, an open book and burnt candle atop it, the only signs of life in this dull space. Kalon helps me to the bed, and I lay back. A weak cough escapes me, the sound wet, the bitter taste of copper lingering. Kalon's face pales.

He rushes to the wall, grabbing some white cloth and looking over at all the vials.

"Where is it? Where is it?" He repeats to himself frantically. I watch him panic, searching the rows of liquids. A shudder of agony grips me, I squeeze my eyes shut. When I reopen them, three figures span through the room, all looking around. I blink in confusion, staring between the three of them, but they all have the same short black hair.

My head spins. I focus on my breathing, aware of my hallucinations but not able to do anything about them.

"Found it." Kalon's voice is triumphant. My eyes flutter open, finding myself surrounded by even more Kalon's. I gawk between the five of them, unsure who the real one is. My eyes zero in on the one reaching out to my side.

Gripping the shaft of the arrow, he looks at me, his expression serious.

"Ready?" he asks. I nod back, my head moving imperceptibly.

"Just get it over with." I croak out.

He pulls the arrow out swiftly, the numb relief I felt disappears, replaced by excruciating fire. I bite my tongue, cutting off my scream. My mouth fills with copper. He twists open the vial and drips a few drops into the wound. Steam hisses out. My back arches involuntarily as my skin boils. This time, a scream escapes me.

My fingers start tingling, signaling the return of my magic. But it doesn't stop coming. My powers burst out of me sporadically. Flinging across the room. Kalon shelters himself against my accidental attack.

As the antidote burns through me, I begin to control my powers. My body seizes uncontrollably as I fight to remain conscious. I gasp through the pain, the scorching agony fading to a dull ache.

"What is that?" I finally manage to choke out.

Kalon stalks closer, relief evident on his face.

"Jewelweed extract. It counteracts poison." he informs me, wrapping the injury.

I stare at him in shock. "How do you know that?"

He shrugs sheepishly. "There's not much to do when you are in hiding. Books offer an escape as well as new knowledge. They kept me from going crazy."

I smile at his candor, mentally agreeing with him.

"Thanks," I mutter to Kalon.

Then, a panicked thought enters my head. "The attack was from Enid. They saw Lyra."

"We had to risk flying out in the open. We must've gone outside of the magical concealment though." His jaw clenches. "I'll take care of it." My gut churns at the unspoken words. He tears his gaze away.

My eyes droop heavily from the loss of blood. I feel Kalon brushing my hair back, muttering comforting words. Feeling safe, I let myself drift off to sleep.

Chapter 22

Soren

"Her guardian?" I echo back to Eiran.

"We are beings sent from the Arae to ensure prophesied beings are watched over. Although limited in how we can interfere, we help as much as we can."

Anger rises in me.

"So you watched while she bled and called it destiny?" I ask crossly.

Eiran shakes his head, guessing where my thoughts had gone.

"Sadly, I was unable to interject when her mother did those things. Those moments have helped shape who she is today," Eiran tries to reason.

I scoff, turning my head away in disgust.

"No one deserves that torture, especially someone that young."

Eiran sighs.

"Yes, well, we cannot go back and change the past. We can only look to the future."

I ignore his words, even though they make sense.

"What exactly can a guardian do?" I inquire, curiosity getting the better of me.

"Since guardians are not from this world, we possess a different magic—a magic that can counter powerful attacks. In a way, we are more powerful than any of the Stregoni here. But we are unable to do anything that is not related to the individual we are tasked to guard. This puts limitations on us."

"What have you done to help her?" I ask, trying to keep the judgment out of my tone.

He sighs like I'm disappointing him.

"You are asking the wrong questions."

Internally, I roll my eyes.

"And what are the right questions?"

Raising an eyebrow, he says, "I cannot tell you that."

"Of course you can't," I mutter to myself.

Louder, I ask, "What can you do to help her now?"

Eiran shallowly dips his head.

"Better. Right now, I am sending you to her."

"That's it? That's all you're going to tell me?" Disbelief colors my tone.

"Have you ever dealt with a higher being before, boy? You must read between the lines," he says, exasperated, leaning back into his wooden chair.

"Why must there always be riddles?" I counter.

"To defy the Arae would be a dire mistake. Therefore, we are bound from sharing certain knowledge."

"Now, we don't have time to dawdle. We must get you to Adira." He emphasizes the *you*, giving me a pointed look.

I sigh to myself. "This is one of those read-between-the-lines moments, isn't it?"

He hums but doesn't say anything. My mind is as exhausted as my body, so I don't even try to interpret his hidden meaning.

Bustling around the room, he grabs supplies, shoving them into a backpack. He passes over some strips of linen and I wrap my wounds. A hiss escapes me as I tighten the bandage, a wave of dizziness overcoming me. I grab the table, steadying myself. Once I feel sturdier, I settle back into the chair. Eiran just tuts like I'm an annoyance and goes over to the wall of mystery liquids. He hands me the backpack along with a small vial of dark blue liquid.

I eye it distrustfully, not taking the vial. "What is that?"

He sighs like my questions irritate him. "It will speed up your healing process."

"And I'm supposed to just trust you?"

He smacks the side of my head. "Boy. With everything I just said, what would killing you do?"

Shoving the vial in my hand, he turns away, muttering to himself.

I scrutinize the swirling liquid. *Trusting strange men in trees wasn't on my to-do list today... but dying here sounds worse.* I reason as I lift it to my mouth, shooting it back. I gag slightly, not having prepared for the earthy taste.

He observes my reaction, rolling his eyes.

"A little warning would have been nice."

"Did you expect it to taste like candy?"

I just shrug, ignoring the tinge of embarrassment at his words, because I am the King's number one assassin and couldn't school my features.

He motions for me to stand before ushering me out of the tree opening. I lift myself up, surprised at the ease. My wounds now ache with a low thrum of pain instead of a steady, sharp sting.

"What was that stuff?"

"Something you cannot find in this realm, so never you mind. You need to get going."

I huff out my irritation.

"You aren't coming?" I ask, looking at his empty hands.

"I will come for part of the journey. Then I must leave you."

Of course.

He gestures to the bag. "Your pack contains provisions and fresh clothes."

"Okay," I sigh out. "Thank you for your help."

"Come on, Soren. We are only a day and a half away from her."

My heart races at the thought of seeing Adira again. Focusing on the forest around me, I follow Eiran into the bush. I let the familiar scent of dew wash over me, calming my senses.

Soon, princess. I'll see you soon.

* * * * * * * * * * * * * *

Night begins to fall when Eiran abruptly stops.

"This is as far as I take you."

I glance around at the greenery, not noticing anything out of the ordinary.

Shrugging to myself, I stick out my hand. He shakes it.

"Thank you again," I tell him, wishing I could ask him more questions but knowing it would give me no new answers.

He nods his head in acknowledgment.

"That path to the left," he starts, pointing to it. "It is a faster way to the top. You should get there around mid-day. I will tell you to remember *alterum dimidium*, but that is all I can do. I wish you good fortune, Soren."

"I appreciate it. But can you tell me what the term is for?" I respond, not recognizing the words.

He turns to go but stops, spinning back.

Staring me in the eye, he says, "I cannot. You will know when to use it. But know this—you *must* help Adira fulfill this prophecy."

I shiver at the intense look in his eyes but nod at him.

"I will."

Without another word, he slinks back into the forest.

Turning toward the path, I start my ascent.

I try to contemplate his parting words, but my mind keeps slipping back to Adira. Wondering what she will think when she sees me. *Will she be angry? Will she send me away? Will she stab me?*

I wince at that last thought, hoping it hasn't come to that—to the point of no forgiveness.

The steep incline is grueling. My breathing comes in short huffs, my heart rate following its quick tempo.

Before I know it, I've reached the peak. I scan the open area.

It's empty. There is nothing here.

Heaving a sigh, I start slowly scanning the area, studying all the surfaces.

The sun dips lower in the sky, casting an eerie glow.

Leaning against a large rock, I tilt my head to the left, looking out over the alluring landscape. Hours have passed, and night starts descending on the area. A faint whisper drifts to my ears. My hand flashes to my dagger as I listen closer.

I follow the sound to the right, keeping my steps quiet. The whispering cuts off. I frown, straightening, scouring the area slowly.

A quick flash of silver catches my attention. I rush toward it and notice a faded symbol in the rock—two wings and a heart.

This must be it. But how do I get in?

Eiran's face flashes into my mind.

I chuckle to myself. *Of course.*

"*Alterum dimidium,*" I speak aloud.

A thud echoes. The ground trembles slightly. One of the massive stones slides sideways, revealing an entrance.

Cautiously, I step into the dark tunnel. A sliver of light appears in the distance.

Walking forward, I almost reach it when a sharp sound cuts through the air—the sound of metal sliding against a sheath.

My hand flies to my sword, but not quick enough.

I pause just as a blade is leveled at my throat.

The man holding the blade steps into the light.

"Who are you?" he demands.

Before I can respond, a gasp echoes through the chamber.

"Soren?"

My heart stops at the voice. My name is a disbelieving whisper from her lips.

"Adira?"

My chest tightens, heart beating faster. *I can't believe I actually found her.*

The sword falls away. I take an unconscious step forward. The man turns to Adira.

"You know him?"

"Yes, I do, Kalon." She pats his arm reassuringly.

I scowl at their closeness, but my scowl fades as I lock eyes with Adira. For a heartbeat, neither of us moves. Then her name slips out—half prayer, half apology.

"We need to talk."

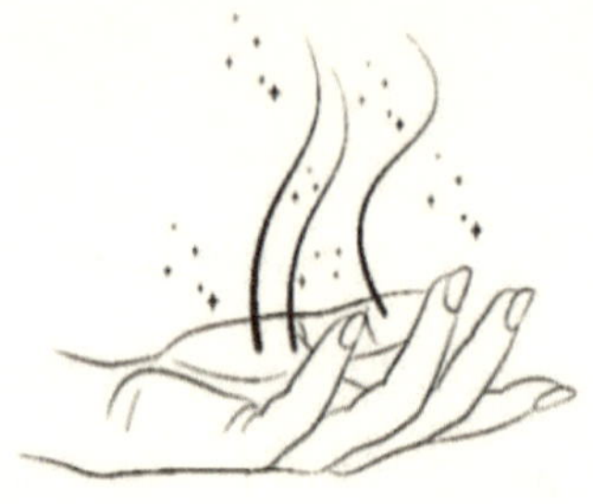

Chapter 23

Adira

Oh my goddess. He's really here. I never thought I'd see him again.

My hearts beating faster than normal. My fist connects before I think. The jolt sends pain through my side, but it's nothing compared to the ache that's been there since he left. He grimaces, stumbling back a few steps. I wince, my hand automatically going to my side to stop the sting.

"I deserve that," Soren admits with wide eyes. "But gods, you've gotten stronger."

"You deserve more than that." I respond flatly, ignoring the stronger part. *Unlocking my reserve must've increased some of my other abilities.*

His stare drops down to my side, and his expression hardens.

"What happened? Did this guy do something to you?" he asks harshly, shooting a glare at Kalon.

Kalon lets out a scoff. Before he can retort, I cut him off.

"No. Enid soldiers managed to shoot me with a poisoned arrow yesterday. Kalon saved me," I tell Soren, raising an eyebrow.

He takes a hesitant step forward and stops, like he's holding himself back from physically checking the wound with his own eyes.

"As long as you're okay."

A flash of pain shoots through me at his concern, followed by a rise of anger.

How dare he show up here, acting concerned after everything?

I cross my arms, avoiding the instinct to punch him again.

Kalon catches the look, taking a step forward.

"Is this the guy that betrayed you?"

Soren scowls at the question.

"Yes," I admit.

"Say the word, and he's gone." He offers.

The scowl on Soren's face deepens, looking between the two of us. Heaving a sigh, I relent, "No. We need to talk."

There's obviously a good reason he came all the way here. Damn logic.

I uncross my arms, forcing some of the tension from my stance. Kalon still stands rigidly beside me, prepared to attack.

I grab his arm and slowly lower it. He sighs, sheathing his sword.

I give Kalon a reassuring smile and hear Soren snarl. I turn toward him, his jaw flexing as he glares at Kalon. For a heartbeat, the air feels charged—not with danger, but something unspoken.

"Let's go," I say to Soren. Twisting on my heel, I lead him through the array of tunnels to the dining room. Once I'm facing away from them, I let out a shaky breath.

As we walk, I sneak another look at him, using my hair as a curtain. He looks tired, but still unfairly handsome. My heart skips, I turn my attention back to the path, ignoring my body's deceit. I tuck a piece of loose hair behind my ear, my trembling hands betraying my nerves.

We enter the room. The scent from our morning coffee still wafting through the air. My stride doesn't break as I head over to the table.

Sitting on the bench, Soren takes the seat across from me. Kalon slowly lowers down beside me. Soren tracks the movement with a hard expression.

My hands twist in my lap. I plant them on the table to still them.

So many questions swirl around in my mind. Logic curls around my heart, offering a barrier for my emotions.

"Why are you here? How did you find me?" I ask with a flat tone.

"It's a long story," he starts.

"I'm here to help you. I found you with the help of Claude and someone else," he says cryptically.

I can't stop a small smile at the thought of Claude.

"You went to see Claude? When? I was there about a week ago."

He turns his face away, but I catch a glimpse of sorrow that flashes across it. My blood freezes.

"Tell me," I demand hoarsely.

His gaze finds mine as he hesitates. I hold my unyielding expression even though I'm already breaking on the inside, knowing what he's about to say.

"He told me where you had gone before letting me stay the night. That same night, his house was attacked by four Enid soldiers. I managed to kill three of them before the fourth sliced through Claude's neck. I tried to save him, but the wound was too deep. I'm sorry, Adira. He's gone," he tells me regretfully, his eyes shooting up to mine with a contrite expression.

My heart twists painfully, shock numbing my senses. I dimly hear Kalon asking me if I'm okay, but it doesn't break through the cotton in my ears.

"No," I stammer out. "He can't be gone."

Soren's hand begins reaching my way. I wait for his comfort, unsure whether I will accept it or not. He seems to sense that, curling his hand back into a fist as he withdraws.

"His last words to me were to keep you safe."

A choked sob escapes me. The air feels too heavy, pressing down on my chest. I quickly stand and flee the room.

Running up to the more secluded training ground, I call to Lyra. Seconds later, she lands next to me.

What is wrong, little one?

My friend, who I thought of like a father, was murdered.

I am sorry to hear that.

It just hurts so much. My sobs echo through the chamber. Loneliness claws at my chest. *He was all I had left.*

I know it doesn't feel like it, but the hurt is good. The ache you feel is proof you still belong to the living. Those without pain forget how to be whole. That's when beings turn into twisted monsters, when there is no thread of emotion tying them to humanity.

I know it's a part of life. But in moments like this, I understand why some beings turn corrupt and heartless. To be able to avoid this pain… let's just say I can understand.

My breath stutters, each one I take laced with sharp agony. I can't seem to get enough oxygen.

Lyra snaps her beak angrily.

No. You cannot say things like that. You are too powerful and important to even talk about losing yourself to your emotions.

The world would not survive it, she ends off quietly.

Anger rises up, pressing through the grief.

Well, fuck the world! I never asked for any of this. Why must it all fall to me?

I know it is not fair. But that is what the Arae have chosen. You must be strong enough to endure what is to come. That means you will lose more of who you care for.

I let my head drop.

It's too much.

"I know, princess."

My head snaps up at the soft voice. *Did I say that out loud?*

I will leave you. You are in good hands, Lyra states, flying away.

My eyes track to the left. Soren watches her go, a wary look on his face, mixed with a flash of... fear? I remember his childhood stories and how they made the Teràstios appear as if they were monsters. I guess his apprehension is valid.

Huffing to myself, I turn my body slightly toward Soren. *Good hands? Right.*

He slowly drops down beside me.

"I am so sorry, Adira. I know how much he meant to you."

My heart cracks again, more of me bleeding out. I squeeze my eyes shut, but all I see are his wise gray ones.

My lids snap open, locking on Soren's troubled expression.

"I want to see," I tell him. Resolve rolling through me as I wipe my tears away.

"You don't want to. Trust me."

"Trust you?" I huff bitterly.

A flash of pain crosses his face, but he quickly schools his features.

"I've never given someone memories before. I'm not sure how to," he admits, grabbing the back of his neck.

"Just focus on the memory, then pull from your power to create a bubble. Surround that memory and fire it down a thread of energy to me."

He nods slowly. "Are you sure you want to see?"

I remember all those times Claude and I sat by the fire, talking well into the night. Playing the card game Cross. Shaking his head at me as I beat him, again and again. *I need to see how it happened. I need to see who was responsible for ending his life.*

"Yes."

Soren nods at whatever he finds on my face. He closes his eyes in concentration. A few minutes go by before he figures out how to do it. Another wave of grief rolls through me, I try not to succumb to it. Then, I feel a thread of power poking at my barrier. I let it fall, and his memory spills into me.

My eyes fall closed as it plays through. Feeling a tear drip down my cheek, I wipe it away. My chest tightens with emotion. *I'll never see him again.*

Opening my eyes, I look at Soren, concern evident in his expression.

"Thank you for showing me. And thank you for trying to save him." My voice breaks from the weight of the words.

He grunts out, "It wasn't enough to save him."

"I could feel your guilt in the memory," I mutter out weakly. "It really wasn't your fault. As much as I would like to blame you."

His jaw ticks as he breaks eye contact, turning away from me.

"Believe me or don't. But you don't have to carry that around with you." I shrug, too heavy to care what he chooses. The silence stretches, during it, I focus on locking down my emotions.

"That's not the entire reason I feel guilty," Soren admits softly.

I still, preparing myself for a terrible confession. I turn toward him, and he holds my gaze. I swallow sharply, reminding myself not to fall victim to his alluring eyes.

"I kept thinking about how lucky I was that I got to Claude before Enid did. Because if I didn't, I wouldn't have been able to find you."

My heart jumps at the admission, his eyes revealing his remorse.

Stupid, treacherous heart.

"I truly did come to help you, Adira. With whatever you need."

I force a scoff. "How will I know you won't just betray me again?"

He stops for a moment, before twisting fully to face me. We lock eyes.

I tear my gaze away from his. His stare is heavy with promise and hope. Two things I don't trust anymore.

"I can take a blood oath."

A gasp escapes me, and my head whips back to him. He nods his head as if confirming with himself that it's a good idea. I gape at the sincerity in his expression.

"But you—you were just freed from one. Why would you willingly take another?" I stammer out, confused.

He leans forward and takes my trembling hands. I let him, the shock distracting me.

"I don't deserve to swear it, but if it keeps you alive—I'll bind myself anyway," Soren vows.

I shake my head, trying to clear the swirling thoughts.

Why would he offer this? Betray me just to sign over his free will? It doesn't make any sense.

My mother's hard voice flies through my head, *if an opportunity arises for help, use it. Just make sure you cannot be hurt in the process, always protect yourself first.*

Despite the fact that I don't fully agree with her words, they do make a bit of sense.

Nodding my head, I whip out my dagger. I regard him slowly, my eyes swollen from crying. His earnest expression never changes.

"Okay then. You can swear a blood oath."

Soren pulls up his sleeve and grabs the dagger.

"I promise to protect you, Adira Selcouth, and aid you in fulfilling the prophecy. I will serve you willingly, until death takes me." he swears, his blue eyes searing into me. An emotion twinges deep inside me.

He slices into his forearm, and a thin bead of blood follows. Grabbing the dagger back, I wipe it on my pants. Slicing through my own arm, I place it directly on top of his.

"I accept your oath."

Chapter 24

Kalon

How did he even find us? And the first thing he tells us is that Adira's friend is dead?

Gritting my teeth, I strain to hear what her and the betrayer are talking about. *He lasted two minutes after she ran off before he followed. And she's letting him talk to her.*

One minute. I'll give her one more minute before I go in after her.

Leaning against the wall, I count down from sixty.

Twelve... eleven... ten...

The door creaks open. I straighten at the sound.

Soren walks out first, and Adira follows shortly after. I take in her tear-stained cheeks.

"Are you okay? Did he hurt you?"

She shakes her head no, as he shoots me a glare.

Let him glare; I've endured worse.

"We need to finish talking," Adira reminds us, leading us back to the dining hall. Her gait is tense, like she's physically holding back her emotions.

I follow behind them, tracking Soren's movements. Ducking, I step under the low archway to the room. The firelight casts shadows across the space. Adira makes herself a cup of tea while Soren and I take a seat. I make sure to sit across from him so I can be ready for any sudden moves he makes. The mugs clink as she shakily grabs one. Adira joins us, her gaze tired but sharp.

"Continue," she sighs, motioning at Soren. He runs a hand over his face before replying.

"Right, well, after I left Claude's, I managed to get over to Modereo. I stayed in one of the towns and tried to hear any news about the prophecy. In the forest, I was ambushed by a group of Enid soldiers. They took me to a village they created. It's about fifty feet off the forest floor, hidden among the trees. They've spanned a huge area with solid wood and built a civilization on top. It is pretty impressive, even if they tortured me."

I notice Adira's hands clench tighter around the mug at his words. A roll of irritation runs through me. *He betrayed her, and she's still worried about him?*

"I had help escaping—someone who claims to be your guardian. He didn't tell me much, so I figure it's fine to tell you." He shrugs.

"My guardian?" Adira repeats, confused. Shock flickers through me.

"His name is Eiran. He told me that all people who are prophesied obtain a guardian assigned by the Arae to ensure the prophecy stays on track. It's all very confusing, he can help with some things, but not others. Apparently, there are rules in place about that knowledge, so he was frustratingly vague."

Adira mulls this over, sipping her tea.

"I've heard of them," I chime in. "It's said that they hide within your lives and nudge you toward things that will further your path to completing a prophecy."

I had all but forgotten about guardians. My father had pointed them out in an ancient text when I was younger. But as prophecies are rare, I pushed the information to the back of my mind.

Adira straightens like she just realized something. "Do you think he was the one that sent Esper to us?" Her hands grip the mug tightly.

Soren grimaces. "That would make the most sense."

"He sent her to die!"

"I thought that too," Soren admits quietly.

Adira rubs her chest, a look of sorrow on her face. I decide it would be too painful for me to ask about Esper, so I keep my mouth shut. I run a hand over the coarse wood of the table, bitterly accepting that I'll never have stories of my own adventures to recount.

"That's so messed up. I can't even fathom how someone can just willingly send someone else to their death." Her words falter as she looks at Soren. Shaking her head, she turns her attention back to her mug.

"I know, princess. It's not normal." My eye twitches at the nickname.

Adira sighs and shrugs. "Well, fuck him. But... hopefully he will continue to help?"

"That's it?" I ask with a hint of disbelief.

She slants her head toward me, eyes narrowing.

"What do you want me to say? I hope he doesn't help us because I disagree with his methods? I don't have any control over what he does anyway. He can't answer a question straight and can't interfere directly. So I'm choosing not to think about it right now. I have more important things to worry about." She snips.

I clear my throat, my cheeks heating. "Fair enough."

Soren snickers quietly. Twisting my head, I shoot him a glare.

"Guys, please," Adira says exasperatedly, rubbing her temples.

"We need to work together. You know the whole world relies on this prophecy being fulfilled," she states bitterly.

Anguish passes over Soren's expression at her claim. My brow creases, realizing the pressure she faces.

"I know. I'm sorry, princess," he says quietly.

A scowl covers my face when she doesn't snap at him. She sees my look, and a flash of an apology crosses her face. A tightness coils in my chest. I bury it beneath duty, feeling my chance at a mostly normal existence slipping away. *I won't get the girl, and I will still be stuck here. In this mountain. Alone.*

"How did you get away from King Dahak, anyway?" she asks, turning her attention back to Soren.

A half-grin covers his face. "King Dahak was told a false prophecy."

Adira inhales sharply. "Really? What was he told?"

"He was told it was, '*In darkness lies dominion. The heart is the prize. But beware... those who know will kill to keep it from you.*' So, he is worried that Enid is working to stop the prophecy, and he wants it to come true. He tasked me with stopping Enid, no matter what."

"But you wanted to kill him? Wasn't that your main goal?"

Soren's face softens before he leans forward to grab Adira's hands. She hesitates, then lets him. I watch them, shifting uncomfortably. At that moment I knew I would have to go against my duty to let another person leave this mountain alive, risking the knowledge of the Teràstios.

"It was my goal... is still my goal. But first I needed to make sure you were okay. After learning about Enid and the knowledge they appear to have on you and the prophecy, I knew I needed to be with you." He clears his throat. "Protecting you, I mean."

Choosing to ignore the flare of jealousy, I let my thoughts travel back to the false prophecy. *Who is trying to betray King Dahak? And why?*

Adira breaks contact with Soren, flushing guiltily. I let my obedience drive out the envy, pushing my budding feelings to the side.

"Let's focus on the real prophecy."

"*The child born from two realms, must bond back the creatures that fell. To find out the truth, you must venture back to when divinities were youth. To rebalance what was torn apart, you must forfeit the life of which you hold closest to your heart.*" She recites.

I still at the words.

"This is the prophecy? Are you certain?"

She turns a confused look to me.

"Yes. This was told to us by the goddesses themselves."

"You've heard it differently?" she asks as I feel Soren staring into the side of my face.

"Slightly. It was almost the same." I huff out a laugh.

"It doesn't matter. It ends up the same."

Adira eyes me for a moment, then shrugs. Her and Soren launching into plans of where to go next.

I offer insight where I can, but I know I cannot leave this safehold to help them. To protect the Teràstios is instilled into my very will. The mountain's magic pulses under my skin, a silent leash that reminds me where my duty ends—and hers begins.

Chapter 25

Soren

Kalon shows me to my room. Which, to no surprise, is further down the hall from Adira's, while his is right across from hers.

I push him out of my mind and settle onto the hard bed. Staring up at the curved ceiling, I let myself smile. *No matter if she continues to hate me, we are together again.*

Lifting up my arm, I stare at the new scar. *And bound together forever.*

I wait for the panic to accompany that thought, but it doesn't fill me with dread. With Dahak, I was forced into the oath and bitterly carried out his bidding. But with Adira, I would happily give my life for hers.

Feeling more content than I have in weeks, I drift off to sleep.

****

I rise early, heading down the hall to Adira's door. I knock on it and wait. She flings it open and eyes me warily, hiding her emotions. None of the vulnerability she showed me yesterday is present.

That's okay. I knew it would take time to gain her trust back.

"Ready for this next part?" I ask.

"Do you think that the cliffs are the right place?"

I think back to the book I read, shrugging, "Not sure. But all the history books say that it was where the Arae landed and later split the world. I figure it's a good place to start. Especially since Enid knows you are here and seem intent on harming you."

I made sure to research the past as much as I could before I left Enelon. I didn't want to show up with nothing to offer.

"I suppose that makes sense. We better leave soon."

She slips past me and heads toward the dining hall. Shrugging her bag off her shoulder, she drops it to the ground. Grabbing some fruit and bread, she shoves it into the pack.

Biting an apple, she turns to me and says, "I just need to say goodbye to Kalon first."

I attempt to hide my disdain, but she catches it.

Rolling her eyes, she tells me, "Whether or not you like it, he helped me a lot while I was here."

"What do you mean 'a lot'?"

She raises one eyebrow but doesn't respond.

Walking toward the door, she stops beside me. She pats my chest and leans in closer, "Nothing I do is any of your business now."

The sting of her words slice into me. I shift to hide my expression, grabbing some fruit for my bag.

I walk out toward the hall with the rooms and wait. I hear muffled voices and a second later, she strides into view.

Kalon follows us as we walk to the entrance of the mountain.

"Thanks," I say to him gruffly.

He just gives me a shallow nod in return, barely acknowledging me. I bite my tongue to stop my retort.

I turn, walking out before I catch Adira giving him a hug or kiss goodbye. *If she kissed him, I think the part of me still clinging to redemption might die right here.*

She joins me a moment later and we wordlessly start trekking down the side of the mountain. My pulse syncs up with each step I take, drowning out my lingering envy. Every few moments she giggles to herself as her beast flies around us.

They must be able to communicate. I reason with myself. Giving her a glance, I notice she looks different, fiercer. I wonder what else she learnt on that mountain.

The crunch of the leaves is the only sound between us. I push my nervous thoughts to the side at her muteness. After almost a day of silence, I can't take it anymore. *You're an assassin, stop acting so weak.*

"Adira, look. I wanted to apologize. And maybe try to explain myself."

Her expression darkens over as I wait for her to tell me it's okay to bring it up.

"You hurt me."

I recoil at the pain in her words.

"I know I did. And I am so incredibly sorry, princess."

She flinches at the nickname, staying silent for a moment before nodding slightly.

"Okay. You can try to explain."

I blow out a breath. *Here goes nothing.*

"When I was younger, someone came to me, someone who was dead. They told me that the prophecy could not come true." I tell her.

"Who was it? Did they say why?"

I wince. "I can't say anything else. I'm bound not to. If I try, my airway blocks itself off."

"That sounds... painful and a bit convenient," she murmurs.

"I know you don't believe me. But please. Believe me. If I could tell you, I would." I swear to her.

She scrutinizes me from the corner of her eye, I keep my expression open and honest. *If I could, I would trade my plans of revenge for her forgiveness.*

"I believe you," Adira tells me after a moment. Relief floods through me, I let out a breath I didn't know I was holding.

"But," she continues, "you still deceived me. You proved what I meant to you when you lied."

My heart drops to my feet.

"That's not true. I had to do it." I tell her desperately, grabbing her hand to stop her.

"Soren, I almost died. Multiple times. You could have prevented it."

A stab of pain hits my gut at her words, because she's right.

"I know I did. And I will have to live with my guilt for the rest of my life. I can't go back and change the past. But I can try to make it right by ensuring you have a future. With or without me."

Grabbing her cheeks, I stare into her eyes. Hoping she can see the truth there.

"You mean more to me than anything else in the realms."

A blush reddens her cheeks before she pulls away.

"Those are just pretty words."

I bite my cheek, holding in a response. *Words failed her once. I'll find a way to make the truth louder than words.*

Chapter 26

Adira

As Soren and I walk down the road, I fight the urge to talk to him. I kick at loose stones, watching them roll ahead.

Should I tell him about my newfound powers? I must project that thought because Lyra answers.

They are not just newfound powers; you are a higher being.

It just seems impossible. I don't feel any different. Other than the stronger hum of magic inside me.

Lyra chuckles lightly. *You do not feel any different because you have always been a semidea, you were just not aware of it.*

I peer up at Lyra's flying form. *I don't know much about semidea's. Do you know anything about them?*

They are strong, fast, and possess an otherworldly beauty. You will have almost no limitations on your power, and you are difficult to kill—not impossible, but difficult.

Do you know what can kill me?

Yes. The potential cause of your downfall is a metal called Iridium. It came from another planet when the Arae arrived, mixed with the meteors. It exploded onto this planet, scattering the material all over. Therefore, they are rare, but it is possible to find.

Noted.

And, Lyra continues, *you will need to practice control again. Thus far, you have ignored the call of your new powers, but you must become familiar with them.*

My sigh is audible. *I know. I will.*

Thank the realms. Now, I cannot ignore the pangs of hunger any longer. While I am away, do not let pride become your undoing, little one.

No promises. I huff out with a laugh, stealing a glance at Soren.

Wait. I stop her, my mind shifting to the journey ahead.

Yes, little one?

How will you come to Enelon? Can you travel through portals?

A long pause stretches out.

Do not place your worry on me, Lyra says cryptically. *I will find you in Enelon.* Then, she lets out a screech and twists to the right, flying deep into the forest.

I guess we all have our secrets. I tell myself, forcing my mind away from the immediate suspicion I feel.

"Where is she going?" Soren asks.

"For food." I clip out, my words coming out sharper than I mean them to.

He nods at my short tone, turning his head back to the path. My gaze finds the brown and red leaves beneath my feet. I breathe in the beauty of autumn, the intoxicating earthy aroma surrounding me.

Dammit, Adira, don't be a bitch. He's trying. Plus, you need to practice your powers, so you'll have to talk eventually.

"We are coming up on a village called Willowcroft." I offer, suddenly aware that I've been silent for a long while.

Soren perks up at that.

"I passed through that village when I first came to Modereo."

Before I can ask him when he came to Modereo, the village comes into view. Bile rises in me at the sight.

The land is decayed and wilted. An eerie silence settles over the barren land. Not a single Stregona appears to be here.

Soren drags a shaky hand over his face, as though trying to bring forth a different image.

"There was so much life and happiness," he half-whispers to himself.

He turns to me, concern on his face. "The Vormr doesn't kill people, does it? It just kills the land?"

I wince slightly. "At the beginning, yes. But now, as it feeds off the land and grows stronger, it's becoming almost sentient. I sense the remnants of magic here. It fought the Stregoni... and won."

Soren takes a deep breath. The air of dread around us thinning the oxygen in the sky.

An almost panicked look flies across his face. His gaze darts around. "Is it still dangerous? Should we get you out of here?"

My lips twitch at the concern. I hide the emotion.

My eyes roam over the charred plants. Wisps of eather float aimlessly through the sky. "There's no danger now, but let's not linger. The portal is just outside the village."

He nods, relaxing. We both start forward, trying to keep our attention away from the destruction left behind. As we reach the edge of town, I relax a bit more.

Biting my lip, I decide that now is as good a time as any.

"There's something I should tell you," I start.

He straightens at the sound of my voice.

"What is it?"

"When I bonded with Lyra, I had to go through these trials. But to go through the trials, I had to be at my fullest power."

"Okay," he says, nodding along in understanding.

"Turns out, I wasn't at my full power yet. But I am now." I tell him, summoning my eather to my skin.

The energy sparks around me, filling my vision with a whitish tint, making the whole area appear otherworldly.

His eyes widen in awe. "Holy gods."

Laughing lightly, I pull it back. The world turning to its former vibrant green.

"I'm a semidea," I admit, watching his expression for any signs of fear.

"A semidea? What is that?" His nose crinkles in contemplation. *The sight is not adorable, nope, it's unappealing.* I focus on my thoughts instead of my feelings.

"It's the child born from a god and a Stregona. Or a goddess and Stregone."

"Holy gods," he says again.

"Is that all you have to say?" I raise an eyebrow at him, keeping my tone friendlier than before.

"I mean, this is good, right? This should help you fulfill the prophecy?"

"In theory, yes. But I can't help feeling that I've just put a bigger target on my back."

"How so?"

"Semidea's are rare. Everyone will either want this power or want to eradicate it."

His face hardens. "I won't let that happen."

"Yes, yes, I know. The blood oath." I wave him off dismissively.

Soren shakes his head, exasperated.

"Not just the blood oath, princess. You. I want to protect you."

My chest tightens at his words, and I turn to focus on the terrain ahead. The use of the nickname causing a pit in my stomach. The bare trees save me from answering as we move around them.

"Are creating portals part of a semidea's powers?" Soren asks, clearly thinking of the abrupt way I left Enelon before. I let out a quick breath, relieved at his subject change.

"I think so? There isn't much information on semideas. All I know is I was instructed never to tell anyone." I wince, used to keeping this a secret.

I kept a lot of things a secret.

"No matter where it came from, that's a handy ability to have."

I wrinkle my nose. "It is, but there are limitations. I can only portal to places I've been before. And it lets out an energetic pulse, announcing to people the location. It's not used often."

He tilts his head, absorbing that.

"Which god is your father?"

I bite my lip. "Either Conri or Tiamat."

He whistles under his breath, staring at me with a new sense of wonder. Clearing my throat, I say, "We're here. A natural portal to Enelon."

"About before..." he starts, "I meant what I said. I want to protect *you*, not because I feel obligated, but because your life is worth so much to me."

I stay silent, letting the words stretch around us. Soren just stares at me patiently, waiting for me to comment on his confession.

I let out a frustrated breath. "I told you before. I can't just blindly trust you, just because you are saying all the right things. I fell for it once before."

Nodding, he replies, "Okay, then." He turns and starts walking toward the portal.

What in the realms? That's it?

I push after him, striding quickly. A twinge of emotion latches onto me at his dismissal.

"What do you mean 'okay, then'? You are just going to let it go?" I ask, trying to keep the hurt out of my voice.

He stops and turns just before the portal.

"Of course I'm not going to give up on you." Leaning in closer, he brushes a hand across my jaw. "You are everything that is good in this world. Everything worth fighting for."

My breath hitches and I instinctively lean into his touch. His mouth twitches up into a soft smile.

My mother's voice ruins the moment. *Never trust anyone, Adira. You are alone in this world. There may be others who can aid you, but don't give them your trust.*

Pulling back, I run my hand through my hair, the pendant burning as though my mother was warning me.

"We should go," I say, shattering the moment.

"Anything you want, princess," Soren replies with a smirk before he steps into the portal.

Hope flutters in my chest. I tilt my head to the sky just before I step through after him.

You've been wrong about a lot of things, mother. Why can't you be wrong about this?

Chapter 27

Soren

I barely react to the coppery taste from the portal, feeling lighter after the encounter with Adira.

There may still be a chance for her to forgive me.

Breathing in the air, I notice it does have a heavier quality from Modereo's atmosphere.

Adira steps through and sways. My hands automatically shoot out, steadying her. Warmth spreads through me at the simple touch.

"Thanks."

I shoot her a smile in response.

Glancing around at our surroundings, I notice we are only two days out from the kingdom. The trees here seem to press in on us.

I scan the forest around. *It's quiet... too quiet.* I strain my ears, but I don't even hear a bird chirping.

"Something's wrong," I whisper to Adira.

She freezes. "What is it?"

"The forest is too quiet."

"I don't sense anything." She frowns.

We start walking forward, moving slowly. Minute by minute passes in tense silence. The air thickens as we walk, like the forest is holding its breath.

Adira stops suddenly, the leaves crunching beneath her boots.

"Shit. We are in a dead zone," Adira murmurs.

My stomach twists with dread as the silence presses in.

The crack of a branch pulls my attention around the area, but I can't discern which direction it came from.

Movement from the left catches my eye, I twist that way, my hand flying to my sheath.

The men seem to appear out of thin air, jumping down from trees, materializing around bushes. They quickly fill the clearing. *How could we have missed all of them?* Two large Hunters silently stalk through the guards, their large mouths making them look more creature than human. A shudder works its way up my spine from the sight of the soulless creatures.

We both have our weapons in hand. My sword reflects the low light as I palm a dagger in my other hand. I glance over at Adira, and we share a look, conveying to each other that there are too many of them to risk fighting.

My hand itches to launch the dagger into the Hunter's throat. I see the same violence reflected in Adira's eyes. I let out a sigh, shaking my head. Adira reluctantly agrees, setting her daggers on the ground. I follow suit, dropping my weapons and raising my hands in surrender.

We'll have a better chance at planning an escape rather than fighting a horde of guards.

The two Hunters stroll forward and grab us, tying our hands behind our backs. Adira hisses. I turn to see a Makutu chain on her. The blood oath rears up in me at seeing her in pain. I struggle against the bonds, and one of the creatures kicks me in the back. We both lean away from the Hunters instinctively, not wanting them to lose their patience and siphon our power.

I land on my knees with a thud, the dark forest around me mocking my defenselessness. For one fleeting moment, I almost believed Adira's forgiveness could exist. The forest took that thought and swallowed it whole.

I shake my despondent thoughts away, twisting my head back to her. "Are you okay?"

"As okay as I can be, considering we just made fifteen new vicious friends." She smiles sarcastically at the guards. Some of them sneer at her, while others look away in disgust.

"His Majesty is eagerly awaiting your reunion, Soren."

I can't help the fear that creeps into me. All the times I disobeyed the King's orders flashing through me. The punishments I've had to endure. My body aches with phantom pains.

I school my features before eyeing the man in charge. "Who are you?" Glancing around at the rest of the guards, confusion filters into me. "As a matter of fact, who the fuck are any of you?"

He smiles maniacally at me, his eyes flashing with a hint of shadows.

"Did you really think the King's leash slipped so easily?"

I don't say anything.

"Aw. You did. How naïve of you," he mocks.

I tense up but force a bored expression on my face.

He smirks knowingly, then snaps forward, driving a hand into my gut. I double over, fuming from the cowardly act.

"Try not to slow us down, okay?"

I meet his eyes, signaling my bound hands. "Maybe next time you will fight me like a man, instead of attacking a defenseless person."

My mocking tone earns me a glare. He doesn't rise to the bait, turning back to the other guards who are watching raptly.

"Let's go, boys!" he shouts to the clearing. "We got them, and pretty easily I might add." They all laugh at that.

"Time to take our new friends to the King," he says, leaning close to Adira and throwing her a wink.

Pitching forward, a snarl slips out of me.

He cocks his head at me, a grin spreading across his face as he glances between me and Adira.

"Oh my. This is just too good." He laughs to himself.

"The King will be very displeased with you."

"Well, I don't really give a fuck what Dahak is pleased with," I spit out, venom lacing my tone.

They laugh at my words. I try to hide my confusion from the reaction.

Another guard strolls up. "I knew the golden boy wasn't the perfect soldier. Didn't I say that?"

"You did. But it was a little predictable, wasn't it? I mean, the King did have his entire family murdered."

My jaw tightens. *Don't take their bait.*

"Poor little orphan boy." A guard in the back taunts.

"That's enough," the first guard snaps. "It's time to go."

Laughter ceases at his tone, and the guards obey immediately. Two guards flank the sides of Adira and me. The one to my left yanks at the chains holding me when I slow down. The guard to the right of Adira just guides her on the path since the chains have zapped her strength. The guards keep a sizeable step away from the Hunters with weary expressions.

She stumbles, and the guard hisses at her.

Anger rises in me, but I shove it down. Lashing out will only make things worse. I turn, focusing on her. "How are you doing?"

"I'm okay. You know I've handled worse," she whispers to me.

I grimace, thinking about how much of her pain is from me or my actions. *It will be a miracle if she forgives me.* I sigh to myself.

We stop abruptly. I look ahead, spotting a shimmering portal that wasn't there before.

Adira gasps.

"You can create portals," she states, eyeing the first guard. He shoots her a grin, ushering everyone forward. I observe the guard anew, surprised at the blatant use of magic. My mind shifts to Dahak's flagrant need for power and find I'm not shocked.

"You didn't think we'd walk two days with you, did you? Not when your beast is flying around," he says back.

Adira's breath catches. Her eyes start searching the sky.

A screech fills the air, Lyra coming into view. Adira strains against her bonds as if calling out to her.

The Teràstios lands in the group and starts knocking guards aside with her wings. Hope flares through me as she easily bests the men. But then one of them pulls out an oval device.

My stomach drops, recognizing it.

The man presses the small button, throwing it toward the creature. Smoke wafts through the air. Distress takes over Adira's expression as Lyra sways from side to side.

Thud.

Adira's Teràstios collapses to the ground. The earth trembles from the force. Adira screams, a tear slipping down her face. My heart cracks at the raw fear I see. I try to shift toward her, but my chain grows taut. I tighten my fists, fighting the urge to break free.

"Don't worry about your precious creature. It'll be in good hands," he tells her viciously, signaling to three of his men. "You three. Stay behind and contain the beast."

They nod in agreement, stepping back from the group.

A panicked look fills Adira's face.

"She's strong, Adira. We will find a way to save her," I whisper to her, really hoping that my words aren't empty promises.

Disbelief flashes across her face before it twists to determination. "First, we have to save ourselves."

We step through the portal, the power of it feeling more sinister. My jaw clenches, the magic stretching and pulling me violently. The energy cuts into me as it shoves me through to the other side. I land on the grass, my hand cutting into a branch on the ground, adding to the other little cuts that now adorn my body. I ignore the biting pain, noting that Adira also carries new wounds.

She gasps out as she regains her feet.

"Why did that feel different?"

Adira looks at the guard distrustfully. "His magic isn't pure, its laced with something darker."

My eyes narrow on the guard, marking him on my list for making Adira bleed.

My focus shifts as the group moves to the edge of the forest. The trees part to reveal the castle looming in front of us. I take in the deep red bricks and gold trimming. *Gods, it's obnoxious.*

Nerves start to invade when I think about my future. *Well. You won't have one. Simple as that. There is no way he won't kill you.*

My chest clenches as I look over at Adira. *Dammit. I really wanted a future.* Her hand grasps her pendant, a slight wince on her face. Before I can ask her what's wrong, besides the obvious, we reach the castle.

The guards drag us through the enormous doors, leading us in the direction of the throne room. Heat rushes us when the doors slam closed. My nose tickles at the rose scent that drifts through the halls.

The smell so pungent that it buries any lingering scent of blood that is always spilled in this cursed place.

Any lingering hope I had diminishes each step we take in the King's direction.

"I'm sorry," I tell Adira, knowing those two little words don't change the fact that I've put us in this position.

She gives me a small smile. "It's not your fault. Plus, it's not over until it's over."

Shaking my head incredulously, I ruminate over her response. *She's optimistic. Even now.*

The doors to the throne room swing open, the hinges creaking as they move. I stop dead at the sight.

You've got to be fucking kidding me.

Chapter 28

Adira

The sharp cut of betrayal runs through me. Again.

I blink twice at the scene in front of me. *Is this really happening?*

I shake my head, hoping it will change the person in front of me.

Stopping, I lock eyes with him.

Kalon.

"What is this?" I angrily demand, the ire I feel drowning out the burning sensation from my pendant. It doesn't escape my notice that this is the second time it's been reacting to the King's presence.

Soren growls next to me. "You gods-damned traitor. I knew there was something shady about you."

"I had no choice. The prophecy can't come true," Kalon deadpans.

Disbelief courses through me. *He must've told the King the real prophecy too.*

Another thought follows. *Damn. Maybe I do trust too easily.*

"Has this been the plan the whole time?"

Kalon shakes his head. "I only knew about part of the prophecy. When you repeated the entirety of it, I knew you had to be stopped."

"What about Lyra? You're just going to let them hurt her? I thought you were sworn to protect them," I hiss out.

A wince covers his face.

"They promised she would stay unharmed."

My eyebrows shoot up.

"And you believe them?!"

King Dahak holds up his hand, silencing the room. I drag my eyes away, looking over the elaborate decorations. Gilded architecture lines the walls, although hints of decay are present, like the castle itself is protesting against the corrupt male that darkens the throne.

"That's enough," he booms. Once the King begins speaking, the Hunters that escorted us turn and leave the room. As the doors swing shut behind them, a palpable tension breaks.

"Kalon. You have done the right thing."

A scoff escapes me. Piercing eyes whip to me. A faint hum of energy crackles through the space.

"And you. Back where you started. Imprisoned with me. Right where you belong," he tells me wickedly.

Soren steps up. "No. Let her go. Take me instead."

Dahak hisses. "You are a fool. Be fortunate that I'm not ending your treacherous life right now." The shadows around the room move unnaturally at his venomous tone.

"Why don't you?" Soren spits.

My eyes widen at his tone. *He really doesn't know when to keep his mouth shut.*

The King just smirks. "I still need you."

A chill runs down my spine.

"You think I wasted all those years training and feeding you just to kill you? No. You, my boy, will become my shield."

"I will never help you," Soren swears, acid dripping from his words.

The King laughs darkly.

"You will have no choice," he purrs, gliding toward him. Soren thrashes against his restraints. The guards pull tighter, forcing him to be still.

The King grabs Soren's jaw, pushing his head up. The temperature drops, the hair on my arms warning me of danger.

"Do you know how mind enslavement works?" he hums calmly.

We stay quiet, my blood freezing at his question.

"First, you will try and fight back. Then you will be pushed deeper and deeper into your memories, diverting your attention from reality. They will consume you. When you finally get a handle on them, you will find yourself locked up in a corner of your mind. With no free will, every command I give, you will oblige. The best part is you will be able to see everything that is happening but will have no control over any of it."

Horror fills me at the description. I glance at Soren, seeing a look of concern flash over his face.

"I will be able to feel your frustration and anger but hear none of your pleas for release." He chuckles darkly. "But before we get to the fun, I have something I need to tell Adira, and I think you should hear it."

I beat him to it, recalling the markings from Orlo.

"Why don't I start?" I snap. His eyebrow rises in amusement.

"By all means."

"I know," I tell him, looking him in the eyes, "I know your name isn't Dahak. You are one of the six beings the Arae created. You are Conri Aamon."

Soren whips his head to me and then to Conri in surprise.

I wait for the shock to appear on Conri's face. He keeps an amused smirk pointed at me.

"What else?"

"Wh-what else?" I stutter out, confused by his reaction. Or lack thereof.

"Yes. You made it seem like it was going to be some terrible secret. But honestly, it's pathetic. Do you know how long I've been here? Hiding in plain sight? I'm almost embarrassed for the foolishness of people."

Shock filters through me. My fingers itch to touch my pendant, but I resist the urge, needing to keep one more secret.

"How did you manage to hide your magic all this time? I couldn't sense anything."

His lips kick up in a wicked smile while lifting his hand. "This beauty." He twists the large magenta ring off his finger, displaying it to us. "It's spelled to hide magic signatures. Very simple, actually."

My fists clench, wanting to wipe the smug expression off his face. I grasp onto his history, hoping to draw the hurt out of him.

"I also know you plotted against the other gods and goddesses. But your brother disagreed. He betrayed you, telling the others your plans. Then he tried to stop you by weakening your powers."

His jaw ticks, the only sign of his annoyance.

I push forward.

"Instead of trying to fix it, you dug your heels in, swearing to them that you would come back for revenge. How is that working for you? Seems to me that you went into hiding and you didn't come out." I let my lips curve up mockingly.

Rage flickers in his eyes, the torches in the room sputtering with the reaction. I wait for him to snap, but he cools his expression before responding.

"I'm immortal. You think a few hundred years mean anything to me?" He scoffs.

"I am in no rush. My plans have been in the process for a long time. Longer than you've been alive. So you can shut your mouth. I will get my powers back, and I will successfully rule over this world." He sneers, his eyes flickering wickedly with that promise. Kalon's expression flashes warily, as if he is just now realizing their goals don't align and he's being lied to.

"And you." Conri turns to Soren. "Why do you suppose I had your family killed?"

Soren's jaw clenches. My heart beats faster for the man who stole it. Because in the face of death, all the past arguments suddenly seem so pointless.

"It's because I knew Cain was going to them, feeding them lies and secrets about me. So I sent my guards to end them. Imagine my surprise when they came back with you. They told me they couldn't kill you, some unseen force was stopping them."

My eyes widen as pieces click together in my mind. *This is what he couldn't tell me. A god was coming to him.* I think back to his broken explanation in the forest, my half-hearted belief solidifying with the facts. My mind races back to all those times he looked like he was about to say something but instead shook his head in frustration.

Soren's eyes widen in shock, as if it were news to him.

"I knew you had to be important. So, where better to keep an eye on your enemy than right under you." Conri finishes smugly.

"My family was working with Cain?"

Conri sneers. "Yes. They appeared to be important people in the rebellion, so my own brother was betraying my trust and informing them about me. Pathetic."

Conri spits the last word out, his energy crackling with barely contained rage. Soren tries to school his features, but I catch the slightly glazed look in his eyes. He shakes himself out of it.

I turn my head, locking eyes with Soren.

"I'm sorry," I tell him. "I should have trusted you."

"It's okay." He replies with a sad smile, disbelief still apparent in his eyes.

I see a goodbye echoing in his expression, and my heart clenches painfully in my chest.

"Now. Time for the fun part."

Soren pales, trying to draw back from Conri.

He clucks his tongue. "Now, now. Don't make this difficult."

"No. Please, stop." I beg, choking on a sob. The chains rattle as I shift forward. A guard tugs me back, pulling a pained whimper from me.

Conri just smiles cruelly at me and grabs Soren's head. The air thickens. I gasp through the pressure in the room, my trapped magic straining to be released.

His eyes roll back, pain etching deep into his forehead. He flails against Conri's hold. My chest squeezes painfully.

No, no, no. "Keep fighting, Soren!" I shout to him. A guard slaps me across the face. I welcome the sting, letting it tear me away from my anguish. Power hums out of Conri, the magic tinted with malicious intent. Wrongness seeps into my skin, my own power yelling at me to stop this immoral act.

Minutes tick by before Soren falls motionless.

"No!" I cry out. "Soren?"

He stares straight ahead, a blank expression on his face.

Conri smiles maniacally.

"Turn to Adira, Soren. Show her how empty you are."

His body slowly turns toward me, and I latch onto his eyes.

But all I see is a deep emptiness. My hope snuffs out.

He's gone.

Chapter 29

Soren

The throne room fades. Blood becomes memory as the weight of a sword is dropped in my hand.

The air whistles beside me. I shift, blocking the attack coming from my left. Stepping back, I turn and slice through the man's stomach. My gut twists, the scent of iron filling the room. He falls to the ground, clutching at his innards. Another man screams in rage, charging at me. I whirl my sharp blade around, cutting his scream off.

His head thuds to the ground. Silence fills the room.

I take in the bodies littered around me, trying to shove down the guilt. I harden my heart, reminding myself the purpose of it. Revenge. Revenge for my family who were brutally slaughtered by these men.

"I refuse to show these monsters any remorse," I say aloud to myself, latching onto the suppressed anger I carry.

I clean the blade because it's easier than cleaning the memory. Shaking off a strange sense of déjà vu, I turn to leave the room. There's no turning back now, I think as I leave behind the men that were the first to mark my soul black. I exit through the door, my feet falling out from under me, dragging me from the flashback.

I struggle against my memories, trying to force my mind back to reality, back to Adira. Another memory swallows me like a tidal wave. I fall into it with the euphoric sound of her laughter.

I blink at the new scene, at the dimly lit forest surrounding me.

Adira's giggle trickles through the trees, pushing my dark thoughts away. The earthy scent of the ground signaling a long overdue spring.

I turn toward her, taking in her smooth hair and radiant eyes.

Gods, she's beautiful.

She stares at me, waiting for my response. "So?" Adira prompts.

"What?" I ask her.

She rolls her eyes playfully. "What's your favorite food?"

My face scrunches up. "Who cares?"

She bumps her shoulder against mine.

"I do. I want to know," she replies softly.

Feeling myself soften, I consider her question.

"Umm, I guess chocolate cake. I haven't had it in forever, but I've always enjoyed it," I tell her.

She smiles brightly at my answer.

"And what's yours?" I ask, suddenly needing to know more about her.

"That's easy. Caramello. It's a soft, dense sweet." Her eyes are closed like she's envisioning it.

I file that information away, peering over at her. She's smiling up at the sun, letting it soak into her. Warmth fills my chest at the image.

"Noted," I rasp out.

Her eyes open at my voice, and we stare into each other's eyes.

The sun gets brighter, whitening my vision. I shield my eyes, Adira's presence fading. I feel Conri's power trying to coax forth another memory. Gritting my teeth, I push back, fighting to clear my thoughts.

It's working! I think as my surroundings start to come into view. Focusing inward, I notice that I can't move throughout my mind. *Shit. It's happening just like Dahak said. Or should I say, Conri. That vile liar.*

I bang around the invisible barrier, trapping me inside my own mind. Adira's voice has me focusing forward. It feels like I'm looking out of someone else's eyes.

"Soren." My name floats to me. I try to turn toward it, but I can't move my body.

Conri commands me to turn. My body obeys. Adira comes into view, staring at me with wide eyes.

I'm here! I shout, but my mouth doesn't move.

Her eyes shutter in pain at whatever she finds on my face.

I'll come for you, Adira. Don't worry. I will always come for you. I promise, projecting it out to her.

Conri nods at a guard behind Adira. He steps up and smacks her across the temple. She crumples to the floor.

NO. I shout, beating against the barrier.

I watch helplessly as they drag her across the room.

Chapter 30

Kalon

I look away as a guard drags Adira to the center of the room, where a small post sits.

They decided to try and get some information out of her before taking her to a cell. I'm standing behind Conri, a guard next to me. He keeps his hand on his pommel, because no matter what Conri says, he won't trust me.

Not that I'm surprised.

"You may enter, Adder." Conri speaks loudly.

The doors part. The largest man I've ever seen walks in. He has an angry scar along his cheek that draws a line to his black eyes—eyes that have a deranged look in them.

He wordlessly strides over to Adira. My gaze snags on the black-roped weapon in his hand.

They are going to whip her.

My stomach turns so hard I have to swallow twice to keep it down. I force myself not to squirm as he readies the whip.

I peek a glance over at Soren. His unnatural stillness causes a shudder to run through me. I stare into his eyes, waiting for any movement, finding nothing but a blank expression.

I wince to myself; *this is going to be painful for him.*

Adder jerks Adira's hands up to the post, tying them tightly, cutting off her circulation. She wakes from the motion, looking disoriented.

He pulls out a small dagger, swiftly ripping through her shirt. I see the realization enter her eyes. She glances up at Soren, and a flash of agony crosses her face. Then she turns my way, anger filling her expression. I flinch at the disappointment that accompanies her ire. The guard beside me tightens his grip on his pommel at the motion.

I grip the back of my neck. *How is this the right thing?* I plead to my father. My pleas summon his last words to me.

You must protect the Teràstios at all costs. You will be forced to make some tough decisions, but you must not stray from our destiny. Do you understand, son? I remember nodding to him even though the last hope of my freedom slipped away with that promise. I let his words wash over me, using them to harden my resolve. *I had to do this. I had no choice.*

Conri steps forward.

"Good. You're up. I will be needing some answers from you to aid me in my noble quest to conquer the realm."

She snorts at his haughty tone. His hostile gaze fastens on her.

"I am already aware that you've met with the goddesses recently."

"If you already know that, shouldn't you know where they are?" her tone holds dark amusement.

Conri locks his jaw, his boots clicking against the floor as he approaches her. "You already know my treacherous brother stole away some of my powers. I believe the goddesses know how I can get it back."

He squats down in front of Adira, rage flowing off him in waves.

"I will stop at nothing to regain what I had. Where are those snakes hiding?" he demands.

She smirks. Fucking smirks.

"Go fuck yourself." She spits—voice steady, eyes glistening.

Fury flashes across Conri's face before he covers it.

"Fine. Perhaps you will be more forthcoming after some lashes. How many do you reckon, Adder?"

"Your Majesty," he murmurs, testing the whip's weight. "Twelve should remind her what pain can teach."

Panic enters her eyes. Conri's lip twitches as he strides back to his throne, lounging on it as if he were watching a show.

"Twelve it is. You may begin."

Seeds of doubt grow as I observe his ruthlessness.

Adder grins maniacally, raising the whip, his muscles flexing with the motion.

He brings it down quickly, and a wet slap echoes in the room.

He broke skin on the first lash.

He pulls it back immediately, his eyes showing his excitement. My nails dig into my palm while I physically hold myself back.

"Stop—" my half-muttered pleas are cut off by a guard's glare.

My gut rolls with each wet slap of the whip. Adira stays silent, biting her lip to hold in her screams. A tear drips down her face, her body's natural response to the pain.

With each swing of the whip, Adder's smile grows while my wrath increases. As he brings it down the seventh time, I avert my eyes, unable to watch.

You coward. I tell myself. *You did this to her.*

Turning my attention back to the scene, I force myself to watch. With each crack, my guilt digs into me further.

Chapter 31

Soren

They are up to lash nine. Her back is a bloodied mess. The floor around her smeared red, the torches shadows making it look like a massacre.

Rage encompasses me, blinding my sight for a moment. My body doesn't reflect the emotion, it stays unmoving and unexpressive. I keep my attention on Adira, trying to silently project to her that I'm here and she's not alone.

Footsteps echo toward me. Conri leans in.

"I can feel your rage. It's quite potent." He taunts quietly with a chuckle. "This must kill you. Not being able to help her."

"After this, she will be tossed into the filthy dungeons below, bleeding through her back. Will she succumb to her wounds? Or will she make it through a fortnight of torture? Because at the end of the fortnight, she will be entered into combattere fino alle morte."

My blood freezes at his words.

NO. You monster. I seethe, pounding against the barrier. Hoping he sees the promise of his death in my eyes.

He keeps talking, seemingly unaware.

"You already know how this ends. I'm only letting you watch."

He shoots me a wink before turning back to Adira. He frowns as the torches flicker dimly. "Now, that won't do. We need to be able to see everything clearly."

He waves a hand, and the torches turn unnaturally bright, revealing the details of every lash and emphasizing the blood on the floor.

My stomach turns over, my eyes unable to look away from the brutality in front of me.

Lash eleven. She whimpers, hanging limply. The torturer, Adder, smiles cruelly, like he gets off on other people's pain. I grit my teeth, promising to repay him back for the pain he's caused Adira tenfold.

Lash twelve. She sways, looking like she's fighting for consciousness.

My brave princess.

I will get you out of this, I vow to her.

A guard steps forward, undoing the chains, her hands drop to the ground. Without giving her a second to rest, another guard steps forward to haul her up. They grimace when they step in the pool of blood.

She stumbles but tries to walk on her own as they drag her from the room. Bloodied footprints follow their path. My wrath feels like a living, breathing thing as she turns, and I see her mangled back. Blood drips down from her, landing on the clean tile.

"Adder," Conri calls. He turns obediently to the King.

I focus on the bastard who held the whip.

He will die first.

"You will stay in the dungeons with Miss Selcouth for the entirety of her stay." He chuckles darkly when he uses the word 'stay'.

"I will send down a list of questions that you must extract from her. Use whatever force necessary but keep her alive."

"Of course, Your Majesty," he responds with a slight dip of his head. Once the doors swing shut behind Adder, Conri turns his attention back to me.

"Turn and face me," he commands.

I lock down on my movements, my body trembling in protest for a split second. My minimal control snaps. I obediently turn.

The smug smile doesn't leave his face.

"Now kneel." I narrow my eyes at him, fighting for some semblance of control.

My knees land against the cold tile, the abrupt motion jarring. I glare up at him with hatred, my loathing momentarily breaking through the hold he has on me.

"It's about time you learnt some obedience," he says with distaste.

"Follow me," he commands, turning and striding out of the room.

My body obeys even as my mind screams.

Chapter 32

Conri

The steady sound of footsteps follows me as I walk down the hallway, steps that do not falter. I breathe in deeply, letting the feeling of power wash over me. I look back at my new pet, his face blank, though I can feel the ire rolling off him.

I smirk, amusement trickling through me.

We come up to a woven tapestry with a creature as black as night, shrouded in mist. My lips twitch at the lack of subtlety. Two guards shift it sideways and press open the door. The air immediately smells of stale incense and rot. My nose wrinkles in disgust, but that is the price you pay for being innovative.

Not paying the guards another glance, I step onto the cold stone stairs. A thrum of excitement filters through me as I near my creations. Chains clank in the distance followed by bone-chilling wails.

I chuckle inwardly to myself, recalling Adira's shocked face. *She thought she could surprise me? She has no idea what I know. She has no idea what is about to come. I will get my power back, even if I must battle the goddesses to do it.*

Screeching blares through the stale air as we walk toward the end of the dim hallway. I push the door open and step into my necromancer's post. Two creatures are chained and rapidly swinging their large heads around, trying to break free. The stench of rusted metal fills the room.

A sense of pride rumbles through me at the wild look in their sickly green eyes. I imagine them tearing through the land, helping me finally take when I deserve. Starting with Querencia, the kingdom who has grown far too complacent.

I will stop at nothing to conquer this world.

Chapter 33

Soren

If my mouth could drop open, it would be gaping wide right now. I'm staring directly into the eyes of a monster I've never seen or heard of before. My stomach turns, the putrid scent of rot overwhelming.

Its savage green eyes are sunken into its face. My gaze is wide, not leaving the beast. Its mouth holds rows of rotting teeth. The beast's breath is so hot that the air is thick with condensation. Its body looks as if it's trying to grow fur but can only manage to cover half of its pinkish-red skin.

A snarl escapes the one I'm looking at, the sound spurring the other to growl. They whip around in their chains. I gape at the rusted metal, hoping it can hold them. The dread in the air mirrors the feeling in my gut.

I watch in horror as one of them bites the head of a guard trying to contain it clean off. The headless body thuds to the ground. The air thickens with the scent of copper, the floor turning a deeper shade of scarlet.

Silence stretches through the room before Conri lets out a sigh, like this is a minor inconvenience to him.

"Why are they not under better control yet?" Conri demands, his stare fixed on the Stregone with crazed eyes.

"It's the new sandstone, Your Majesty. The properties are more durable than the past stones, which reflects in the strength of the beast," the necromancer stammers out. I listen with rapt attention, hoping to learn something that I can use against the god.

Conri narrows his eyes.

"I didn't ask about their strength. I asked why they were not under control yet."

"Your Majesty, strength does not only refer to their physicality; it can also refer to their mentality. In this case, they are even more stubborn than the last batch." The wiry man bends into a nervous half-bow, afraid of Conri's reaction.

Conri stares at him for a long moment. A bead of sweat drips down his temple from the attention.

"Very well. You have until the month's end."

The necromancer stiffens. "But, Your Majesty, there is less than three weeks left."

Conri's gaze hardens.

"Then start. Every moment you breathe is a moment wasted."

"Ye-yes, Your Majesty."

"Good. I will check in with you in a few days."

Conri turns and walks out the door. My useless body follows. The last thing I see before we leave is the necromancer's shaking hands.

Chapter 34

Adira

Pain wakes me.

Fire coats my back as I shift slightly. Lifting my head slowly, I take in my surroundings. I'm laying on my stomach on the floor of a dirty cell. In the corner sits a grime-covered pot.

I will absolutely not do my business in that. I think with disgust.

The wall to my right has thick chains attached to it. At the end of the chains are bones.

I push myself up and promise myself that will not be my fate. The Makutu chains weaken me as I shuffle to a less vulnerable position. I lean my shoulder against the wall to my left, letting it hold me up. My body trembles from the effort, my breaths coming out faster than they should for such a miniscule movement. Splitting pain races down my back, pulling at the open wounds.

My blood dripping on the floor is the only sound. The silver lining is I no longer feel the sharp pain from my pendant; now it's drowned out by all my other wounds.

Footsteps sound in the distance, walking closer. My shoulders tense.

The man who whipped me comes stalking into view. *Adder, that was his name.*

He doesn't seem surprised to see me awake.

"It's about time," he purrs, squatting down next to my cell.

I refuse to let my fear show, so I tilt my chin up.

"What excitement do you have planned for us today?" I ask with a smirk.

His gaze darkens at my haughty tone, and he stands. He removes a key from his pocket, slipping it into my cell door. It clicks and swings open, the hinges groaning from the movement.

I stare up at him as he strides in, hiding the need to shudder.

"Do you know what I enjoy most about torturing someone?" He asks me as he turns, his stare intense.

Internally, I roll my eyes. "No. But I'm sure you're going to tell me."

He flashes me a quick grin, laced with dark promise.

"It's when they refuse to talk. Silence is a good tutor. It always teaches me something new."

Dread crawls in, but I force myself to maintain a bored expression.

"So," he continues, "when I went to Conri with an idea, he jumped on it. The price was worth it."

Before I can respond, he pulls a dagger out from behind him.

My lips part in shock.

It has an onyx black handle with an intricate design of a skull. But that's not what catches your eye. It's the blade—semi-transparent, with blazing flames swirling inside, looking like it's alive.

I draw back instinctively. Distantly, a group of barking sounds echoes, like the dark energy woke the nasty creatures that chased me the last time I was a prisoner here. The Umbrai. I pale at the echoing barks.

He notices, his lips turning up.

"What is it?" I ask.

"It's a blade that was forged from the pits of hell. With the smallest scratch, it will fill you with an agony so great, you will think you are dying. And wish you were actually dying... just to escape the pain." He pauses, tilting his head. "Or were you talking about your friends? They still have your scent and are impatiently waiting to see you again."

Terror seizes my vocal cords, their deep red eyes and snapping teeth entering my memory.

Adder squats down in front of me, bringing the blade to my face, using the edge to lightly brush my jaw.

"You *will* tell me what I need to know," he states confidently.

"Are you ready?"

Steeling myself, I summon up the little courage I have left.

"Do your worst," I respond, smiling wickedly. *My body may be weak, but my mind is as strong as ever. And I'll be damned if I let this asshole break me.*

He matches my smile. "Oh, I will."

Adder moves the dagger to my collarbone. He traces the area lightly before pressing down. As the blade breaks my skin, searing flames follow in its wake.

A scream rips out of me.

Holy goddess, I've never felt anything like that before. I look down, unable to help myself.

The new wound looks like it's glowing, like it lit a fire within me. Smoke billows out as my skin burns. He repeats the process, carving new lines in my skin. My vision blurs. I try to stay conscious, but the pain drags me under.

****

I awake bleary-eyed. Adder leans against the wall, flipping a dagger. When he notices me awake, he strides over.

"How did you enjoy that?" he asks mockingly.

Smiling through the haze, I respond cheekily.

"Barely felt it."

He backhands me across the face.

"Stupid bitch."

My head snaps to the side from the impact. A ringing sound echoes.

"Question time," he says, pulling out the cursed dagger. Its beauty rivals the agony it promises. A shudder escapes me at the sight of it, knowing the pain that follows.

He smiles at my reaction.

"Where are the goddesses? We know you were in Enelon when you found them."

My surprise must show on my face because he elaborates.

"Conri felt their echo cross the veil. You left fingerprints. So, I'll ask again. Where. Are. They?"

I narrow my eyes at him, not tempted in the slightest to reveal anything. Especially anything that would help that corrupt god become more powerful.

A nervous thought drifts through my pain-ridden mind. *Could Conri be my father?* Disgust latches onto me. *Goddess, I hope not.*

His steely eyes enter my mind, I latch onto the fury that accompanies the sight of him, letting it clear my head. Magic swirls in my gut, the feeling reminding me that I am stronger now.

A thread of energy vibrates within me. My heart rate kicks up with it.

Little... one? ...you okay?

My body relaxes in relief, and I have to force myself to keep the tears at bay. I don't know how it's possible to reach her while I'm a prisoner to the Makutu chains, but I don't waste the opportunity.

Lyra. Are you okay?

I'm fine. They... trapped me... escaped. Wards thick... hold your mind steady.

Relief rushes through me as I piece together her broken words.

It's okay. You're okay, that's all that matters. I'll figure a way out of this, I tell her, trying to muster up some hope. Her voice dims, seeming to pull away. My momentary energy drains with it.

Thread... weak.

I have lots of drugs in my system. I also keep losing consciousness, so the pain probably severs, if not weakens it.

I hear a pained growl.

Don't forget... strength comes... mind.

The bond starts weakening. Whatever reprieve we had, either from my stronger magic or our bond, fades.

Thanks, Lyra. I hope I can see you soon.

Don't give up... waiting... you.

The thread goes silent. I slump down, drained from the short conversation. The power I was able to summon falling from me rapidly.

Cold steel pulls me back to the present.

"Well, are you just going to sit there? Or are you going to answer?" Adder growls, pressing the blade into my skin.

Your mind is strong, I remind myself. *He can break my body, but he can't break my mind.*

I pretend to think about it.

"Hmm, I choose to not answer."

"Have it your way."

He breaks skin with the vicious blade. My body vibrates with pain.

Inch by inch, he slowly drags the blade all over my body. I'm assaulted by the smell of charred flesh spreading through the cell. My stomach twists violently. Pushing down the nausea, I decide to stop fighting the pain. I give way to the numbness and let the shadows embrace me.

Chapter 35

Soren

I stare ahead in horror, my hands covered in blood.

That's the fourth person Conri has made me kill. The fourth person who has begged for their survival. They all seemed innocent. My soul darkens further at that thought.

It's been a week. A week that they've tortured Adira. I haven't been able to see her, but Adder will stroll in with updates. They are always the same. He's used Belial, and she fades in and out of consciousness but doesn't talk.

Pride and anger mix together when I think about how strong she is. *But she shouldn't have to be,* I think broodily, cursing Kalon.

Also, Belial? The demon? Does he have an object from hell, or is the actual demon carrying out her torture? The latter seems too absurd to even entertain.

"Soren. Look here." A voice commands. My head whips to it.

Conri steps expertly over the bodies.

"Next, I need you to retrieve someone. Adder will go with you."

He's leaving Adira alone? Relief spreads through me.

Conri's face hardens when he feels it.

"It won't take long. Adder will be back torturing her before you know it."

I brim with concealed wrath at his blatant tone. *I will kill him.*

Conri carries on, ignoring my ire.

"Since I won't be there to direct you, I will loosen the restraints temporarily. Make no mistake, Adder will stop you if you try anything."

He locks eyes with me; his swirl with power.

"You will go with Adder to retrieve someone for me tonight. You will not try to escape or harm Adder. Once you complete the task, you will immediately return back to me."

The command washes over me. My body merges back with my mind. Pinpricks slide through me at the abnormal feeling.

I bite my tongue to keep from cursing at him. The last thing I need is for him to remove this freedom before I can figure something out.

He stares at me a moment, then dismisses me. I walk slowly to the weapons room, my feet carrying me there. I glance around frantically, knowing this will be the only time alone I get.

I turn the corner, spotting a lady strolling down the corridor toward me. As we get closer to each other, I recognize her as Emma, the lady that befriended Adira during our short visit.

Knowing I can't stop to talk, I whisper-shout to her.

"Emma. You won't recognize me, but I'm Caspian. Alona is in the dungeons. Please go help her."

Her eyes widen. She stumbles a step and stops. I stroll past her, pleading with my eyes.

A confused look stares back at me when I refuse to stop.

"Please," I say again.

My body turns the corner, and she disappears from sight.

I hope that was enough. Hopefully, her curiosity will be begging her to explore.

Twisting the handle on the door in front of me, I open it. Adder stands by the weapons rack, waiting for me.

"Let's get this over with," he tells me, disdain covering his tone.

"Like I want to work with you either," I bite back, hands clenching.

"If Conri didn't explicitly tell me not to kill you, you'd be dead right now," I state.

He just chuckles.

"Come on, lover boy. We have something to collect."

He strides out the door. I have no choice but to follow him.

****

We step into the loud tavern. The hearty aroma of savory stew wafts through the air, mixing with the scent of freshly brewed ale. A band plays a low, sensuous tune. Guests rub their bodies together as they sway to the music. I avert my gaze as a man thrusts his fingers into one of the servers.

Looking around at the lowered inhibitions, I wait for Adder to lead us to our target.

I don't have to wait long, as he walks over to a server with short black hair. She turns toward us, and I notice that her eyes flash silver when they catch the light. When her attention slides to Adder, her gaze widens in recognition.

She drops the tray, bolting toward the back.

Adder chuckles and tracks back through the front door, walking leisurely. I follow a few steps behind, unable to stray too far from him.

We get out on the street, her figure darting between buildings, sprinting farther away from us. I tilt my head at Adder, but he just keeps strolling along, whistling.

The movement stops ahead, but Adder remains unworried. Still gallivanting through the cobbled streets. A few minutes later, he stops and sniffs the air. Understanding dawns on me.

He can scent others.

It explains his blasé attitude during the chase.

Pushing open the door, we walk into a rundown house—if you could call it that. The roof has caved in, moss dripping down the walls. A musty dampness fills the air as we walk deeper.

A slight scraping sound reaches my ears. Adder smiles to himself.

"Found you, little lamb," he taunts.

Adder motions for me to go first. I step through the door and get the wind knocked out of me. I bend in half, catching my breath. My movements appear to be a second delayed as my body and mind adjust to being back together.

She hit me with a piece of wood. Amusement trickles in. Good. At least she's defending herself.

Adder steps into the room, smirking at me. I narrow my eyes in irritation.

"Bastard. You knew she was going to attack."

His lips twitch up. "I had a feeling."

I straighten up, noticing that she has backed herself into a corner, holding the jagged piece of wood toward us. I eye her terrified expression, feeling a twinge of regret at aiding in her capture.

"Stay back," she tells us with a shaking voice.

Adder lifts his hands mockingly. "You don't even know what we want."

"I know you work for the King. I won't have anything to do with that monster."

My eyebrows raise at her open defiance. Adder's expression falls flat, seeming done with the conversation. He shoots forward, easily disarming her.

I can't help but think of Adira and the women in Modereo. *At least in their realm, they are trained, so they could at least defend themselves if need be.* I quickly tie her hands together and let Adder steer her out of the door.

"Please," she pleads. "You don't have to do this. I will fake my death and leave."

Confusion causes me to eye her. *Does she know why she's being taken to Conri?*

Adder jerks her body to shut her up.

"Stop talking. You know why the King needs you. You are far too valuable to release."

She whimpers but stays silent.

I wonder what she can do.

****

Once we get back, Conri is waiting in the throne room. As soon as we enter, a pleased smile crosses his face.

He stands and moves to the quietly weeping girl.

"My dear, I've searched everywhere for you. You almost slipped away up north, but you came back, made the capture so much easier. Thank you for that."

Fury flashes across her face, but she keeps her head down.

"I have a task for you," he coos, caressing her cheek. She shirks back in disgust.

Unfazed, he turns to us.

"You're dismissed. I need to speak to my new pet alone."

Anticipation runs through me. *Maybe he will forget to command me.*

Adder and I walk toward the door, and the guards start pulling them open.

"Oh, and Adder? Keep Soren with you."

Fuck.

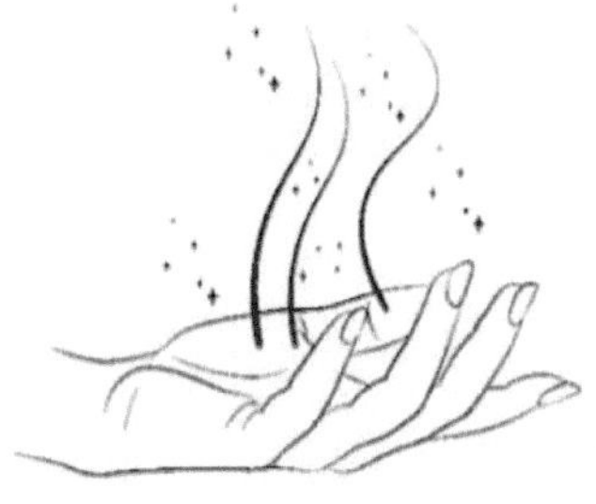

Chapter 36

Adira

"Alona?"

A voice pulls me from the depths of my pain. My senses kick in first, the salt-iron smell tickling my nose.

Lifting my head up, I blearily see a figure. I blink a few times before the image becomes clear. The court lady from our stay before. My eyes widen. Her face is filled with uncertainty.

"Emma?" My voice croaks from disuse.

Confusion floods her expression as her gaze roams over my face—the face that is not Alona's. She takes a step back.

"Wait." I rasp. "It's me. Alona."

Doubt mars her brow. I shift forward, the chains rattle from the movement. My next breath gets caught as a spasm rolls through me.

"The Alona you met wasn't real. It's always been me. My name is Adira."

"Adira." She repeats slowly, processing the information.

"Yes. Adira Selcouth."

She frowns for a moment, then her eyes widen.

"I know that name."

Now I feel confused.

"How?"

"My mother kept journals. She wrote... about a friend. Emilia. She... she was kept apart. Not like the others."

A gasp escapes me. Emmas' shock mirrors mine.

"Emilia Selcouth. My mother. She was the King's mistress?" Shock barrels through me at the revelation. *I had no idea.* My gut tightens at the thought of her being under Conri's control.

"She wasn't his normal mistress. She was..." Emma cuts off, twisting her hands. I wait for her to continue, holding my breath. The slow drip from the ceiling the only sound in the silence.

 "Always locked up. She tried to escape several times, until one day she did."

My heart twists. I glance around at the bloodstained walls. A crack in the stone letting in a damp cold. *Was she kept in a cell like this?* Emma looks at me with sympathy.

"She confided in my mother. Emilia told her that she had fallen pregnant and didn't want Dahak to know."

"What?" I croak out, disbelief coursing through me. My pendant flares with heat, I ignore the sharp sting, focusing on Emma's sullen expression.

"If you are Adira Selcouth... then King Dahak is your father."

Bile fills my mouth as Emma confirms my suspicions. I place the back of my hand to my mouth, ignoring the grit under my fingernails. *I can't believe that monster is my father.*

I take in the cell, its damp walls, the moss sprouting out between the old stones. The smell of stale air assaulting my senses. A huff of a laugh escapes me. *My own father placed me in this cell.*

You knew it had to be one of the gods, I tell myself grimly.

My mind flashes back to my childhood. To my mother making me swear that I would never take an assignment in Enelon. I remember laughing, telling her those undercover assignments were for senior guards. Her intense expression didn't crack until I swore it.

My hands tremble, the shock dampening the ache of the Makutu chains. I look to Emma, not believing my luck. "How did you find me?"

"A man passed me in the corridor. He said his name was Caspian even though he looked nothing like him, and that Alona was in the dungeon." She shrugs sheepishly; her earlier fear having lessened. "I had to come see."

I bite down hard on my lip, a metallic taste entering my mouth. *Conri must've loosened his control.* I press a hand to my chest, not daring to hope.

"His name is Soren. Did he look alright?" I ask her somewhat desperately.

Her nose wrinkles. "Fine, I guess. He whispered to me as he was walking by and didn't stop."

Tension leaks out of my shoulders.

"Why don't you know who he is? Soren was Dahak's number one assassin."

Emma lifts one shoulder. "Perhaps anonymity? I imagine being an assassin would require discretion."

I frown at that. "I suppose, but surely he's been recognized before. Even we have renderings of him in Modereo."

Her expression darkens. "King Dahak has talked about many enemies that he has, so I presume Soren would have been spotted a time or two. He probably lived mostly out on the streets instead of in the castle."

"I guess so..." I respond, still not convinced. My back unexpectedly seizes, drawing Emma's attention downward.

"What happened?" she asks, her voice shaking slightly as she takes in all the blood dried around me. Her eyes lingering on the single pot in the corner.

"It's a long story. Let's just say the King is not who he appears to be, and I found out, so he is punishing me and Soren."

Her hands cover her mouth, eyes glistening with unshed tears.

"This isn't right."

"Nothing in my life seems to be right." I mutter bitterly.

"Does he know you are his child? Maybe he'll let you out?"

I jolt forward, an ache sliding all the way down my body. "No. He mustn't know, Emma. Please tell me you'll keep it a secret."

She nods slowly. "I won't betray your trust. Your mother trusted mine with her secrets, so I will offer the same to you."

I give her a small smile at the show of empathy.

"Maybe I can help you get out of here?" She ends it as a question, seeming scared that she suggested it.

"It's okay, Emma. I don't want you to get in trouble."

She straightens up, summoning courage.

"No. I can't leave you down here. My mother would have wanted me to help Emilia's daughter. Maybe I can sneak you some food? Will that help?" she asks hesitantly.

As if it heard, my stomach growls. The last thing I ate was mushy gray porridge yesterday.

I smile sheepishly, the move causing me to wince.

"That would be great. Thank you, Emma."

She nods. "I'll be back as soon as I can."

We both pause at the sound of footsteps. Mercifully they echo in the opposite direction. We let out a collective breath.

My worried gaze finds Emma. "Just don't get into trouble."

"I wouldn't want your guard to worry." I add with a wink, lightening the moment.

She huffs out a laugh, turning to go, her eyes darting nervously up and down the corridor before taking off.

****

I get an hour of blissful silence. At least I think it was an hour. Heavy footsteps stride down the corridor. My ears strain. *Wait, there are two sets of footsteps.*

Adder strides into view, Soren walking behind him, a tortured look on his face. My breath hitches in my throat as I scan him for injuries. My hands shake in relief when I don't see anything.

"Hello, witch," Adder greets, flipping the horrid dagger.

Soren steps forward frantically when he spots me. He clutches the bars. "Adira? Gods, are you okay?"

Tears spring to my eyes. My chest lighter than it has been in days. "You're you."

An anguished look fills his face.

"Don't cry, princess. I'm me for now. But Conri barred me from touching him." Soren finishes with a dark look at Adder.

My mind grasps onto what he means, and he voices it a second later.

"I won't be able to stop him when he tortures you," he croaks out, his eyes shining as he looks helplessly at me through the bars.

My gut twists painfully. *This won't be easy for him to watch.*

"I'm sorry," I say.

His eyes snap to me. "You're sorry? Princess, I'm sorry. I failed you."

My heart warms at the tender tone that accompanies the nickname. I watch his gaze scour my cell, his lip curling up in a snarl when he spots my 'bathroom'.

I shake my head, the movement drawing a ragged breath from me. "You have nothing to be sorry about."

Adder steps forward, the nearness of the blade causing the hair on my arms to rise. "That's quite enough. These sweet words will make me vomit."

Soren clenches his fist but stays silent.

Adder whips a key out of his pocket, opening up the cell.

Soren rushes in first, crouching down in front of me. He brushes back a piece of bloodied hair, but before he can say anything, Adder drags him away. Since Conri demanded he not harm Adder, his body spasms as it fights his natural instincts.

Grabbing one of the chains, Adder shakes out the bone that's in it. It clangs against the floor. The sharp white is jarring against the soot covered stone.

He snaps it on Soren's wrist.

"Just in case you get any ideas," he tells Soren with a malicious smile. Soren's eyes darken with a promise of death. Adder just stands, unbothered by the unspoken threat.

His cold eyes turn on me. I try not to shrink back, but when he pulls the dagger out, my body lets out an involuntary shiver.

They both notice. Soren tenses, while Adder's smile grows.

"It's okay, princess. I'm here with you," Soren soothes.

I try to summon a smile, but my face feels frozen. Numb as it waits for the pain that is to come. Adder crouches down in front of me.

"Ready to talk?"

I spit at him. "You know the answer to that."

"Great answer," he replies, bringing the dagger up. My pendant burns at the nearness of the blade. The scent of fear fills the small cell. My eyes latch onto the swirling flames, pleading with it.

Adder senses my desperation. "All of this pain can be avoided. You only need to tell me what I want."

He presses it against my arm, grazing it lightly. Teasing. I stay tense, waiting for the inevitable pain.

"Not going to happen." My voice shakes, betraying my nerves.

"That is a shame." He purrs.

Finally, he pushes down, breaking the skin. I clench my teeth, fighting a scream. He keeps dragging it down the length of my arm, prolonging the pain.

A scream bursts out of me, and I vaguely hear Soren's yelling mixed with chains rattling. Adder removes the dagger, the agony lessens slightly. He quickly moves to my other arm, trailing down from shoulder to palm.

My vision blurs, black spots dance in front of my eyes. *Yes, darkness, please take me,* I plead with it. As if Adder can hear me, he removes the dagger. I slump down, sweat stings my lashes, my body shivering from the aftershocks.

"You've been harder to crack, I'll give you that. Perhaps I've been going about this the wrong way. What would happen if I were to focus my efforts on your boy?" Adder taunts. He stands up, turning toward Soren.

Soren's eyes are trained on me, his gaze full of anguish.

My heart catches. Horror momentarily seizing my vocal cords. Soren sits up straighter, his expression daring Adder to come closer.

"No. Leave him alone," I rasp out desperately. "Are you bored with me already?" I end with a mocking smirk.

Soren snarls. "No, Adira. Let him."

He glares up at Adder with thick hatred.

"You're already dead," Soren promises him, the dark threat clear in his eyes. "So do your worst. Because when we get out of this, and we will, you will be the first person I come for."

My heart flips at his words. Adder's face tightens angrily.

"We'll see about that."

He brings the dagger up to Soren's chest, ripping easily through his shirt. Heat presses down in the cell as the blade moves closer to his skin.

He wastes no time. The instant Soren's skin breaks, agony flares in his eyes. He keeps quiet, though.

I whimper as beads of sweat appear on his brow.

Adder hears the sound and turns.

"Ready to talk, princess?" he arches a brow, his tone taking a mocking lilt at the nickname.

Soren shakes his head at me, his eyes telling me not to say anything. I can feel my resolve crumbling as his body shakes violently.

His breathing turns ragged, the chains clinking as he tugs on them. I don't allow myself to look away from the torture that he's taking for me. The torch crackles, the dim light showing the strain in his neck as he keeps quiet.

After what feels like an hour, Adder stops. My heart batters rapidly like I'd been the one being tortured. Sweat and blood drip down Soren's face, his eyes droop as he fights for consciousness. Adder sighs, like he's disappointed in us.

"That was your last chance," he tells us.

"We have found another way to get the information, so you are essentially useless, Adira."

Soren's eyes widen with panic.

Fear mixes with hopelessness. My odds of getting out of here diminishing at his words.

Adder unties Soren, dragging him to his feet and through the cell door. He slams it shut behind them. Soren sags against the wall, using the support to keep himself upright.

"What happens now?" I ask with a resigned sigh.

Adder smiles widely.

"Now. The King's pit. A fight until one stops breathing."

Dread rises up. With those parting words, they walk away.

Chapter 37

Soren

I sit numbly in the throne room, barely listening to Conri spewing lies to the people around. Then my ears catch the words that have been haunting me.

"Combattere fine alle morte." Excited shouts ring out through the room. I twist toward him.

"We have a new contender." He turns, winking at me when he says this. My stomach twists painfully.

"Tonight, my champion will go against a witch!" They all cheer and boo at the word witch. Animosity fills the air, making the room feel dangerously charged.

Clenching my fists, I scan the faces around me, the ones I should have paid more attention to over the years. The court people I thought were mindless bores all have crazed grins on their faces; not a single one looking remorseful that Conri is sending someone publicly to their death.

I hope Emma can help her, I think to myself, though doubt lingers when I imagine the gentle court lady.

"The Stregoni are vile, unnatural beings. None should be allowed to live!" A yell of agreement sounds through the room.

Disgust fills me. *All of these people are monsters. They don't know anything about the world, only what Conri has poisoned them with.*

After the clapping dies down, Conri lazily glances over the crowd.

"You are all dismissed. The festivities start at the ninth hour."

Everyone starts dispersing out of the room, taking the frenzied energy with them.

Conri turns to me.

"Once the little witch is out of the way, you will stop fighting me so much and just succumb to your fate."

I try to keep the sneer off my face, knowing that angering him won't help anything.

"I will never give in."

He shrugs, not believing me.

"Seeing her die will cause you to break. I'm not worried."

My stomach flips at his casual talk of her death. He turns to Adder.

"Go get her ready for tonight."

He bows his head before strolling away.

"You just sit here until I come back and get you." He smirks, standing and walking out of the room.

Silence fills the space, leaving me with my bleak thoughts.

****

Hours later, he returns with a wicked smile.

"Follow me. It's time to watch your girlfriend die."

I glare at him, but my legs start walking forward.

He leads us through the long corridor and up a set of stairs. Two guards pull the doors open as Conri nears. As they open, the shouts get louder, rumbling the area, showing their excitement for the bloodshed about to happen.

Conri steps out onto the white-stoned balcony, striding to the railing. He raises a hand and the crowd silences. The rancid smell of blood and sweat fills the air. My nose wrinkles in distaste. *They never properly clean the arena.*

I let my eyes trail over the circular stadium, taking in the full seats. I can't spot a single empty one. The ground in the center was brown, now it's tainted with dried blood, making it look more maroon.

"Let justice be served tonight!" Conri booms out.

The cheering intensifies, shaking the structure. Conri smiles at the reaction, as if he's happy they are as bloodthirsty as he is.

"Give it up for my champion!" Conri shouts while waving a hand toward a barred entrance. The guards beside turn the lever, and the grate rolls upward. Heavy steps stomp out. A massive body follows, pumping its arms up to the crowd, riling them further.

I gulp at the sheer size of him. *Adira's strong, but she's weak from being tortured.*

"Now, the moment everyone has been waiting for... the witch!"

Guards roll up the lever to another entrance. Adira strolls out, head held high.

The crowd boos, throwing things down toward her. I'm assaulted by the smell of rotting fish. I notice her eyes narrow slightly. Despite the situation, my lips twitch to a smirk at her defiance.

Her eyes shift to her opponent, a flash of imperceptible fear crossing them. He roars out, pointing at her with death in his eyes.

I have to do something, I turn frantically.

Conri senses my agitation.

"Sit and don't move." He demands.

My body obeys as my mind fills with hopelessness.

I'm sorry, Adira.

Chapter 38

Adira

The sound is deafening. The chanting crowd reaching a decibel so high that the ground seems to hum. I glance down, noticing the dried blood has produced a hard mud.

My gut churns from both the smell of the rotting fish and the fear of what is to come. My magic stays dormant within me, almost like this whole arena is one big dead zone. I shift my feet. *Of course he would build this death chamber on land that doesn't allow magic.*

Humid air suffocates me, aiding in my panic.

It's okay, you can breathe. I force my heartbeat to slow, taking controlled breaths.

I look up toward the small balcony, finding Conri staring down at me with a smug smile. Beside him sits Soren, a tortured expression on his face. I shoot him a small, reassuring smile, even though my body is twisted with nerves.

I'm not as weak as I would be right now since Emma snuck some food to me yesterday evening. *Good timing.* And they did remove the Makutu chains for this vicious display.

Scanning the crowd, I try to find Emma through the angry faces. My gaze snags on a silver dressed lady hovering near an exit. Her face twisted with worry.

I shoot Emma a quick smile, hoping she doesn't carry any guilt for where I ended up.

I face my opponent, sizing him up. He is a large man, his arm muscles the size of his legs. A long-jagged scar runs across his cheek, making him look even more menacing. I don't let panic overtake me. *Use speed, not brute force,* I remind myself.

He struts forward, not looking worried in the slightest.

I smirk despite the current predicament I'm in. *Cocky males.*

"Kill her!"

"The witch needs to bleed!"

I scoff at the bloodthirsty comments while keeping my eyes trained on the giant in front of me.

He charges at me without warning. I slip into my fighting stance, watching his body for any sign of direction. When he's a foot away, he shifts slightly to the left. I wait a moment, then shift left, spinning out of his path. Digging his heels into the hard ground, he turns with a snarl.

A couple of chuckles roll through the audience. He stops for a moment, eyeing me as he realizes it won't be as easy as he originally thought.

Dropping into his fighting stance, he snaps his hand forward. I duck back, leaving my ribs open. He lands a swift kick to my right side. I groan at the pain but quickly push it down, bouncing back to reorient myself. The pain pales in comparison to Adder's torment.

He moves quicker than I realized he could, knocking me onto my back. The air huffs out of me when I slam into the rough ground. I wheeze, trying to fill my lungs. He straddles me, pulling back his fist. He brings it down hard on my face. A ringing fills my ears as he lands punch after punch. My nose throbs from the blood spilling out of it, and my eyes start to swell shut.

Panic takes hold of me. *This is it. I'm going to die.* Regret fills me. I think about Soren and what could've been.

My face snaps sideways from a hit, my eyes trying to find Soren one last time. I stifle a sob when I realize I can only see blurry outlines.

My mother's voice cuts through my bittersweet thoughts, ... *always something near you... there is no impossible situation. Look... Adira—look.*

A groan escapes me, but I force my heavy eyes open. The behemoth of a man having paused his pommeling to amp up the crowd. He raises his hands, signaling them to cheer louder. *Bastard.*

Splaying a hand out, I reach around the ground, remembering the rocks that littered it. Deep wrenching pain causes my body to twitch, but I keep going. My fingers brush against something hard. The scar-faced man has turned back at the movement, disbelief showing on his face.

I grasp it with my hand, using all my strength to drive it into his head. He grunts in surprise, releasing some pressure off my body. I twist my hips with a scream, shoving him sideways. I roll the opposite way, twisting onto my feet.

He stands with a growl, blood dripping from his temple. I sway slightly, dizziness threatening to knock me down. The stench of copper stings the air, the crowd's roaring a distant buzz in my still-ringing ears.

My teeth stay clenched, forcing myself to stay conscious. Blood drips down my face, obscuring my vision. I quickly wipe it away.

"She's still standing!"

"End her!"

More lovely sentiments reach my ears. I tune them out, keeping my energy focused on staying upright.

If you are against an opponent that has the upper hand, there is a pressure point that can knock them out. My mind replays the memory, my training kicking in. I bring my fingers up to the side of my head. Glancing at his bleeding temple, I decide the right side is the best spot, hoping the injury will make it easier.

He races toward me, an ugly snarl on his face. I jump to the side and quickly release the rock. It careens through the air, striking him against the temple. His head jerks to the side from the motion. He drops to his knees but stays conscious. *Damn it. I didn't hit him hard enough.*

I bolt forward, adrenaline coursing through me. Bringing up my leg, I twist it sharply toward his head. I release a yell as I make contact. His head snaps to the side and his body spins from the motion. He falls down, unconscious. My legs shake from exertion, I go down hard onto my knees. Sweat and blood drips down my body, soaking into the muddy ground, taking my energy with it.

Dragging in ragged breaths, I peer up the balcony. Conri has a tight expression on his face, the disbelief he's trying to hide shining through. Soren's face holds relief.

My lips tilt up into a teasing smirk. Conri's expression darkens.

"It is called a fight to the death for a reason," he says sharply, his voice slightly muffled from the blood filling my ears.

I tilt my head at him. "You want death? Fine." I rasp out, my voice hoarse from disuse.

I crouch down next to the scar-faced man, wrapping my hands around his throat. I squeeze, cutting off his airway. My arms shake, the adrenaline from the fight wearing off. Threads of guilt threaten to overtake me as I choke an unconscious person. *He tried to kill you, Adira. It's you or him.* I sigh against the logic, keeping a tight hold.

His pulse thrums weakly under my hands. He's almost gone.

Just before I can finish the job, I hear a shout, the voice rising above the chatter of the crowd. My eyes instantly look to Soren.

His expression is panicked, his eyes locked on something behind me. Before I can turn, I'm hit by a blunt force. A sharp pain ricochets through my head. My body sways, darkness leaking into my vision. I hit the hard ground.

Then, nothing.

Chapter 39

Soren

Even if Conri hadn't commanded me to stay in this spot, I still would be frozen. My eyes stay locked on Adira. Her body looks so small in the large arena. Blood soaks her clothes, leaking onto the ground around her.

A guard leans forward, saying something to Conri. My heart is pounding too loudly for me to hear anything. A wave of animosity hovers over the balcony. I rip my gaze away from Adira, looking at Conri. His nostrils are flared in annoyance.

A spark of pride runs through me at his obvious frustration. *She's stronger than you think.*

My eyes trail back to her. Guards have come out and started dragging both Adira and the other contestant's body away. I grip the handles of my chair tightly.

"What are you going to do with her?" I ask Conri, hiding the shakiness I feel.

"She shouldn't have won." He shakes his head as he says this.

He turns to me, his face twisting into a fake smile.

"Now, we tell everyone she was cheating and hang her in the morning."

My eyes widen. He grins cruelly at my reaction.

"You can't."

"Boy, I can do anything I want. I am the King."

I spit at his feet.

"You are no King of mine."

He just stares lazily at me.

"Stand," he commands.

I stand.

"Turn in a circle."

I grit my teeth at the ridiculous command, but my body turns. He chuckles darkly, moving in closer to me.

"Looks like you don't have a choice."

I bite back the slew of insults I want to say. He seems to notice my sharpening gaze because his face clouds over.

"Report back to the throne room. I will deal with your insubordination later."

My feet turn, striding off the balcony. I glare at the guards around, noticing them laugh at my lack of control.

My thoughts drift back to Adira. Panic overtakes me.

What am I going to do?

****

Once I'm back in the throne room, the command lifts. Tension eases out of my limbs, giving me back my control. I pace around the room while I wait, trying to come up with a viable plan before the day ends. I grab my hair in frustration, powerlessness surging through me.

But you're not powerless, I remind myself. *When you aren't under command, you can still get inside people's heads.*

A spark of hope flutters within me. Before I can devise a plan, the doors creak loudly. They swing open and Conri strides in with a confident swagger.

He spots me, raising an eyebrow when he catches me staring.

"You can go sit in the corner, pet."

I breathe deeply, biting my tongue. My body leads me to a corner with a chair. I plop down onto the hard wood. He smirks at me.

The throne room starts filling up with people inquiring about political nonsense. I drown out the voices.

Eventually, everyone clears out of the room, their heavy footsteps echoing down the long corridor, getting fainter with each minute. Conri sighs heavily.

The silence doesn't last. Frantic footsteps pound closer, approaching the throne room. A frazzled-looking courier runs in.

He bows immediately. "Your Majesty. You have received an urgent message from J."

Conri straightens at the name.

Interesting.

"Bring it here," he barks.

The courier stands on shaky legs, walking forward with the letter extended. Conri snatches it from his hands.

"You are dismissed."

He goes to open it, then pauses.

Looking behind him at the guards, he scowls, "You are dismissed too."

They bow and quickly stroll out of the room.

I hold my breath, realizing he may have forgotten me, hoping this is a chance to learn something about him, something I can use as leverage to free Adira.

Conri's head snaps up, like he could feel the hope flittering through the room. His gaze narrows on me in the corner.

"Go back to your room. Report to me first thing tomorrow," he sneers out.

My body obeys, moving me toward the door.

A sense of loss fills me as I leave the room, my gut telling me that staying would have told me something important. A secret he doesn't want to share. *Who is J?*

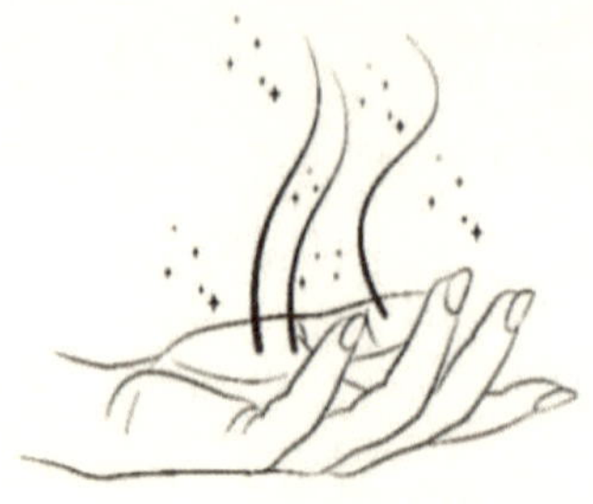

Chapter 40

Adira

The pounding in my head wakes me. I groggily open my eyes, wincing at the dim lighting. The smell of damp stone mixed with fear surrounds me.

I'm back in the cell.

The Makutu chains once again holding me captive. Anger rises quickly. *That lying snake. I won the challenge, and they knocked me out.*

Footsteps sound rapidly down the narrow hall. A shadow grows larger as it gets closer to me. I freeze, staring at the silhouette, pleading that it's not Adder.

The figure rushes into view. The tension leaks out of me, but concern rises up at the kind face.

"What are you doing down here, Emma?"

Her troubled gaze scans my body. She gulps audibly at the sight of the dried blood.

"I had to make sure you were alive. I couldn't leave you here," she whispers.

I give her a weak smile, remembering her worried face in the arena.

"I appreciate that, Emma. But after the fight, I can't imagine I'll be here much longer. There's no reason to keep bringing me food. And please don't feel guilty."

Her face sharpens.

"Fuck that."

I choke on a laugh, surprised at her language, the words so opposite from her delicate demeanor.

"You need to escape. Tonight. The King announced your hanging for tomorrow at dawn."

Any humor I had felt disappeared. I close my eyes at that news, trying not to dwell on the fact that I've been too close to death multiple times. Panic snares me once again, the feeling more familiar than joy.

So that's it. Everything is over. A low bitter laugh wheezes out of me. *This fucking sucks.*

My body slumps further to the ground, my remaining energy disappearing with my hope.

"Here," Emma whispers, glancing around. "Take this."

She slides a rusty key through the thick bars. My eyes widen at the sight.

"How did you get this?"

"I have my ways." She winks, a blush rising up on her cheeks. *Ahh, her guard.*

I smile warmly at her. The cuts on my face pulling at the motion.

"Thank you, Emma. Thanks for giving me a chance. I will never forget it."

She smiles shyly.

"It seems like fate that our parents were friends. And friends don't need to say thank you." She waves off my gratitude. My heart swells at her words.

I clasp her hand through the bars, a jolt of pain running through me from the motion. I ignore it, looking at her earnestly.

"Then I won't say thank you. I'll say that I'm lucky to have met you. You have been a friend to me in the darkest circumstances. I hope that the Arae bless you. I hope you and your guard get the happiness you deserve."

"Thank you, Adira," she responds, sounding choked up.

She clears her throat. "I only wish we could have gotten to know each other better."

I squeeze her hand before letting go. "In another life maybe."

"I hope for you to get out of this and live a content life," she says softly.

I give her a smile that's more like a grimace.

"I don't know if that's in the cards for me. But I wish that also," I admit to her, contemplating the prophecy.

A clang sounds down the corridor. We both freeze.

"You need to get out of here," I tell her urgently. "No matter my fate, don't spend too long worrying. Live your life to the fullest. Also, have your guard up around the King."

She nods, but tears track down her cheeks. Standing, she gathers her skirts in one hand and quietly rushes off down the hall.

I watch her go, hoping it's not the last time I will get to see her. Loneliness presses in on me as she disappears around the corner, a single tear sliding down my face. I force the distracting emotions away, gripping the rusty key. I hide it in the bucket that I'm meant to do my business in, gagging slightly at the putrid smell of old urine.

I move away from the bucket, leaning against one of the hard stone walls as I wait for the guards to do their rounds. Hope flutters from what Emma selflessly did.

She gave me a chance.

****

A steady gait draws near. I tense, then force myself to relax. Adder walks into view, behind him a timid boy carries a bucket. He unlocks the cell and ushers the boy in. The boy places the bucket of water down in front of me with shaking hands. The water sloshes over the side.

Adder's face twists. "Useless. You can't even carry a bucket of water without spilling it."

The boy shakes, eyes downcast.

Adder snorts with disgust. "Get out of my sight."

The boy scampers off. I sneer at Adder.

"Are you so insecure that you feel the need to attack a child?"

Adder turns, slapping me across the face.

"Shut up, witch. I don't answer to you."

He gestures to the bucket. "You need to clean yourself up." He looks me up and down with revulsion. "People need to be able to see your face when you are hanged tomorrow."

An involuntary shiver travels through me as I casually hear about my death. He smiles at the reaction.

"Soon enough. I won't have to deal with you anymore."

I narrow my gaze on him, refusing to show him any more of my nerves.

"And I guess neither will Soren."

I flinch at his name.

"Maybe that's where I'll go now. Just to remind him that come tomorrow, you will be gone. For good."

I grit my teeth. "Leave him alone."

"So sweet. Too bad you can't stop me."

I look away from his sharp stare, drawing in a painful breath as I think about Soren.

"I'll come collect you at dawn. Try to look presentable," he says with doubt lacing his tone.

With that, he turns, walking out of the cell. He slams the door shut, the bars rattling from the force. Slipping a large key in the lock, he latches it. The click echoes through the dim cells. He smirks at me one last time before walking away.

Once he leaves, I put a plan into action. The guard on duty strolls past my cell. He glances in, noticing I haven't moved to clean myself yet.

Banging on the bars, he shouts, "Clean yourself up."

I cringe, pretending I'm afraid of his anger. He snickers at my feebleness and strolls away. When he's out of sight, I push the bucket over. Water sloshes over the muddy stone, spreading the dirt and blood around.

"Guard. My bucket spilt. I need more water," I call out to the corridor.

I hear his angry steps before his face comes into view.

"You worthless witch. Why should I get you more water?"

"The King sent it for a reason. I'm sure he wouldn't appreciate your inability to control a prisoner on your watch."

He sneers down at me, hatred in his eyes. The indecision clear on his face. Finally, he relents.

"I'll be back in two minutes," he says harshly.

When he walks out of sight, I drag myself over to the other side of my cell. Turning away, I reach my hand into the foul bucket, grasping the key. I shove to a standing position, the Makutu chains dragging on the floor. Shakily, I gather up the chains, holding them to my chest. My body sways, black spots enter my vision, but I let the adrenaline force them out. I reach through the bars and turn my wrist. The key slides into the lock easily. I twist, leaning heavily against the bars.

My breath comes in ragged pants. The lock turns. I push the cell open. A whimper of relief escapes me, the feeling quickly chased away by panic. *Will I make it?*

My sluggish limbs press forward, ambling down the corridor in the opposite direction of the guard. The path splits in two ways. One way has an ancient door with a brass image on it at the end, while the other is longer and dark. Not remembering the ancient door, I turn right, taking the dark passage.

Shouts echo behind me. A second later, barks bounce off the walls, signaling the pursuit of the Umbrai. An involuntary shiver mixes with the déjà vu of the situation.

My pulse thrums loudly, blocking out the sound of my footsteps.

I move faster, pushing my body to its limit. My power pushes through the restraints of the chain, dredging up anything it can. The sight of the stone door causes me to weep. *I'm almost there.*

I get to the door, pressing against the cold stone with shaking hands. My legs give out. I fall to my knees, allowing the sting of the rock to jar me away from unconsciousness.

The door gives easily when I press against it again. Shock and uneasiness fill me. I glance down at my hands in bewilderment. Shouts sound again, closer this time. I tamp down my confusion and scurry out the door. The door slams shut behind me, the distinct sound of a lock clicking. Instead of worrying, I thank the goddesses and escape forward.

I pass the treeline, the forest blurring around me as I run, my sole focus on getting away.

Then, a figure steps into view.

Soren.

His steady strides fill me with apprehension. I freeze at the sight of him, gulping at the apologetic look on his face.

"Run—please. I can't—"

All my optimism trickles out at his words. Defeat weighs heavily on my shoulders.

"I'm too weak. I can't outrun you."

His face twists into a tortured expression.

He gathers me up into his arms, the chains clink between us. Even with a tight grip, I relish his warmth.

Another figure steps out from behind the trees.

Adder.

"I got this, Soren. You can let her go."

"No," Soren responds. Adder just smiles at the blatant refusal.

"Let me rephrase that. The King allowed me a thread of eather to command you with when he is unavailable." Soren freezes at that.

"You will let her go. Now." His warmth moves away at the command, his fists clenching as he tries to fight the compulsion.

Adder steps toward me.

"Now, before we take you back, why don't we have a little fun?"

I step backward at the crazed look in his eyes.

He runs a hand down my arm.

"You are a pretty little thing. Should I find out for myself why you are so obsessed with her?" Adder taunts Soren.

"Don't you dare." Soren spits out, venom coating his words. Adder ignores him, bringing his face closer to mine.

Bile rises up at the implication. "I would rather die."

His face twists in anger.

"Fine. Have it your way." He whips out Belial. The swirling blade of flames pulls at me, yearning for my pain. Heat crackles through the clearing.

"You ca-can't kill me. The King wants me alive to make a spectacle," I stutter out, fear causing me to falter the words.

Adder just shrugs.

"Accidents happen."

I break out into a cold sweat. *I'm going to die.*

Soren senses the shift of energy in the air.

"Don't, Adder. Please, I-I'll do anything," he pleads as he twists in place, trying to beat the command. My heartbeat pounds in my throat as Soren's voice cracks.

Adder smiles evilly. "You already will do anything."

Turning back to me, he wastes no time, pressing the blade onto my skin. My muscles seize, the pain numbing my motor senses.

Soren is shouting at Adder.

Adder slams the blade into my gut.

My body tenses; blood drips out of my mouth. A numbness settles over my whole body. My gaze finds Soren's, his eyes distraught.

"NO," Soren shouts.

A blast of energy fills the area. I fall sideways onto the ground. Soren charges at Adder. *Impossible. Am I already dead?*

They land on the ground in a tangle of limbs. Soren holds out a hand, his eyes glowing slightly. A string of eather appears, shooting into Adder's chest. Adder's eyes widen, the startled expression frozen on his face as he falls to the ground.

Dead.

Soren hurries over to me, horror overtaking his face as he presses down on my wound. My heart beats sluggishly, knowing the end is close.

"It'll be okay. You'll be okay. I won't lose you now."

Tears leak out of my eyes, my breaths coming in short wheezes.

A glow works its way down Soren's arm and through the hand covering my wound.

Thump……. Thump…….. Thump.

The wound gets hot, the skin feels like it's stitching itself together. My body tries to shift away from the unnatural heat, but I stay unmoving.

Thump… Thump… Thump.

Soren's stunned eyes match mine. *How is this happening?*

Thump. Thump. Thump.

The wound closes. My heart beats faster, the adrenaline and magic mixing in my system.

He sits back, unbelieving eyes scanning my body.

"Y-you healed me," I stammer out.

"How?" he half-whispers, his eyes wide with incredulity.

I sit up shakily, wincing against the stiffness of my body. Facing Soren, I stare at him, trying to figure out how it's possible.

"I don't know," I murmur back.

A snap of thunder sounds above. Gray clouds roll in swiftly, but no rain falls. I stare up with a frown at the unnatural weather.

A crack of lightning reverberates through the air. The sound reaches us before the blast does.

We don't have time to panic as a bolt of lightning shoots down, striking us. My vision goes white, a searing feeling grabs at my chest. My hair blows back from the force of it.

Energy caresses us, forming a small funnel of magic. The searing lessens to warm heat. The air hums, causing the earth to momentarily shake. My Makutu chains vibrate before falling to the ground. I whimper in relief.

The power whips around us a few times before it dissipates, my vision returning to normal. The area turns lighter, we look up at the now clear sky, not a single cloud remaining.

I scrutinize Soren, trying to find any injuries.

"I'm okay," he says with a dazed voice.

"So am I."

My hand flies to the heat that still lingers on my chest. My eyes widen, and I grasp at my shirt, pulling it down to see the spot. Only when I find his matching mark do I understand.

Holy goddess.

An eternal symbol crosses over a heart, the rare symbol shining on our bodies.

Our eyes meet.

We are true mates of heart.

Chapter 41

Soren

My heart beats erratically. Shock numbing my senses. I stare into her eyes, the ring of violet pulling me in. Her features appearing more defined than before. I run a trembling hand through my hair, trying to ignore the cold sweat that broke out after I somehow healed Adira.

The leaves rustle with leftover power, the forest itself seeming sharper in color.

My mind spins from a sense of fullness, or perhaps the use of magic. I stare down at my hands, the lingering feel of power still resonating in me.

How is this possible? I've never known...

The thoughts are dizzying, but they trail off as Adira grips my hands.

"Are you okay?" she says with a breathless tone.

My gaze takes in her beaten figure. Reaching my hands out, I embrace her tightly, holding her swaying body upright. An echo of pain throbs my body, the same places she's hurt.

"I don't feel the command to capture you anymore," I tell her, my eyes widening at my new freedom. Dogs bark in the distance, we tense but loosen up when we realize how far away they sound. *They must've gone the wrong way. Thank the gods for that.*

"Are you okay? How did the chains come off?" I repeat the question back to her, seeing the Makutu chains lying on the ground beside us. Her injuries from before still adorn her body. *I should have healed all her wounds. But how?*

She smiles weakly.

"Physically, everything hurts, especially my ribs. But..." Her hand rises up to my face, grazing my cheek. "I've never felt more complete. And I think... the divine energy broke through the chains."

Her hand trails down to my chest. She holds it over the new symbol, as if she can't believe it happened. I cover her hand with my own.

"I've always known there was something here. I just didn't know it was *this*. I have never felt this way about anyone before you," I admit to her gently.

Her eyes soften.

"Me too," she agrees.

Leaning down, I kiss the top of her head. She sighs and presses into my arms. A sense of contentment fills me from the feeling of her in my arms. Nothing has ever felt as right.

"What does this bond mean? I don't know much about it." I admit.

She lifts a shoulder. "There aren't many recorded cases of true mates of heart. Each one states something different happening... so I suppose it differs for each couple."

I consider that for a moment. She shifts in my arms, causing a dull ache to flare up my body. My eyes widen.

"I think I can feel your pain."

Her mouth drops open.

"It's just a dull ache right now, but it's all over my body." My jaw works as I say this.

"That's... I was going to say impossible, but I suppose that word shouldn't be in my vocabulary anymore."

"Why didn't the blast heal your wounds?" I wonder aloud, glancing down at the broken chains.

"I can't even begin to understand the thoughts of the Arae..." she trails off, falling silent with a look of concentration. Then, she goes rigid. I pull back.

"What's wrong?" I ask, scanning her.

Her eyes are wide.

"Speaking of impossible. How did you do it? Where did that power come from?"

The power swirls around in my gut, as if it likes being the main topic.

"I don't know... I've never felt anything like that before. I can still feel it within me. Do you think it was the Arae when they blessed us as true mates of heart?"

She shakes her head.

"No. It's said that true mates of heart occur when both beings are at their fullest power. Maybe that power was hidden within you the whole time?" She ends it off on a question, but what she says rings true.

"That must be it." I nod slowly in agreement. "I've always felt more comfortable in the forest, surrounded by nature." My mind spins, failing to fully grasp that I've had power my entire life.

A twinkle sparks in her eyes as a grin spreads across her face.

"Let's see it then."

"What?" I respond dumbly, my eyes lingering on her bright smile.

By the gods, she's beautiful. I didn't think I'd get to see her smile again.

"Show me your magic. Call it up."

"Are you sure? I don't know how to control it," I say skeptically, even as my power coils inside me excitedly. The air seems to fall denser in anticipation.

"I trust you." She waves off my concern. Warmth erupts throughout my body at her words. *She finally trusts me again.*

I squeeze her hands, unsure how to voice what I'm feeling.

"Thank you." My voice comes out thick with emotion.

She smiles softly. "Now, show me what you've got, pretty boy."

A chuckle escapes me at the use of the old taunt.

Pulling my hands from hers, I close my eyes. *Okay, magic... come up? Show yourself?*

I swear I hear it chuckle at me. It doesn't move though. I frown, concentrating on it. *Earth,* it seems to say. I press one hand into the soft ground and hold the other upward. The ground trembles beneath my palm, energy rushing up through the dirt to the surface.

I hear her soft gasp and open my eyes. Hovering over my palm is a ball of whirling energy. A heady tingle covers my body as the eather crackles within me. It sparks out sporadically, flashing through the forest. The air crackles with energy, raising the hair on my arms. Adira chuckles slightly at the chaotic display. I focus harder, and it settles back into a ball.

Her eyes are filled with awe. The flare of my magic lighting her face, giving her an ethereal glow. My lips part at the sight of her beauty. My thoughts derail and my power dissipates. I forget about the distant barks and voices, captured by Adira's gaze.

I step forward into her space, grabbing her waist with my right hand. Her breath hitches. I tilt her head back, grasping the back of her neck. Our lips crash together in a surge of desire. I deepen the kiss, pressing my body into hers for more contact. Her hands come up, grabbing greedily at my back. My hand slides higher on her back, touching a warm wetness. I freeze, remembering her other injuries. Stepping back, I look at my hand. Blood coats it.

Squeezing my eyes shut, I curse at myself.

"I'm so sorry, princess. You're injured," I croak out shamefully.

She smiles lightly. "Never apologize for kissing me."

My lips twitch up at her words. I lean forward, giving her one more peck on the lips.

"Can I heal you?" I ask, ignoring my exhaustion.

"You should be able to with the new bond."

"Okay, let me try." I caress her cheek.

A blush covers her face.

"Okay," she agrees.

I grab her cheeks, resisting the urge to lean in and kiss her again. Closing my eyes, I feel around for my magic.

Uh, hello. Can you help me out? I want to heal her. It swirls around but doesn't rise. A wave of frustration flows through me before I realize my mistake.

"I forgot I, uh, need to be touching the earth."

She squeezes my hand, dispelling the overwhelming emotions that were rising. She gracefully sits on the ground, pulling me with her. My back burns as I sit, a wince crosses my face knowing it's not my injury. Reaching down, I sink one hand into the soil while the other grazes her cheek.

Heal her now. I command.

It responds rapidly to my tone, rising up to the surface of my skin. I direct it toward my hands, and it moves into Adira. A bead of sweat mars my brow as I concentrate on keeping hold of the power.

It's energy just like your mind magic, Soren. You can do this. I tell myself.

Images emerge in my mind, her injuries appearing up close. My jaw clenches at all the images it shows me. She must be in so much pain, more pain than what I'm feeling from her.

Yes, heal all of those.

It heeds my orders, rolling over the wounds, leaving unmarred skin in its wake. I breathe out in relief, my shoulders releasing a tension I didn't know I had. A light throbbing starts in my temples.

My power starts receding from her body, working its way back up to my arms. Once it settles back into me, I gently remove my hands. I slump down, feeling like I just got beaten up. My head pounds, momentarily drawing out any thoughts. I let my hand rest in the earth, hoping its energy will counteract the dizziness.

"Thank you," she whispers to me, wrapping me in a hug.

"Anytime, princess," I tell her, resting my head on top of hers.

"So, you are an earth wielder." Adira voices it out loud with a cheeky smile.

I shrug with a half grin. "I guess so."

Shouts ring out in the distance, this time moving in our direction.

Shit. How could we have forgotten we are being chased?

"We need to go. Are you okay to run?" I ask her, rising unsteadily onto my feet. Her features sharpen with determination. My own persistence rising up to meet hers.

"I'm ready." Pride flows through me at her strength.

We turn away from the voices, facing the ominous forest. Taking a deep breath, we surge into it. Running as fast as we can, while keeping our steps as silent as possible. I leap over a fallen log. Adira jumps gracefully over it a second later. A bird crows loudly, like it's warning us to move faster.

After what feels like hours, the voices behind dim before disappearing altogether. We've reached a dense part of the forest. Trees lean over us, their gnarled branches reaching to us desperately. I put my hand out to stop Adira.

"I think we lost them. We can stop here for the night. Use those bushes to shield us," I say, pointing to an overgrown area of bushes.

She nods, catching her breath. Fatigue lining her eyes.

I curse to myself. *I shouldn't have pushed her so hard; she needs time to fully heal.*

We settle onto the ground, my body heavier than I realized. *Damn, I guess I need time to heal too.* Nature envelops us, its natural energy sinking into us.

I pull her against me. She rests her head on my shoulder.

"I found out that Conri is my father." She whispers to me. Shock takes hold.

"I always thought my father would come save me from my mother's lessons when I was growing up." A choked sound escapes her. "If I got my wish, I'd probably be imprisoned or dead."

I squeeze her tight, refusing to think about a world without her in it. "I'm sorry, princess."

She laughs dryly. "That monster sired me. Part of him is inside me."

I tilt her chin up, looking into her eyes. "I know what you are thinking and you are nothing like that monster."

She smiles weakly like she doesn't fully believe me. "But what if I turn into that one day?"

"Impossible." I shake my head. "There's too much good in you. It will always drown out the bad."

Her eyes glisten at my words. She settles back into my side. Silence descends on us. *I can't believe that monster sired her. That seems impossible.*

Adira's uneasy energy crackles through the air, drawing me from my thoughts.

"What's wrong?" I ask her.

She gulps audibly.

"The prophecy."

"What about the prophecy?"

A tear leaks out of her eye.

"The last part... it's about sacrificing who I hold closest to my heart."

My body freezes, already coming to my own realization.

She looks into my eyes, hers brimming with tears.

"It's about you."

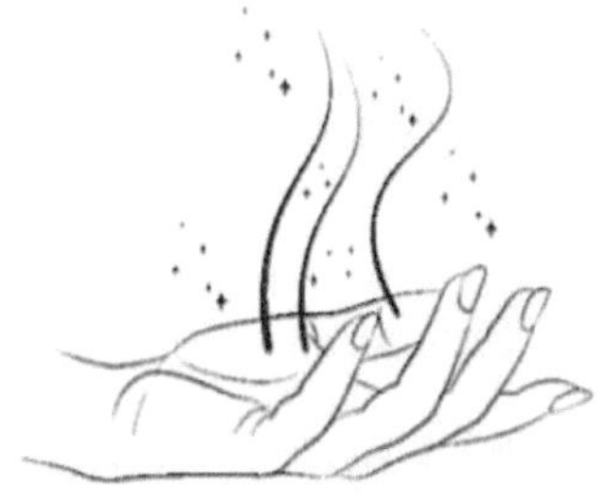

Chapter 42

Adira

Shock and pain steal my breath. His eyes shutter at my words, then he pulls me close.

"Let's not worry about that now."

I pull back. "What? How can we not worry about it? The prophecy says that I have to... have to... kill you." I whisper the last words, feeling my heart shatter from even uttering them.

"Maybe we misinterpreted it," he tells me, though his voice reveals his doubt.

"It says that I need to sacrifice the life which I hold closest to my heart." I whisper out, pressing my hand onto his fresh mark.

He covers my hand with his. "Maybe there is another way."

My mate mark aches. I take a deep breath, inhaling the crisp pine.

He grabs my chin, turning my head toward him. We lock eyes, his blue ones showing an emotion I've never seen.

"Let's focus on the next part before we worry about this."

"Okay," I agree readily, grasping onto anything that will take my mind away from it.

"Okay." He smiles at me. I relax slightly. "Should we explore the ancient ground?"

Our earlier plans suddenly seem so foolish.

"I had lots of time to think when I was in that cell."

Soren gulps audibly at my words. His arm tightens around me while he waits for me to continue.

"The next part is '*To find out the truth, you must venture back to when divinities were youth.*'"

His brows mar in confusion. "How do we venture back? Is there a way to time travel?"

I chuckle slightly. "Maybe, but that's not how we will do it."

He silently urges me to continue.

"There's two ways we can do this. One is finding the last living member of the Sage family. They know the true history, but this person hasn't been seen in years. The other way is that there is a legend about an object that lets you see into the past. You can see anything you want to know."

He frowns slightly. "Both sound difficult."

This makes me laugh outright.

"Nothing is ever easy for me, so this doesn't surprise me."

He rubs my shoulders, sensing the bitterness hidden within my words.

"We can ask around, see what will be easier to try."

I smile up at him, liking the sound of *we*.

"Now, get some sleep," he says, placing a quick kiss to my head. I melt into him, letting my exhaustion pull me under.

****

I stretch my arms over my head, feeling ten times better than before. Soren's head shifts down when he realizes I'm awake.

"Are you feeling better?"

"I am. I don't think I've ever slept that well before," I admit softly.

"Me either," he replies, his gaze intense.

I push up, ignoring the stiffness of my body. Every pain pales in comparison to that wretched blade. I shiver at the thought.

"Cold?" Soren asks, pulling me close.

I go to say no but instead burrow deeper into his arms. Warmth and contentment drown out my lingering thoughts. *I could get used to this.*

My mother's unwanted words trickle into my mind. *I'm sorry, my love. Nothing will come easily to you. Everything you have will disappear, everything you want will be ripped away. Use the coldness of the world to harden yourself. You will need to be ruthless to survive.*

I sigh, knowing some of what she said is true.

"I'm fine," I tell him, pulling out of his arms. He frowns slightly but doesn't push it.

A thread of energy flows into me.

Adira? A voice echoes in my mind.

Relief floods me. A sliver of guilt follows when I realize I should've contacted her right when we escaped. *Lyra! Are you alright?*

I should be asking you that, little one.

I'm okay. We escaped. Where are you?

I was trying to get help. I'm on my way to you now. I will be there before sundown.

We will wait for you and then head over to Modereo, I tell her, excitement filling me at the thought of seeing her again.

I missed you too, little one. Hang tight, I will be there as fast as my wings can carry me.

I send a burst of warmth down the thread, letting her know how I feel.

I clear my throat. "I can make a portal to Modereo. But Lyra is on her way—we can wait until sundown."

An embarrassed grimace covers his face. "With everything going on, I forgot to ask about her. I'm sorry."

I shake my head. "Don't worry. I couldn't reach her before; the thread connecting us was weak, but it's back now. Before we leave, I-I need to make sure she's alright."

"I understand, princess." He places a kiss on my head.

A loud roar reverberates through the air, the noise sounding extremely close to us. I whip around, unsheathing my dagger. The forest stays unmoving. Then, a large object flies over the trees, landing in front of us. Trees and bushes crush beneath its feet when it drops. It opens its mouth—sharp teeth line its jaw. The smell of rotting meat blasts out at us. I gag at the scent.

Ignoring the nausea the beast's last meal gives me, I focus on the creature, trying to find any weaknesses. Its deep red fur makes it look like it's bathed in blood. Its eyes focus on me, Soren, and a path to our right. *Yep, that's right—it has three eyes.* Its wings are tucked away, but they appear thick and strong.

"Go for the wings," I tell Soren.

He nods, and we split up, slowly circling the beast.

Its eyes track us, backing up with the motion. *Intelligent little beastie, aren't you?*

Now, I shout to myself in my head. I leap forward, seeing Soren do the same. I call upon my magic, trapping its wings in tight. Soren manages a slash through the wing while I stab its joint. It rears out, knocking me back. I fly through the air, my back slamming against a tree.

Adira!

I shake my head, certain I just heard Soren. Looking up, I freeze. The beast is a foot away from me. Its three eyes staring down at me. I hold my breath, trying to stay still. It doesn't matter to the beast. I call upon my power, ready to blast this thing in the eyes, when a crackle of energy comes from behind it.

It sniffs the air and turns, offering me a view of Soren. He's running up behind it, chest heaving. I remember the bond as I spot a pained look on his face. I can't help but marvel at his strength as he slides down on the ground, one hand trailing through the earth. A soft glow of magic surrounds him. He screams out in rage, sending a blast of eather at the beast. The beast leaps back—but not fast enough. It catches him in the shoulder. It screeches, my ears pop from the sound. A drip of blood trickles out. Soren smoothly jumps back up, getting out of the way of the now flailing beast.

I don't hesitate, I shoot out my own blast, aiming for the wing. It punches a hole through it. It screams again, its head twisting between us rapidly. Sensing it won't win, it limps back, disappearing into the trees. I go to summon more eather, but the pain in my back distracts me. Wincing, I try to move. Nothing. *Shit, something must be broken.*

Soren's head whips toward me. He runs to my side.

"What's broken?" I twist my head at him in confusion, checking that my barrier is up.

He doesn't wait for my response. He calls upon his magic, sending it into my broken body. A flash of brief bewilderment flies across his face, the disbelief of his new power evident. A minute later, his warmth travels to my back. A loud crack echoes through the trees. I jolt at the sharp pain, but it quickly fades to a dull ache. I shift upward, moving on my own. I look at Soren, his relief mirroring mine.

My mind drifts back to my thoughts.

Can you hear me?

He startles, glancing up.

"Yes. Is your barrier down?"

No, it's up.

He pauses for a moment, thinking about something.

How is that possible?... Can you hear me?

Yes, I can. And I don't know. It must have to do with true mates of heart. The ability to talk mind to mind.

He grins, not at all disturbed by the information.

I glance at him incredulously. "This doesn't bug you?"

He shrugs. "Why would it?"

"Because you'll have no privacy."

He leans toward me, dropping his forehead to mine.

"With you, I don't need privacy. I trust you, and I don't want to ever hide anything else from you again. Now, I can't." A layer of relief underlines his words.

I bite my lip, nodding despite my uneasiness. He senses my discomfort.

He gives me a soft kiss on the lips.

"It will be fine."

I embrace his words, willing myself to believe him.

Maybe this will be fine. But soon enough, the prophecy has to be completed. And I can guarantee I won't be fine when that happens.

Chapter 43

Soren

The sun sinks lower in the sky. Adira is fading off against a tree as we wait for Lyra. Exhaustion threatens to drag me under, but I fight the pull, keeping my gaze on the forest.

My mind trails back to my new power. I latch onto the feeling of fullness instead of the panic that comes with it. A bitter laugh escapes me. *Of course I would gain power and finally be with Adira just to meet my end.*

At least I will get to see my family again. I rub my chest, thinking about them. *It's been too damn long.*

I decide to use this time to familiarize myself with my new power. I call it up, practicing with the different threads I see. Just as easily as the exhaustion tugs at me, it dissipates, replenishing through the terrain.

I lose track of time, then the sound of beating wings reaches my ears. It gets louder. I stand up, hand going to my weapon in case it is an unwelcome surprise.

"Princess." I whisper. "Wake up."

Her eyes snap open at my voice. She scans the surroundings before her gaze lands on me. A deep throb pounds in my chest at her alert reaction, the wariness that's always been present in her life.

"What is it?" she asks me, rubbing her eyes.

"Listen." I tell her.

I fall silent, letting her hear the sound. A grin spreads across her face. I swear the sun flashes brighter at the sight.

"Lyra!"

She goes silent, probably communicating with the Teràstios in her mind.

Curiosity tugs at me. *I wonder if I'll be able to hear their conversation.* Closing my eyes, I concentrate on the thread connecting Adira's mind and mine. I follow the pulse of eather down it. Nothing but silence reaches me once I'm in her mind.

Hello? I test out.

She flinches. *Soren, what are you doing?*

I wanted to see if I could hear you and Lyra.

Her nose wrinkles. *Well, tell me before you do that.* A sheepish look crosses my face at her words.

Then, she pauses.

Did it work?

Nope. Nothing but silence. I guess I can't hear other bonds you have.

She huffs. *Bond traffic only goes one way. You get me, not her.*

I shoot her an apologetic smile. Her irritated look fades.

"Okay. Are we ready to go?" she asks aloud.

Lyra snaps her beak in confirmation. Adira nuzzles her neck, the relief evident on her face. I take a weary step away from the large beast. Images of terrified villages with beasts flying above enter my mind.

"I'm ready. But won't someone sense your portal?" I ask, remembering her earlier words.

"We have to risk it. I don't want to linger in Enelon when we have a whole slew of guards and a god after us."

I concede. "Good point. Let's take our chances in Modereo."

Adira heaves in a deep breath and holds out a hand. A blast of swirling eather shoots out, all the colors of her magic mixing together. The ball stops a few feet in front of her, then it starts expanding out, creating a whirling doorway.

My jaw drops in awe as I get a closer look at it. The surface is iridescent and looks as if it's barely contained mist. It swirls around, inviting us in. It appears different than the other portal I went through.

Adira grabs my hand before turning to Lyra, speaking aloud so I can hear her. "We'll meet you in Modereo. Tell me if you run into any trouble." Lyra nods her beaked head.

We step forward into the mist. The scent of copper lingers in my mouth and my head spins as my body feels weightless.

A second later, we're through. *Woah, it didn't feel like that before,* I think to myself with confusion. A tingle sparks in my stomach. *It must be my new power. Or Adira's.*

I take a breath of air to clear my senses. As it enters my body, it hums, seeming fresher and full of energy. I feel lighter than I have since I was a child.

"Okay." Adira says. "There is a village called Ashenridge about thirty minutes from here. They are known for their gossip and knowledge."

"Let's go get some information." I respond back, flashing her a charming smile.

Before we exit the forest, Adira leans down, scooping up a handful of dirt. "Keep this in your pocket. You never know when you'll need your magic."

I give her a kiss on the forehead. "Good idea, princess." Her features soften.

We get to the village quickly. Lyra slinks deeper into the forest, hiding from view. Adira pulls her hood up, shadowing her face. I frown, about to ask why she's hiding, but someone bumps into me. The stench of sweat distracting me.

I notice a rundown building with a sign hanging over the door. *Tavern,* it reads. *Perfect,* I tell myself, *taverns are the best places to get information.*

I nudge Adira with my shoulder, pointing to the building. She nods and we head in that direction, passing all sorts of vendors along the way. A glint of emerald green hangs on display. A power pulses from it, beckoning me closer. My nerves flare at the familiar feeling. I remember the mesmerizing amulet from Willowcroft.

I shake myself out of it, turning to Adira.

"What is that?"

She follows my line of sight, seeing the amulet. Her eyes widen.

"That amulet contains the power to enslave someone to do anything you want. Once they put it on, they can't take it off unless allowed by the wielder or by death. It's difficult to find and even harder to make. Not many exist," she tells me, eyeing the necklace.

"I saw some in Willowcroft."

She frowns. "Really? Usually the King restricts those types of vendors."

I wince. "The King doesn't seem too worried about the villages."

A quick flash of anger passes across her face. "As soon as the Vormr started getting worse he has been hiding out more. Leaving the people to fend for themselves. It's pathetic."

She whispers that last part, eyes darting to the sparse guards.

She shifts her focus to me. "Like I said, the people of Ashenridge are very informed. They trade mostly in secrets. It is the highest currency in this village."

"Should we... at least learn how to spot the real ones?" I ask tentatively, still stuck on the mesmerizing power. "I don't want either of us shackled by some trinket."

She shakes her head. "No. The way to make it uses forbidden magic. Those who create it and those who use it must surrender to a dire punishment chosen by the twisted power."

A shiver works its way up as the lingering power trails up my spine seductively. I let my own magic rear up, pushing it away.

"It seems wrong that they blatantly ignore it." I say, eyeing the blue uniformed men.

Adira looks at the guards with disgust in her expression. "They are essentially useless. The realm appears to be plunging further into darkness and there is nothing anyone can do about it."

Her voice is sullen. I knock her shoulder with mine. "Don't give up, princess. We'll stop the Vormr and I'm sure things will start looking up."

I cling onto my unnatural optimism, hoping to the gods it happens. Adira deserves a land that's thriving, not covered in shadows.

The door to the tavern swings open just as we reach it. A drunk patron stumbles out, slurring something about teasing women. I twist out of the way when he almost runs into me. The sharp scent of liquor wafting from him.

Before the door can slam shut, we press into the building. The pungent smell of alcohol fills the air. A loud band plays in the corner. Round wooden tables span across the floor. The table in the middle is surrounded by cheering patrons, the seated people playing some sort of game.

An empty table sits to the right. We make our way over to it and sit with our backs to the wall. Only two servers move through the space, both running around to fill orders. We sit there for ten minutes before impatience takes over.

"I'm going to get us some food and drinks," I tell her. She nods as I get up, moving through the dense crowd to the bar.

A tired-looking man stands behind the counter.

"Hello. Could I please get two bowls of stew and two beers?"

He nods before shouting the order to the kitchen behind.

"The stew is down to its bare bones." He warns me. "The Vormr killed the farms surrounding us, nothing has grown for months."

I tell him it's okay, looking out into the busy crowd. He grabs two large tankards and fills them to the brim with frothy beer.

"Is it usually this busy?" I ask him.

He shakes his head wearily.

"No, not usually. News that the Vormr is almost upon us spread to the villagers. Most panicked at first. Some ran, some stayed. The ones who stayed decided to stop trying and just have fun before it hit us. Hence the busyness of my tavern."

An emotion I haven't felt in ages creeps in. Sadness. These people weren't just celebrating life, they were racing from famine.

I dip my head in acknowledgment, and he hands over the pitchers. I slide some money across the sticky counter before spinning back around. My eyes find our table immediately and my body freezes. Hot whips of jealousy thrash in me when I see another man leaning over our table, leering down at Adira.

She seems unbothered, but I notice her smile is tighter than usual. I stride over, my anger rising as he reaches out for her arm. Slamming the tankards down on the table, I grip his shoulder.

"What do you think you're doing?" I seethe out.

He glares at the intrusion.

"Talking to a pretty lady."

He turns a smarmy smile on Adira.

Her lovely voice flows into my mind. *Calm down, Soren. I'm fine. I was using the situation to get information from him.*

And? Did you get it?

She hesitates a moment. *Yes. There's a woman named Maelle—says an old 'looking-glass' lays within the King's reserves.*

I nod once.

"Time for you to leave."

"Fuck off, man. I was here first."

You really don't trust me, do you?

I shoot a glance her way.

Of course I do. It's him I don't trust.

"Want to take this outside, pretty boy?" he sneers at me. I reach into my pocket, feeling the small grains.

I let my power float up, the anticipation causing it to crackle around me. My vision tints the world white. The patrons nearest to our table freeze momentarily. Then, they shrug, scooting their chairs further away, as if this was a normal occurrence. The man audibly gulps, then hardens his features.

He scoffs, responding to his unanswered question. "Whatever, man, this bitch isn't worth it." He spits in her direction, shooting her a vile look.

I see red.

My magic thrashes in me, my control on it slipping as rage replaces it. Adira's power slips out, coaxing mine back down. The man grunts something unintelligible before walking away. Her hand grasps mine, tugging me down onto the chair beside her.

"That was unnecessary, you big brute. I can handle myself just fine," she grumbles at me.

My gaze softens at the look of embarrassment on her face. "You're right. I'm sorry."

She looks surprised at my apology. I squeeze her hand, tugging her closer to me.

"I know you can take care of yourself, princess. You are the strongest person I know." I rub at my chest. "Maybe it was the bond, or maybe it was just the fact that another man was close to you, and I was jealous."

Her eyes widen when I admit it.

I smirk. "I admit it. I was jealous. I only just got you back. I don't want to lose you again—especially to some magic-wielding flirt."

A small smile covers her face.

"You should know, I'm not that easily won over." She brings my hand up to her heart, hers thumping steadily beneath me. "Let this symbol give you comfort. I'm done fighting what is between us. I forgave you. And the Arae knew we were meant to be. No one else would ever take me away from you."

I gulp at her words, a hint of vulnerability showing through. I didn't know how much I needed to hear that she was in this until she admitted it.

"But." She continues. "You'll need to work on controlling your emotions, the hold on your magic is weakest when you lose control."

I wince, trying not to think about the fact that I was about to blast that guy with gods know what. I could've killed him. I shake off the discomfort that accompanies killing. *I've never had this moral dilemma before. What happened?* My body answers before my brain can, I lock eyes with Adira. *She changed me. She makes me want to be better.*

"I'll do better." I promise her. She smiles slightly in response.

Our stew arrives, the soup made up of basically only broth. As we eat, our eyes clash together, the silence letting our thoughts run wild. When she finishes, her heated gaze meets mine. Grabbing my hands, she pulls me up gently.

"Let's get a room for the night...to rest." She says with a devious smile.

My lips twitch up. "Rest is important."

"We'll leave tomorrow, mid-morning. I don't want our hasty departure to be noted." I nod at her words, though my concentration is hanging on by a thread as she places a soft kiss to my mouth.

With a wink, she draws her hood up, slinking to the bar to acquire us a room. We head up the wooden steps hidden around the back of the rowdy tavern. She unlocks the door, swinging it open. I'm surprised to find that it's clean and tidy, the opposite of what is below.

She grabs my shirt with a glint in her eye, pulling me into the room after her.

The door snicks shut.

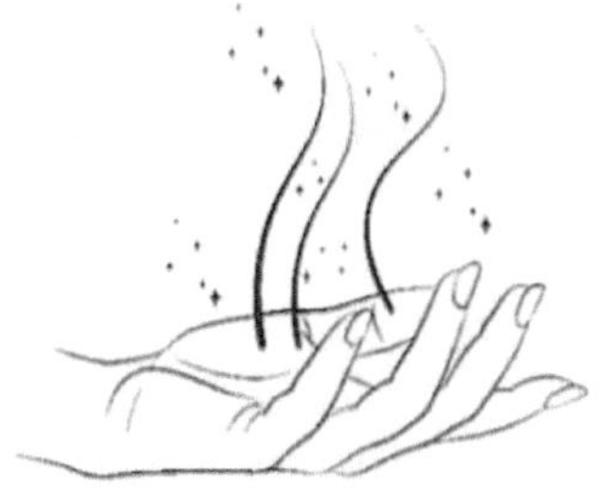

Chapter 44

Adira

I tug Soren forward, latching my lips on his. A groan reverberates through his chest as he deepens the kiss. He walks us back toward the bed. My legs hit the edge. He pulls back slightly, drawing my shirt up gently. His hands careful in all the places the world was not.

His eyes lock onto mine, swirling with an intense emotion. I don't shift my gaze. I let the emotion spread through me. His hands caress my body, leaving behind a tingling sensation wherever they touch.

I yank his shirt up, desperate to feel his skin. I revel in his toned body. His control snaps as I trail my hands down his back. He hisses, eyes flaring with heat. Giddiness spreads through me. *My touch did that to him.*

My thoughts spiral as he kneads my breasts. My eyelids flutter as his rough hands roam my body. Heat rises. I quickly shuck off my pants; he does the same. We stand naked in front of each other, both of us staring with hooded gazes.

Soren steps close, tugging me toward him. Our lips meet passionately, the sensation drawing sounds from me I didn't know I could make. He lowers me down onto the bed, hovering over me.

A charged energy fills the room, as if our powers know this is more than just sex.

I gulp down the emotions threatening to overtake me. He kisses his way down my body. My breath hitches when he plants a kiss on my inner thigh, a shiver of anticipated desire rolling through me.

My hips lift up as his tongue finds my center. He holds my hips down while he works his tongue in and out of me, swirling it around, bringing me to the edge. My breath comes in quick pants as he brings me closer. I curl my fingers in his hair, needing to grasp onto something. The feeling is almost painful as I climb up and up.

Then, I shatter.

"Soren." My voice catches as I come. Blinking the stars out of my vision, I look down to see Soren with a smug smile. His hair is mussed from my hands. He crawls up my body, giving me a soft kiss. When I deepen the kiss, I can taste myself on him. He groans and shifts his body down. His hard length pressing up against me.

"Need you. Now." I pant out, rolling my hips.

He lines himself up with my entrance and pauses.

"Are you still..?" He trails off, thinking of the right word.

I nod. "We're safe." He breathes out his relief, shifting up. The tip of him slides in. He stops, groaning. My body aches for all of him, so I wrap my legs around his back and press up. He slides in easily.

I gasp from the size of him and move my hips, adjusting to the intrusion.

He waits, his eyes on my face. I bring a hand up, trailing it across his cheek. Locking eyes with him, I give him a nod.

He starts moving, driving me closer, his gaze never straying from mine, steady and sure. My control slips, the sensation overpowering me. My fingers knot the sheets, grasping onto anything solid.

My magic rushes to the surface, tinting my vision. I sense Soren's new powers darting up to meet mine. The power springs from us, circling around our moving bodies. Awe and euphoria capture me as a mix of purple, blue, and white fill the space. The magic caresses our bodies, driving our pleasure up.

"Soren." I choke out, unable to form a coherent thought. His eyes blaze as he keeps a steady rhythm. His features tighten, and I know he's close too.

Together, we fall over the edge. The release so intense that our magic bursts out through the room. Glass shatters. Then it's reeled back into us rapidly, leaving only our panting breaths. He gently pulls out of me, giving me a soft kiss on the lips. Standing, he heads to the bathroom. He returns with a warm wet cloth. My heart swells at the gesture. My eyes sting as he cleans me up.

He slides back onto the bed, pulling me close.

"That was amazing, princess."

"It was," I agree happily.

"I think our lovemaking is dangerous." He whispers amused.

I follow his gaze to the broken mirror, giggling at the sight. My powers must've coaxed his out without him needing to touch his element.

"It does seem that way."

He lets out a content sigh, pulling me tighter against his body. We lay together as our hearts slow down to a normal rate. I twist in his arms, wanting to see his face. He gives me a kiss when I settle back into his warmth.

Soren goes to say something but stops himself. A flash of uncertainty crosses his features.

Say it, I plead in my mind.

Okay, I will. His response shocks me.

Shit, I forgot you could do that. I chuckle, my cheeks heating with embarrassment. I twist my head away, breaking our stare. *Tell me when you're listening.*

Always—if you want me there.

My face burns further at his words. *I always want you there.*

I feel a rush of overpowering emotion from his side of the bond. He reaches out, turning my chin toward him.

"Look at me, princess."

I slowly drag my eyes back to his.

"I love you. I am *so* in love with you." His eyes swirl with a deep emotion.

"You don't have to say it back. I know I probably still need to earn your trust back for betraying you. But I needed to tell you."

My lips curve up into a smile. I hold his cheeks with my hands.

"I love you, Soren," I tell him, sending the warm feeling back down the bond.

His smile widens, blinding me with its beauty. A hint of relief present from my words, as if he was doubting that I could love him.

"Me and you, princess. Until the end."

My heart cracks slightly at the words, knowing the end will be sooner than we'd like.

My eyes well up as I respond.

"Even if the world tries to take you from me, I'll fight it. Me and you. Until the end."

Chapter 45

Soren

Warmth surrounds me when I wake. I tighten my arms, sighing deeply. The clatter of mugs rings faintly from below.

I haven't felt this content in a long time... maybe I never have.

Adira releases a soft sound and wiggles slightly. I groan.

Leaning into her ear, I whisper, "Princess, if you do that, we will never leave this bed."

She shifts again, grinding back into me. All the blood rushes down my body.

I flip her onto her back swiftly. She squeals at the motion.

"You're trouble."

This time, I take her slow, letting her see the tenderness in my expression.

I can't believe she loves me. Gods, she's gorgeous.

A knock sounds at the door.

"Check-out was thirty minutes ago," a hard voice shouts through the wood.

Adira giggles, her happy expression warming my chest.

"Are you paying for another night?"

I speak up. "Sorry. We aren't staying. We will be right out."

"You better," the voice warns.

We smile to each other with amusement.

Standing, we quickly get dressed before the innkeeper can charge us for another night. I stare at her, thinking another night wouldn't be so bad. But the weight of the prophecy bears down on me.

I rub at my chest. *Death is constantly in the back of my mind. With a job as an assassin, how could it not be? But now that I've found someone worth living for... I can admit, I don't want to die.*

We walk down the stairs, entering the main room. Adira flips her hood up. I eye her questionably. "There's a chill."

I frown at the explanation, only feeling the balmy air.

A few patrons have started drinking early, lounging on the chairs. Their eyes track our movements, causing my neck to tingle with awareness. Adira grabs my hand as we stroll out of the tavern, the sticky scent of alcohol still lingering in the air.

Once we're outside, she tugs my hand, stopping me.

"What's wrong?" I ask, immediately scanning the area.

"I just remembered we didn't discuss the plan." She laughs loudly. "You screwed out all my coherent thoughts."

A burst of air pushes my chest up, a sense of pride and ego at her words.

Smirking, I kiss her forehead. "Worth it."

She shakes her head, but her features stay light.

"I subtly brought up rare magical items, and he started bragging that one of his cousins guards them in Magia, the capital. We need to sneak into the castle to find the object."

"Perfect. How far is that?"

She winces slightly. Before I can question her, a flyer snags my attention. A drawn photo of a woman with dark hair. Underneath reads, 'Wanted for Murder: Adira Selcouth. Reward will be granted.'

My jaw drops. I rip the paper from the post, turning to Adira.

"What is this?" I hiss-whisper at her, scanning all the patrons milling around the vendors before pulling Adira into an alley, out of view. The hood she's been wearing suddenly making sense.

She twists her hands, gaze darting away.

"That is what I was going to tell you."

I narrow my eyes, waiting for her to continue. She sighs.

"I was framed. By the King's mistress, Josephine. I don't know exactly why, but she had the King's most prized guard killed. Which happened to also be one of my best friend's brothers. So, I lost my job, my friends, and was sentenced to death."

I grip onto her tighter at those words. Remembering her mentioning that her friends had forgiven her when she was in the Chamber of Harnew, but I was so distracted by my own guilt I must not have comprehended them.

She gives me a weak smile.

"But I escaped. Twice. I'm certain they wouldn't expect me to return to the castle."

My gut churns. "Maybe we can find another way..."

"I appreciate it, Soren, but I'll be fine. I have backup now," she says softly, gesturing to me.

A smile stretches across my face. I lean down, giving her a quick peck on the head.

"Yes, you do," I reassure her.

"Okay, so that's what we'll do," she breathes out. "Magia is about a two-day walk from here. That's if we push ourselves hard, not allowing a lot of stops. I don't want to waste too much time. Even with my new powers, I can still feel the Vormr trying to drain it from me. It feels like my reserve has a slow leak."

I take her shaking hands in mine.

"Two days. We can do it. But we'll need to mask our footprints, I got the sense we caught the eyes of some of the patrons of this town."

"I felt their attention." She confirms. "But we had to risk it for the information."

I purse my lips, not in agreement that the risk was worth her life.

"This would've been good to know before, princess."

"Sorry." Her tone carries remorse. "I'm used to working alone, it's a hard habit to break."

I sigh, understanding that feeling too well.

"Okay. Let me go buy some food. You stay out of sight."

I approach the vendor stands, taking in the bruised fruit and dried meats. I nimbly leap out of the way when a wheel barrels toward me, children shriek happily, chasing the object. My lips tug up at the joy that kids can feel even on the precipice of famine.

I quickly stroll to a vendor nearby, purchasing some jerky and bread. I hand over Modereo's silver coin. He takes the Ellyr, glancing at me suspiciously, but doesn't say anything.

I eye him back, seeing if he does anything rash. He looks away first. I turn and head back to Adira. She has her pack open, ready to carry the weight of some of the food. I hand her less than half. Surprisingly, she doesn't argue with me.

We leave town swiftly. I glance back continuously, ensuring that no one is following us. The light shifts as we walk, fatigue starting to line our steps. I place a hand on my stomach, wondering if this feeling is due to the disease spreading across the land and draining the magic. My eyes dart to Adira, noting the exhaustion in her eyes.

Silence drags on between us as we focus on keeping our steps light, stepping only on leaves and logs that will leave no trace of us behind.

While we walk, my mind shifts to the prophecy that's unfolding. A sense of foreboding takes root in my gut. The panic not just for myself, but for Adira. The pain she will feel when she completes it.

I squeeze her hand harder than I mean to. She glances up, smiling, not seeing the fear I'm trying to crush.

I heed her earlier words and try to view the situation in a more optimistic way.

Impossible. I huff out.

This won't be a happy ending for either of us.

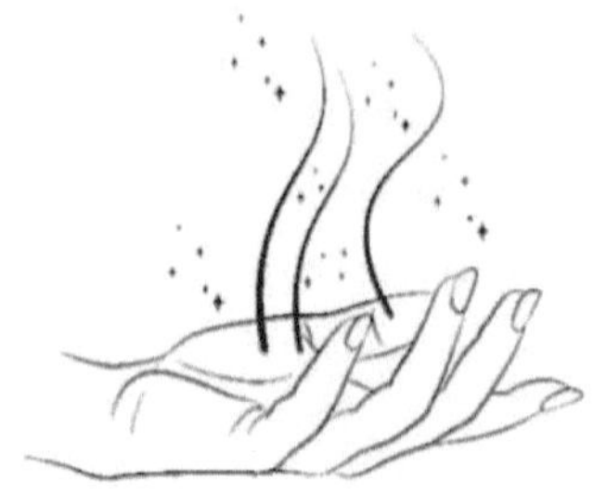

Chapter 46

Adira

Exhaustion weighs us down as we reach the edge of Magia. The two days flew by in a blur of repetition. Walk. Rest. Eat. Walk. Lyra kept watch flying low overhead, allowing us peace of mind while we rested. If only Teràstios could carry two bodies.

A wave of fear and resentment slips into me. My mind pauses at the abrupt change in emotions. Then, I realize it's not coming from me. It's coming from Lyra.

Are you okay? I direct to her.

Do not worry about me, little one.

The air hums the closer we get to Magia, the magic charging the atmosphere.

But I do. I know this place can't hold good memories for you. You can go hide until we are done. I don't want you to get hurt anyway.

She huffs, but there's a thread of relief at my suggestion. *I cannot just leave you.*

You'll cause more trouble for us if you are seen. It makes sense for you to hide. Don't worry, I've lived here all my life, I know the ins and outs of the castle.

I sense her indecision through the bond.

I'll call you if I need you, I reassure her. And next on my to-do list will be *to assimilate the Teràstios back into society.*

She snaps her beak, the doubt spiraling through the bond.

Fine, she concedes. *I will stay close. Call me at the slightest sign of trouble.*

Very well. But stay hidden.

She lets out a squawk and arcs away from us, heading further from the castle. The beat of her strong wings causes my hair to whip around my head. I brush it out of the way, my fingers snagging on the ends and twisting them. *I need to cut my hair.*

Soren grabs my hands, calming my nerves. A frown pulls at his lips as he stares in Lyra's direction. "Where is she going?"

"She won't be safe in Magia. It would also be more dangerous for us if she's spotted," I tell him.

He sighs in understanding. "That makes sense. But the added protection for you would have been nice."

"I don't need added protection. I will be fine." I tell him. My nose wrinkles as I think about how many times I've said that. *Will it be the truth? Or has the phrase lost all its meaning?* I straighten my spine. *I'm stronger now... alarmingly so, but still able to handle more.*

A bundle of nerves settles into my stomach. *I wonder how Saline and Atin are.*

I push down my wishful thoughts and focus on not getting caught. We stay under the cover of the trees, moving deeper into the kingdom. An hour later, the castle comes into view.

Soren's jaw drops as he takes it in.

I turn, trying to see it from his eyes. The castle floats on a large boulder, the air around it shimmering with energy. Gulls circle below the clouds.

A path of floating stones leads up to the front. The magic below them is so thick that the air looks distorted. The thrill of the danger being if you step wrong, you will plummet to the crashing waves below. It holds a vibrant allure from being imbued with magic.

"Wow. I know you told me it was floating, but it's surreal to see it in person."

I smile at his awe. "It is pretty neat."

He nods his head in agreement, his assassin brain taking over.

"How will we get in without being seen? Is this the only path?"

"It is the only path available for guests. All other paths are charmed. But I have a way."

He looks weary. "What's your plan?"

I just grin, grabbing his hand.

"Come on," I tell him, leading him in the direction of the vendor square.

I summon a quick spell to alter my appearance. Showing my face near the castle would be an unnecessary risk. My power flows over me easily. My lips twitch up. *Maybe being a semidea isn't so bad.*

Soren steps back. "Woah, I felt a rush of your power when you did that."

I roll the tension out of my neck. "I hope others can't sense the disguise."

His eyes widen. "Can Stregoni do that?"

"Powerful ones, yes. And ones specifically trained to spot them."

"Wouldn't all Stregoni learn to spot disguises?"

"No. King Elijah only had the guards closest to him taught. I imagine it's because he uses the magic himself for nefarious purposes."

The understanding echoes in Soren's eyes. Power. Spying to maintain control of a kingdom.

We step out of the shelter of the trees, falling onto the worn path.

"Why can't Lyra just take us?" he asks in a whisper as we stroll through the crowd. Soren's gaze snags on the uniformed men as they walk methodically around the area. Wanted posters line the posts, I see my face along with other unknown people among them. I take a wide berth around the guards.

"I'm not risking her. This plan will work."

"What plan?" he asks again. I ignore him, leading him through the whispering merchants. I turn my chin up in confidence, not giving them anything suspicious to speculate on.

The patrons stroll around, a more somber mood than normal settles over the whole area. Terrified words about the Vormr circle the air, the people knowing they can't stop it, yet unable to talk about anything else.

We reach a royal blue stand. The counter is lined with different colored vials. An old lady with a large wart stands behind the counter, an impassive look on her face. I walk confidently up to her.

"Mornin'," I greet. She grunts back.

"See anything you like?"

I lean in close.

"Two shifting vials, please."

Now she eyes me suspiciously, no doubt wondering who I am.

"Which animal."

"Bird."

She stares at me for another moment. A trickle of fear slivers in. *What if she refuses? What if she tells the guards about me?*

She shrugs to herself.

"Sixty Ellyr."

My eyes nearly bug out of my head.

"Sixty?!"

She narrows her eyes, her wart seeming to grow bigger.

"Something tells me you are up to no good, girlie. So, sixty Ellyr."

I bite my tongue and let out a frustrated sigh. Reaching into my pack, I pull out the Ellyr.

I hand it over to her. She quickly counts it and reaches below the counter. She pulls out two brown vials, holding them out to me. I go to grab them, but her hand closes over the vials.

"The spell only lasts for thirty minutes." *Plenty of time.*

"Got it. Thanks."

She opens her hand, and I snatch them up before she can change her mind. A guard nears the booth. I shift my face away by instinct. The woman raises an eyebrow at the move, as if to say *I knew it.*

We melt swiftly back into the crowd, putting distance between us and the woman who could easily call upon one of the many guards in the area. Tension lines my shoulder while we walk through the crowd of people. One counterspell or strong Stregona could reveal me.

Before we leave the main area, Soren spots a booth with daggers.

"I'm going to buy a dagger. I'll be right back."

I nod at him, using the opportunity to slip away to another vendor. I stick close to the edge of the market before delving in toward the booth I seek.

I make it back to the spot just before Soren does. Nodding to the forest, we slip back into it. Once we are back in the seclusion of the trees, I explain my plan to Soren.

"When night falls, we will drink these vials. We'll shift into birds. I'm going to be honest, the process is painful, but it's quick. We will have thirty minutes to fly around the castle and search the windows for the room of objects. I believe it's in the east wing, but it would make it easier to narrow down where," I say, gesturing to the enormous castle.

"After thirty minutes have passed, our bodies will automatically shift back. This is just as painful as the initial shift, so we will have to be careful to stay quiet. Then, hopefully, we can reach the room tonight and I can use some of my fancy new powers to get us in there undetected."

Soren shakes his head in disbelief.

"There is so much unknown in this plan. Like, what happens if a guard spots us? What if we can't even find the room? Will the objects be protected under a spell? How do we leave the castle after?"

I wave my hand. "I work best on instinct. Best not to plan too much."

His face scrunches up at my response. I take in his expression and can't help but feel relief that Poderosa isn't here. The trials we keep facing get more and more dangerous as we go.

I cross my arms, waiting for his argument of the necessity of planning. *He may have a point, but my plans never turn out. Better to stick with what works for me.* Soren lets out a rough chuckle, taking in my defensive stance.

"Can we at least plan how to get out?"

"We can alter ourselves to look like guards and walk out the front doors," I tell him.

"Why in the realms can't we do that to get in?!"

"Because King Elijah is very cautious about who he lets into the castle. He has people monitoring it all the time. What he doesn't care about is who leaves, since they have already been 'checked' when entering."

He grumbles. "Sometimes I hate when you make sense."

I flash him a smile. I survey the lush forest, bushes overflowing with berries. *For now.* My mind drifts back to the dead lands, a renewed sense of determination flowing through me.

"Let's walk deeper into the forest so we can approach the castle from the side. I'll also need to alter our magical signatures to blend in with the wards."

"You can do that?"

I grin easily. "Absolutely. I've been training all my life for insane magical missions."

He chuckles lightly at that.

We walk through the dense trees, stepping over the hard terrain silently. The plants pulse with energy, getting stronger as we near the castle.

Night presses in on us as we come close to the edge of the cliff. I hold my hand out to stop him.

"This spot will work."

I reach into my pack, grabbing the vials. Giving one to Soren, I uncap mine. Magic rolls out of me in waves, blending our magic to match that of the castle. It's not perfect, but it will conceal us if someone doesn't look too closely.

Picking up both of our bags, I hide them in the tall bushes.

"Ready?" I ask him.

He tugs me against him, giving me a deep kiss. Then, he pulls back and nods. "Ready."

I shake off the dazed feeling. He looks pleased at my reaction.

"Bottoms up."

We tilt our vials into our mouths. The taste of dirt and energy creating a revolting combination. My stomach clenches. Soren doubles over, gagging on the ground. The world sways. My body tilts. Pain ricochets up my arm. I realize a second later that I've fallen onto the ground. Soren's eyes are glassy and wide with pain. I want to offer comfort, but the edges of my vision tint black.

My whole body tenses before seizing uncontrollably. The darkness obscures everything. I feel my mind being thrust through a tunnel of eather, my body contorting and arching as I spin around this vortex. Something flashes in the distance. It looks like a silver pool.

It gets bigger and bigger. Panic drowns out the pain as I fly toward it at a vicious speed.

Then, I reach it.

My body jerks at the impact.

Then, nothing.

Chapter 47

Soren

Groaning, I force my eyes open. Panic beats in my chest as I stare up at ginormous trees. A flower stands beside me, my gaze meeting the top of it. The ringing in my ears fades as I blink at it in confusion.

For a moment, I forget where I am and what happened. I force my eyes down, seeing webbed feet.

A squawk draws my attention. An angry-looking bird stares at me, tilting its head.

Are you ready to go? Adira's voice sounds in my head.

I blink in shock, the world appearing more vivid than before.

We're birds.

Yes, we are. I told you this would happen.

I know you said it, but living it is a different thing altogether.

She huffs her agreement. *We only have thirty minutes though, so we need to go. I'll take the east side of the castle, you take the west. Communicate here if you find anything.*

Okay. How do I... fly?

Your body will just know how, she tells me, the amusement evident in her voice.

I trust her, but my nerves still shoot up. She doesn't waste any time—she launches herself up into the air, her wings beating fast, pulling her higher. I take a deep breath that feels strange entering through a beaked mouth.

Then, I flap my wings. I feel ridiculous as I move my arms up and down, my muscles tremoring with the new motion. But the feeling fades when I take off into the sky. The wind whips around me, but I stay steady. I look down, the height both disorienting and freeing.

Bewilderment spreads through me. *I'm flying.*

The castle approaches quickly. I tilt my wings, shifting my body sideways as I soar past the walls, keeping my gaze locked on my surroundings. The bricks hum with energy. Vines wrap around the windows, creating a naturalistic archway.

Noticing nothing the first time, I loop back around and slow down, letting myself cruise through the wind. None of the rooms I pass contain any ancient-looking objects. Hoping Adira has had better luck, I call to her.

Anything?

No, not—wait! I see something. I think I found it. Come around to this side, toward the back of the castle.

Coming.

I turn my small body, flapping my wings for momentum. An odd sensation takes root in my chest. I shake it off, seeing another bird hovering by a window. I fly over to her. She spots me coming.

It's in here, she tells me, the excitement evident in her voice.

The strange feeling latches onto me again.

Do you feel that? I ask her.

Feel what?

Something strange is coming from my chest.

Her voice gasps through my mind. *That evil Stregona. She said thirty minutes.*

My blood freezes at her panicked tone.

The spell is wearing off. We need to get someplace safe.

Is anyplace safe? I ask her, looking around.

She hesitates. *No, but I know a place that's safe enough. Follow me. And quickly. We don't want to be in the air when the spell hits.*

I peer down at the rough waves below. The dark ocean seeming to sing a dark tune. A shiver works its way through my feathered body.

Yes. Let's not fall to our deaths.

Follow me.

She soars through the air, diving toward the ground. She makes a sharp turn, circling around the castle. Stables come into view. I breathe out some relief as we fly over solid ground. She flies directly into the stables, landing in an empty stall.

They do nightly checks on the animals, so try to stay silent when you shift.

Will do, I respond back.

Suddenly, energy seizes my body. My muscles strain against it. A sickening snap fills my senses, then a crushing feeling presses into me. My body screams in agony as my bones shift and contort. I bite back whatever noise would come out of my mouth, unsure if it would be a squawk or a scream. A burning sensation travels up my body, leaving numbness in its wake.

I almost sigh in relief when it gets to my head and drags me into the darkness.

****

I awake groggy. The sharp taste of copper in my mouth. I spit it out. Hay shuffles to my left, drawing my attention. Adira sits up, clutching her head.

"Damn, I forgot how bad that feels," she mutters.

My mouth goes dry as I take her in. She's naked. Noticing my stare, she glances down.

"I forgot to tell you that the shift burns your clothes away."

I shoot her a smirk. "I'm not complaining."

A pretty blush rises on her cheeks.

Her eyes scan my body, her gaze heating as she does. Tension fills the air.

I stay still, not wanting to derail her line of thinking.

She shakes herself out of it, lifting a hand. Energy charges through the air, splitting through the tension. Clothes appear on us. I gasp at the sudden change. The edges of her eyes glisten white with power.

Leaning forward, I take her chin in my hands, ignoring the lingering throbbing from the shift.

"You are breathtaking." I pull her in for a slow kiss. Her body melts into me with a sigh.

Voices sound in the distance. I keep my forehead on hers, whispering.

"We need to be careful in there. Don't you dare get caught. I couldn't handle you being tortured again. It almost killed me." I admit softly, my eyes closing as I recall the horrors she's had to face.

Her eyes soften at my confession. She lifts her hand to my face, caressing my cheek.

"Everything will work out. We'll have each other's backs in there."

I grasp her hand.

"Deal." I give her a quick peck on the lips.

"I love you, princess," I say softly. "Me and you. Until the end."

A tender smile crosses over her face.

"I love you too. Me and you. Until the end."

The voices get louder, shattering the moment. We stand gingerly, creeping toward the door on silent feet. Two guards walk leisurely around the grounds.

Adira scans the area. Her eyes tracking the guard's movements.

"This way," she tells me, leading us toward a small wooden door at the back of the castle.

"How do you know there aren't more guards over there?" I ask cautiously.

"I trained here, and part of our tasks was being assigned to guard duty. So, I know their schedule." She smirks.

"Then, after you, princess." I say with a wink.

She searches the stones and pulls out a hidden key. Her eyes dart around the grounds once more.

Sliding it into the lock, she twists. It clicks open, the sound echoing through the silence of the night. We both pause, listening for signs of any incoming guards who may have heard. When we hear nothing, I sigh out in relief. She presses into the gnarled wood, pushing the door open. It lets out a low groan at the motion.

An empty, dark corridor meets us. The cold air trapped by the stone washes over us as we step in. The hair on my arms stand to attention from the mixture of frigid air and old energy.

We need to move fast. Nighttime is when his guards are the lowest.

I frown at the logic. *Wouldn't it be the opposite?*

The King's magic locks a lot of rooms during the night so there is no need for extra guards.

She starts moving swiftly up the hallway, keeping her steps silent as she moves. I follow her lead. We reach a fork in the corridor. She doesn't hesitate, turning left. After a few minutes, we reach a line of doors. She confidently pushes through the middle one before she freezes, pulling me quickly behind a woven tapestry. We stay stiffly pressed together in the shadows.

A guard passes by, whistling to himself. I feel her heart pounding rapidly.

Shit. King Elijah must've added more guards onto the night shift. Her panicked eyes meet mine. *I was hoping I wouldn't need to do this yet, but I'll need to alter our appearances to look like guards.*

I frown, thinking that was the plan already. My confusion must show because she elaborates for me.

Altering appearances uses a lot of energy. You felt it earlier. Which means that more powerful Stregoni or other beings can feel the spike of energy in the air. I wanted to wait until the end to do it, in case it alerts anyone. But we'll have to risk it.

I swallow down my trepidation remembering her earlier words. I squeeze her hand in support.

We'll just have to be quick then.

She gives me a short nod before closing her eyes. Power rises up around us, curling over our bodies. The tapestry stirs, the torch nearest to us flickers. My eyes widen at the feeling.

I can feel how much stronger you are. I say in shock.

Adira looks down at her hands, not responding to my obvious comment. She snaps out of her stupor, her features hardening. *Let's go.* She steps out into the large corridor. I glance around, noticing the statues of living magic. The air flickers around them, but it stays in one spot, like it's been restricted to that area. The floor shines with a pattern of dark blue and pearly white tiles. I keep my gait steady as we turn the corner.

Adira leads us confidently through the maze of the halls, but some of her nerves sneak through the bond. Eventually, she stops in front of a small brass door. I squint at it and notice an engraved symbol—it's a crown. The body curving with metal, giving it a coiled look.

Adira turns the knob, pressing into the door. It creaks loudly. A single guard stands in the room, her weapon held up toward us. She relaxes slightly when she sees our uniforms, then her eyes narrow in suspicion.

"What are you two doing here? No one was assigned to take over for me tonight."

"Change of plans," Adira says smoothly. "Commander Garan told us to swap with you."

She frowns. "And where were you stationed?"

"Out by the stables."

The female guard mutters something under her breath.

"Commander Garan needs to sort out his schedule. This has happened too many times."

Adira smirks. "He is the most unorganized commander I've ever met."

The girl laughs in agreement before leaving the room.

"We don't have much time. The item should be something with a mirror or glass since it lets you see into the past."

I nod, already scanning the room. Shelves line the walls, energy pulsing from all the objects. Adira moves to one side of the room, while I move to the other. I fight the urge to touch the pulsing objects, trying to focus on the task at hand.

A groan sounds through the air as the door shifts open. My hand drifts to the pommel of my sword.

A middle-aged man with black hair strolls in. He seems unsurprised to see us.

Adira straightens, putting on a suspicious look. "What are you doing here this late?"

He holds up his hand.

"Don't bother, Adira."

She blinks once at that. "You know my name."

He smiles fondly. "I know more than that, dear. I am the last living member of the Sage family."

She gasps.

Are we really this lucky?

Her eyes dart imperceptibly to me. *Only one way to find out.*

"I have been writing about you a lot, Adira Selcouth." He shifts toward me, giving me a sad smile. "You as well, Soren Banrs."

My eyes widen slightly.

"A divine energy led me here tonight, I believe to aid you. The object you seek is the mirror in the corner." He tells us while gesturing to the left of the room.

Adira walks over cautiously and picks up the object that was half-hidden behind glowing orbs. I take a step toward her, finding her holding a small handheld mirror, the glass swirling with a deep pink energy.

"Why are you helping us? Why can't you just tell us of the past?" Adira asks the man suspiciously.

"We all have our part to play in what is to come. I am merely a pawn. I was pleased to have been guided in your direction, but I am unable to tell you anything further. You must seek the truth yourself."

I watch the man closely, looking for any signs of lies.

Well, that answers your question. We are not that lucky. Her sarcasm has me biting back a chuckle.

That's okay, princess. At least we found the mirror.

"I wish you both all the good fortune. You will need it."

With that ominous parting, he slips back out of the door.

"Wait—" Adira starts just as the door slams.

A bell rings out in three short rings.

"By the gods," Adira curses. "That's the alarm. The guard we sent away must've found us out. We need to go."

I rush to the door, swinging it open. We slip out, pulling it shut. She grasps my hand. "This way."

I follow her, keeping my gaze sharp for any attacks. We make it to the end of the corridor without trouble. A breath of relief escapes me.

Then, a blast of air knocks us back.

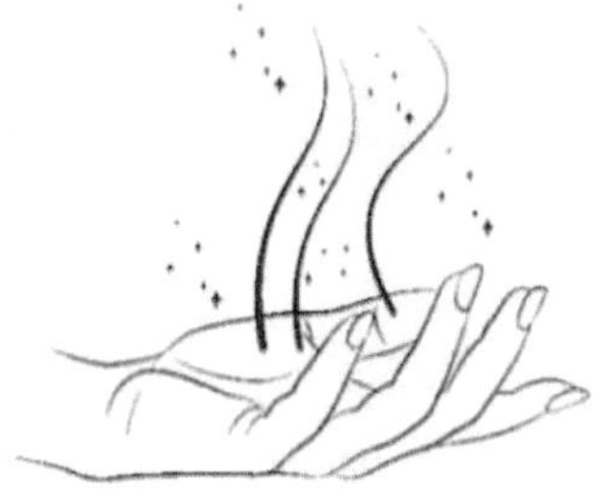

Chapter 48

Adira

My back snaps against the stone wall. I grunt from the impact. Looking up, I notice that the guard is Leo, one of the guys I used to train with. A power sweeps over us, working to remove any spells. I hold tight onto the glamour, pushing my magic against Leo's magic. He can wield earth, fire, water, and has a special affinity for breaking through spell barriers.

I let my magic wash over us, giving him the illusion that his spell worked. Once his magic retreats, he narrows his eyes at us.

"Who are you?" he barks.

I hesitate a moment, wondering how I should play this.

"Leo. It's me. Elena. We met briefly during training. We're new here."

He frowns at the use of his name. He appears to be replaying the last few weeks in his head. I interrupt his thought process.

"We saw someone running that way," I tell him, pointing toward the front doors.

"That's where we were going—to catch the thieves," Soren adds gruffly.

He stares at us for a long moment, debating whether to interrogate us and risk losing the thieves.

"Fine. But I'm coming with you two. Then, afterwards, we can check in with the commander. Together."

His face is still clouded with suspicion.

"Of course. Let's go."

Soren's voice filters into my mind.

What's the plan, Adira?

I'm making it up as I go, but once we are out the front gates, I'll conjure up a shadowed figure and have it attack Leo. Then we can escape.

Should we... kill him? That way he can't report that he saw us.

I glance over at the man I used to train with, his features hardened from the job.

I used to be friends with him. Can we not hurt him?

Soren pauses, as if he's about to contradict my choice. Then, he shakes his head, relenting.

Whatever you think, princess. This is your kingdom.

I don't respond, I just send my gratitude down the bond.

Our footsteps pound noisily on the marble floor. We turn sharply around a corner, and the front door comes into view. Leo pushes it open, grunting at the weight.

I summon up my magic, letting it flow to the side of the castle walls. My head starts throbbing, the first sign that I'm using too much magic.

"Look, there!" I shout, pointing to a place behind Leo.

He turns, spotting the shadow figure. Without hesitation, he darts forward, unsheathing his sword. While his back is turned, I shoot out a small bolt of energy. It hits him in the back of the head, and he crumples to the ground. My gut churns with guilt.

Hopefully, he thinks it was the figure he was chasing, I say to Soren.

If not, it doesn't matter, because we are getting out of here right now.

Soren's words float quietly to me, my magic exhaustion straining the thread.

We take off down the stone path, leaping onto the floating rocks. I keep my eyes on each step, not looking down at the dizzying drop. I feel Soren's nervous energy from the swift pace, but I don't dare to slow down.

A loud screeching fills the air, and the energy shifts. The sound is one I'm becoming increasingly acquainted with. The alarm when the wards detect fleeing magical signatures.

My eyes widen in shock.

"Shit!" I exclaim, looking ahead. We have five more large stones to go. The noise turns shrieking as the power withdraws.

"What?" Soren asks frantically.

"That sound means the stones are going to fall. They know we are trying to escape."

"What do we do?" Panic laces his tone.

My mind flashes back to when I learned I was a semidea. My power was so charged that it lifted me off the ground.

I wonder...

CRACK.

The magic holding up the rocks snaps. The ground beneath my feet disappears. Gravity starts to pull at us. My power rises on instinct, keeping us afloat. My body jerks in the air, coming to a stop. I open my eyes, seeing Soren and me hovering over the coarse ocean.

Okay, great, I tell myself, a bead of sweat trickling down my temple. *Now focus. Take us to solid land.*

My head is pounding now, the sound drowning out the crashing waves below. Much to my surprise, it starts shifting us forward, closing the distance between us and the cliff. My powers strain against me, not used to the amount expelled. I distantly hear Soren, but I don't dare shift my concentration from the solid ground in front of us. My vision blurs temporarily, I blink rapidly, refusing to succumb to my magic exhaustion before we reach land.

I pull us up, bringing us back to the rough terrain. I release my hold and we drop to the ground. I collapse onto the earth, my limbs shaking as if I was just training for a day straight.

"Holy gods, princess. That was incredible," Soren tells me with wide eyes. "Are you alright?"

I blush slightly under his gaze, breathing heavily from the outburst of power. The soft terrain already replenishing my reserves.

"I'm exhausted." I admit.

Voices yell from the castle, and the alarm bell rings again.

"We need to go." My fatigued body gets a shot of energy. Soren looks worried, but doesn't say anything, knowing we don't have much choice. I try to call out to Lyra, but magic exhaustion stops me from successfully wielding the bond. I recall Soren's earlier words, noting that they too faded when my magic was low.

"I could carry you?" Soren offers. I try not to scowl.

I shift my weight, my feet stinging like I'm walking on pins and needles. I give him a determined look. "I'm not some damsel, I can run."

He nods at the determination etched on my face. We take off running into the forest, twisting around the cliff to snatch up our hidden packs along the way, putting as much distance between us and the castle as we can.

****

After running for about a day, we collapse against some thick trees. Soren pulls out his waterskin, wordlessly handing it over to me. I shakily take a few sips before passing it back to him.

Little one? Are you okay?

Relief passes through me from her voice. The bond back to its usual strength after being in the forest all day.

I'm fine. A close call, but we made it out.

I'm coming to you.

I scan the forest for any surprises, happy when I don't find anything.

Okay, I say to Lyra.

Soren tugs me against his side. I lean into him, letting the warmth of his body release the tension I'm holding.

Noticing a bush full of berries, I nudge Soren, pointing toward it. He lets out a small chuckle, no doubt thinking of Poderosa and how excited she would get when she spotted one.

I sigh. "I miss her."

He kisses the top of my head. "Me too."

I sink into his side, appreciating that he didn't try to make me feel better about it, just acknowledged it. Because I know she's better off now, but that doesn't change what I feel. We sit in silence for a moment, both reminiscing about Poderosa.

"So, what's next, princess?"

I reach into my pocket, pulling out the stolen artifact.

"Now, we look into the past."

"What's going to happen?" he asks, staring at the object warily.

I study the ancient object, hoping it will tell me all its secrets.

"I'm not sure. Hopefully, it will be like a magic stamp and show us. But something tells me it won't be that easy."

Soren's lips flatten into a grim line.

"Ancient objects usually demand a price for the use of them. I'm not sure what this one will be."

Without hesitation, Soren grasps my hand. "Whatever it is, let me pay it."

My magic rears up at that, like the Arae are listening and telling me that I must be the one to complete all of the prophecy.

"You don't know how much that means to me. The fact that you are willing to take on any pain in my stead is the sweetest thing. But I must do this myself. The prophecy must be fulfilled by me and me alone."

He sighs, resting his head against mine.

"I would carry the burden of all your pain and this wretched prophecy if I could."

My heart swells.

"I know you would."

Before I can pull it out, Soren stops my hand.

"Can we really trust what the Sage man told us was the correct object? What if he was lying? What if he is working with Conri?"

I sigh.

"There's always going to be 'what ifs'; that's why I choose to rely on my intuition. I didn't sense that he meant us any harm. Plus"—I chuckle grimly—"I can't imagine the Arae would let anything happen to me. Like the man said, we are all just pawns to them."

Soren's grip doesn't loosen as he has an internal struggle. Eventually he releases a heavy sigh.

"Okay, princess. Just be careful."

I give him a small smile. "I always am."

A thud echoes through the forest. A second later, Lyra swiftly pushes through the brush.

I'm about to find out the truth about the past.

She eyes the object. *Be cautious, that's the passato riflesso. The price is usually something important to you.*

Looking down at the wrapped object, I swallow my nerves.

"Apparently, this object is called *passato riflesso*," I tell Soren.

"Whatever it is, it better not hurt you."

I chuckle at that and turn my attention downward. I pull the object out of the cloth it's wrapped in, holding it in my hand. Nothing happens.

Then, the sky flashes purple. A pink mist swirls around us. I watch it in awe.

It rushes forward, coming straight at me. I brace myself for the attack, but nothing comes. I look down at myself, just as the last of it is absorbed into my body. Glancing up, I meet Soren's confused eyes. Tension racks his frame.

"Wha—"

My voice is cut off as the pink mist expands throughout my body. My eyes slam shut until all I see is hazy pink. The mist transforms into a figure.

Will you give up a piece of yourself for the truth? The voice echoes strongly in my mind.

Can you tell me what I'm giving up?

The pink mist flashes deep red for a moment, the voice growing deeper.

NO.

My heart thumps twice as fast. I think about the man beside me and the friends I left behind. *I have to do this... no, I want to do this, for them,* I tell myself.

To the figure, I respond, *Yes, I am ready to give a piece of myself for the truth.*

The anger seems to dissipate from it, leaving the same swirling pink.

You must give us three of your best memories.

I try to hide my relief at the request. *I thought they were going to ask for my firstborn or something.* I freeze at my thoughts. *Since when do I think about the future?* Soren's face flashes in my mind, the hope I feel when I'm with him rising.

How do I know which ones are my best memories? I ask the mysterious figure.

We will pull them from you.

Before I can respond, a thread of eather enters my mind, rapidly shifting through all my memories. It doesn't hurt, but it is extremely uncomfortable. It reaches one and pauses, pulling it up in my mind.

I stand, twisting my fingers nervously as I wait in line to enter the castle. My first day of training, and I can't stop fidgeting.

"Name," a rough voice demands.

I jerk my head up at the sound.

"Adira Selcouth," I tell the man checking us in. He scans the list, crossing off my name.

"The building beside the castle is your lodging. You are bunk thirty-five in building C."

I open my mouth to ask more questions, but he interrupts me.

"Go," he says dismissively.

I shut my mouth and head over to the building that will be my new home. I hear swords clashing, and my gaze finds a training ground right behind our sleeping quarters. My eyes stay glued to the skill the two people fighting possess.

Then, my body slams into another person.

I twist my head toward a girl with a long braid.

"I am so sorry," I tell her. "I wasn't watching where I was going... obviously."

She laughs. "No problem. I can't stop staring either—this place is amazing."

I give her a small smile, not in total agreement with her. Because sure, if you've always wanted to be a soldier, then this is the place for you, but if you haven't, then it resembles more of a gilded prison.

"I'm Saline," she introduces, holding out her hand.

"I'm Adira," I respond with a smile.

She loops her arm around mine.

"I think we are going to be good friends," she says confidently.

A warm feeling fills me at her words.

The memory cuts off, but the warmth doesn't disappear. It spreads through me, causing me to feel different things.

I lay down beside the fire; Soren lays down beside me. I glance at my surroundings, spotting Esper and Poderosa across the glowing flames.

I fight back against it, knowing the memory it's trying to purge. No, *please, not this one,* I plead with it.

It hisses at me, latching onto my head, delving deeper.

Soren turns so we are face to face. The fire crackles loudly around us. Since yesterday, the tension between us has increased. I just don't know if it will shatter into anger or lust.

The silence stretches. His eyes briefly flicker to my lips; I find my own gaze mimicking his. Thinking we should talk about the horrifying visions, I drag my gaze up, hesitating when I see his blue eyes piercing into me.

"Hi," he whispers. His eyes swirl with emotion.

"Hi."

"I was thinking, when this is all over, you can come see what my realm is all about," I say, trying to keep the vulnerability out of my voice.

"I like that idea, princess." He pauses. "And I like you."

My eyes go wide. He has a small smile on his face at my reaction.

I huff out a laugh of disbelief. "Well, shit. I happen to like you too."

The memory cuts off; tears streak down my face. My mind grasps to remember, but nothing appears.

Then, another memory seizes me.

A snap of thunder sounds above. Gray clouds roll in swiftly, but no rain falls. I stare up with a frown at the unnatural weather.

A crack of lightning reverberates through the air. The sound reaches us before the blast does.

We don't have time to panic as a bolt of lightning shoots down, striking us. My vision goes white, a searing feeling grabs at my chest. My hair blows back from the force of it.

Energy caresses us, forming a small funnel of magic. The searing lessens to warm heat. The air hums, causing the earth to momentarily shake. My Makutu chains vibrate before falling to the ground. I whimper in relief.

The power whips around us a few times before it dissipates, my vision returning to normal. The area turns lighter, we look up at the now clear sky, not a single cloud remaining.

I look at Soren, trying to find any injuries.

"I'm okay," he says with a dazed voice.

"So am I."

My hand flies to the heat that still lingers on my chest. My eyes widen, and I grasp at my shirt, pulling it down to see the spot. Only when I see his matching mark do I understand.

Holy goddess.

An eternal symbol crosses over a heart, the rare symbol shining on our bodies.

Our eyes meet.

We are true mates of heart.

I push against the thread trying to pull this one away from me. It tugs harder, another thread zooming up to zap me. I hiss at the sharp pain, losing my concentration. The first thread rips my memory away.

Distantly I hear my name being shouted as I cry for the memories that I've already forgotten.

Chapter 49

Adira

The pink mist swirls in front of me.

"We have accepted your payment."

Before I can ask what happens now, my body and mind jerk, rushing forward. I briefly glimpse dates floating around me, but my disorientation scatters them before I can make them out.

The end of the mystic tunnel nears, and I screech to a halt. A bright light flashes, obscuring my vision. When it fades, I'm looking at the angry face of Conri. For an immortal being, he appears slightly younger in this memory.

He's arguing with Cain about overpowering the others. *Wait, I've seen this,* I say to myself, remembering Orlo's cave.

When they confront the others, the two beings that were unclear to me before have a sharper image. Tiamat and Fadama.

I gasp at the sight, focusing on Fadama.

Or should I say, Josephine.

As I stare at her flawless face, an energy pulls me toward her, dragging me into another memory. *She sits on a blood-red throne, a twisted crown made of gnarled metal seated on her head. A man is kneeled at her feet, his gaze to the ground.*

"Rise, Pheebus," she commands him softly. "What news do you have?"

"There were some human rebels, but we eliminated them before they could cause a riot."

"Good."

He hesitates a moment with a nervous look on his face. "They were rebelling the tithe."

An angry look crosses her face. The air fills with a dark tension.

"Do I not allow them to live on my lands? Could I not purge their foulness from existence if I please? They should be kissing the ground I walk on for their lives."

"I–I agree, My Goddess," Pheebus stammers out.

"Have you heard any word from Conri yet regarding my request?" she asks lightly, though her hands curl slightly around the arm of the chair as she waits for the answer.

Now, a tint of red creeps up on Pheebus' face, followed by a flash of fear.

"Yes, My Goddess. He replied that he was too busy to entertain such fo-foolish requests right now," he rambles out.

Fadama's face hardens at his words. Her magic rushes out of her, swirling around the space in an enraged mass. Pheebus keeps his head down, but I can still see his teeth chattering with fear.

She pulls it all back into her, placing on an icy demeanor, her eyes bright with barely contained power.

"Get out of my sight, Pheebus. I don't want to see you for the rest of the day." Her voice is thick with energy.

"Of course, My Goddess." Pheebus bows quickly and scurries away.

Fadama rises, gliding out of the room. I get a better view of the throne, realizing it was one of the images I saw when I was in the cave of Orlo. Who was Orlo? How did he know so much?

The memory blurs, causing me to sway. Then, it shifts to the side, creating a spiral of colors.

When the world rights itself, I'm in a ruined village. Houses with roofs caving in and holes in the walls line the street. Debris scatters the ground, covered in dust, as if it's been there for a while but no one bothered to move it. A few people stagger along the road with torn clothing, walking in a daze like they don't know where they are. Or don't care.

I spot a castle up ahead, the only pristine building in sight. My feet propel me forward; apparently the memory I need to see is in there. Sadness tugs at my chest as I pass all the starving people.

Stepping into the castle, I eye the banners of unknown beasts hanging from the tall ceilings. I walk down the hallway, the ground made up of a thick glass. Darkness swirls below the floor, waiting to be summoned to attack. My body leads me to a set of marbled doors, the stone on them carved into different beasts. They swing open before I can touch them. I'm met with Conri sitting casually on a dark throne. Cain stands in front of him, a pleading expression on his face.

"Have you looked outside, brother?" Cain asks. "Our people are starving."

Conri waves him off. "If I feed them, they lose their fear of me."

Cain's face twists angrily. "So, you want to rule in fear?"

"Of course, I do. No one challenges fear." Conri sneers down.

Cain just shakes his head sadly.

"You will have no one to rule, brother. Everyone is dying."

Conri pauses at that before his face lights up like he has an idea.

"Then we need to seize more kingdoms."

"More kingdoms? But it's just ours, the goddesses; Tatsuya and Wilhema, Fadama's, and Tiamat's." Cain says with confusion lacing his tone.

Conri smiles wickedly. "Exactly. We need to make the others bow down to us."

Cain blinks once at that.

"But they are our equals. The only other immortals in this world. You would turn them against us?"

Conri shrugs. "We have each other for company, Cain. If we have all the kingdoms, then we will have all the power."

"Is that all that's important to you? Power?"

"Nothing is more important in this world than power," Conri states.

Cain stares at his brother, seeing the change that power has already done to him.

For a brief moment, a flash of thoughts spring to me from Cain. A plan he has. He is going to first warn the others of Conri's plan. Then, he is going to seize his brother's powers before they can consume him and the world.

My mind jumps over the warning scene and lands abruptly into a dark forest.

Cain is hunched over the ground, looking at something.

I walk around him. The thing he is looking at is an ancient book. He speaks something from the book. The ancient words stick in my brain. His power hovers in his hand. A quiet unease settles in around us. He doesn't stop though. He finishes speaking and thrusts the power up into the sky.

The sky flashes a multitude of colors. The air pressure changes, becoming so charged it's hard to breathe. Blasts of purple light come careening toward us. Three to be exact. They crash into the earth, but no mark scars the ground. A second later, the air becomes less stifling, and three figures stand in front of Cain.

I take them in, gasping at the sight. The divine energy giving them away. These must be the Arae.

They are impossibly tall, their eyes a deep purple. You can feel their primitive energy crackling around. I swear one of them looks at me, their eyes threatening to drag me under. A shiver works its way down my spine, I shake it off. When I look back, their attention is on Cain.

"I need a way to seize my brother's powers."

The Arae in the middle regards Cain with a curious expression.

"Are the powers we bestowed upon you too much to handle?" The Arae speaks out, the voice deep and piercing.

Cain bows his head slightly.

"We thank you for the gift of power. But my brother has let the power take control, it is all he craves, all he desires. He will stop at nothing to be the most powerful being in this world. I can't stand by and do nothing."

They stare deeply at Cain, their purple eyes piercing into him, judging his soul. After a long moment of silence, they speak.

"I sense your honorable intentions, Cain Aamon. The path we see for you is to weaken, not remove."

Cain nods his head in thanks.

"While this lifestone sits on your palm, these words must be spoken." The Arae hand over a deep brown stone along with an old piece of parchment. I look over his shoulder, reading the ancient words. "The only way to reverse this spell is to have the child he sired to willingly transfer their power to him."

Cain frowns. "He hasn't sired any children."

"Yet." The Arae say ominously.

The vision melts away. I press a hand to my chest, trying to hold back my rising fear.

I'm the one who can give Conri his full powers back. I almost laugh at the irony of him trying to kill me.

A panicked thought enters my mind.

"Who else knows this information?" I ask the pink mist.

"One other has this knowledge."

Well shit.

Chapter 50

Soren

Iwatch helplessly as tears run down her face. Her body twitches, and her eyeballs move rapidly under her eyelids. I hold her close, hoping the contact offers her some comfort. I feel no physical pain reflected onto my body, that knowledge giving me a semblance of relief. After what seems like an eternity—but is probably only ten minutes—her body finally stills.

I freeze, waiting to see what will happen.

Her eyes flutter open. She groans, shifting into a sitting position.

"Are you okay? What happened?" I ask frantically, searching her gaze for signs of pain.

"I'm alright," she responds. "It showed me the past. I saw Fadama—only she's also Josephine, King Elijah's mistress from my realm." Her face tightens with distaste. "She had her own throne and looked to be lusting after Conri."

"Then I saw Cain meeting with the Arae." Awe fills her voice. "They were so powerful... through the memory, I could feel the energy they radiated." Her eyes glaze over as if she's seeing them again.

Her face hardens. "I know how Cain took Conri's powers. He used a lifestone."

My face scrunches up at the foreign word. "What's a lifestone?"

"It's a stone from another world. It can contain unlimited power. Cain trapped his powers in this stone and hid it. The only way to reverse the spell is if a child Conri sired willingly transfers power to him." She laughs bitterly as my mind catches up with the information.

"Ironic how he almost killed his only chance at getting his powers back."

I don't laugh with her. The thought of losing her weighing heavily on me. I step forward, wrapping her in a tight hug.

"It's not funny, princess. I almost lost you."

She burrows further into my chest.

"I know." She sighs. "But I don't know how to handle all the shit that's happened. Making light of the situation seems to be my method of coping."

I sigh deeply. Then, a thought occurs to me. I pull back to meet her eyes.

"Wait. What was the payment for seeing that knowledge?"

She winces. "They took three memories from me."

"Which ones?" I ask, then immediately feel stupid for the question. She rubs at her chest.

"I don't remember. I just feel an aching loss." She whispers.

I think of her tears. Brushing a piece of loose hair from her face, I caress her cheek. "You were crying when you first went under the object's spell."

"Maybe you'll fill in the blanks if it comes up," she says.

My brows furrow. "I won't know them if they happened before you met me."

A blush rises in her cheeks.

"I don't have many good memories from before I met you," she admits, looking at the ground.

Warmth spreads through my chest at her words. I reach out, tilting her chin up so our gazes meet.

"Same here, princess. I didn't realize I was just going through the motions of life before I met you."

She sighs with content. "I love you, Soren."

My heart jumps at her words. *I'll never get tired of hearing her say that.*

"I love you too, princess."

Her eyes take on a faraway look, a thread of anguish creeping into them.

"Hey." I draw her attention back to me. "Don't worry about the future. Let's just focus on the next step."

She forces a small smile, but it doesn't hide where her thoughts have strayed.

I keep my expression neutral while I ruminate over the prophecy, not wanting my emotions to make this harder for her than it already will be. *But... dammit, I don't want to die.*

A shy expression takes over her face.

"I have something for you."

My eyebrows shoot up in surprise. "For me?"

She nods, reaching into her pack. She pulls something wrapped in a clean white cloth. I grab it from her outstretched hand. Unwrapping it slowly, a small piece of chocolate cake is revealed. My mouth kicks up, and my gaze shoots to her.

"You got me chocolate cake? When?"

A blush covers her cheeks. "You said it was your favorite. I saw it and wanted you to have something good. I bought it when you were at the booth of daggers."

My heart swells at her words. I lean over to kiss her softly. "Thank you, princess. That was very sweet of you."

"Well, go on, eat it!"

I chuckle at her enthusiasm, taking a bite. A groan escapes me from the decadent taste.

"Oh my gods. I don't remember it being this good."

She smiles wide at my reaction.

I'm so lucky to have her.

"Do you want a bite?" I ask her, holding the cake out.

She shakes her head. "Nope. That's all for you."

I finish it off quickly, wishing another piece would magically appear. I grab her shoulders, pulling her against me. She relaxes into me.

After a few moments, the clearing fills with uneasiness. Adira sits up, chewing on her bottom lip. She takes a deep breath, rolling the tension out of her shoulders.

"Okay, we need to find a way to beat Conri."

"How do we do that? I thought that mirror would tell us."

"It did tell us."

I run back through the information she told me, not finding an answer.

"What is it?"

"We can summon the Arae. They will be able to aid us."

A worried look flashes across her stunning face. I grab her hand, unable to stop myself from touching her.

"It's dangerous, but we have to do it."

"Okay. How do we do it?"

"I know the spell. Cain used it in the vision," she admits in a hushed tone.

My eyebrows rise.

"So we could potentially summon them right now?" I ask, feeling rushed.

She gulps audibly. "Yep. Right now."

"Feels a little quick, doesn't it?"

"It does, but it won't change the outcome whether we wait a few days or deal with it now," she reasons quietly.

"That's true," I respond, pushing away the thoughts of my impending death.

Steeling my spine, I straighten.

"Let's do it then."

Adira nods in reluctant agreement, shutting her eyes.

She utters a string of words in an ancient language. Her palm lays open to the sky, her power swirling around in a ball. A white hue surrounds her, making her look ethereal. My mouth drops open at the sight of her beauty.

As she finishes speaking, the ball of energy shoots up to the sky.

It crackles across the clouds, causing the blue sky to erupt in a variety of colors. The pressure in the air changes, becoming almost suffocating. My eyes stay locked on the sky, my magic trying to rise up against the unknown power emanating from it. A flash of purple light catches my attention. Adira looks the same way.

As the light gets closer, it splits into three sections, barreling toward us at an inhuman speed.

Just when I'm about to pull Adira away, it crashes into the ground a few feet in front of us. The world flashes a bright white, and my retinas burn. I can't see anything in front of me.

Then, it fades.

I blink the spots out of my vision and focus on the clearing in front of me.

Before, it was empty. Now, three ancient figures stand.

Chapter 51

Adira

The blinding light fades. I blink a few times, but the scene doesn't change. Three beings stand in front of us, staring unnervingly with deep purple eyes.

I swallow my apprehension, taking a daring step forward. They note the movement, staying eerily still. Soren steps up beside me, his hand hanging loosely near the hilt of his weapon.

Goddess, I hope he doesn't try to use that against them.

"Speak your intent." The Arae on the right says with a tilt of its head. The voice echoes through the trees, creating a harmonious, otherworldly sound.

I snap out of my awe, bowing swiftly. I tug at Soren's sleeve to do the same. He drops down beside me only after a short hesitation, unwilling to take his eyes off any potential threats.

"We have come for your aid. We are hoping for information on how to stop Conri Aamon," I tell them. Then I pause, adding, "My name is Ad—"

They hold up a hand, silencing me.

"We know who you are, Adira Selcouth. As well as you, Soren Banrs," the one on the left says.

The one in the middle gestures gracefully toward us. "After all, we were the ones that have chosen you for this prophecy."

We stand slowly, letting their words wash over us.

I swallow hard at the sheer implication, confirming what I already knew—my life was never my own. All of my choices have been influenced by higher beings. I feel my sense of self begin to disintegrate. *Who even am I? Was anything that's happened to me real?* I shake my head out of that thought. *Of course it was real. You felt those things.* I bite my lip, trying to push my spiraling thoughts away.

"We will aid you."

My head snaps up at that.

"Why?" I blurt out. Soren shoots me a look, trying to get me to stay silent and accept their aid.

"Conri Aamon has been a stain on this world. We created Celestara with hopes of prosperity, but only death and destruction have fallen upon it. The beings of this planet took hold of the power gifted to them and fought for more—Conri being the worst of them. Centuries ago, we tried to restore hope by splitting Celestara into two separate realms. But the truth is clear to us now. Corruption still leaks throughout the realms, poisoning people and nature."

Shock and awe mix together as they casually speak about splitting a world in two.

"Thank you," I half-whisper.

"The past of the brothers was revealed to you. Cain was given a stone to weaken Conri's powers. The stone was made of materials not of this world. Another object was forged. We foresaw you coming to us for aid. We planted the object within your grasp, tasking another with its importance until you came of age to handle it yourself," the middle Arae says.

"The object has been within your possession since birth," another adds.

What? I think in shock. My hand automatically goes up to my pendant for comfort, and I freeze. My eyes snap down to the swirling rock—the only gift my mother had ever given me.

I remember it like it was yesterday.

"Adira." My mother's voice spoke from another room. "Come here."

I followed the sound to the living room, finding her sitting near the fire, her legs crossed patiently as she waited for me.

I took a seat cautiously beside her, ready in case it was another test. "Yes, mother?"

She reached behind her, pulling out an old wooden box. The lock was made of thick iron. She pulled at the string around her neck, producing an old key. The air thickened with disquiet.

I sat silently in confusion, knowing she didn't like to be interrupted.

The lid creaked open, the sound filling the quiet room. A flash of fear and resentment crossed her face. She reached in and pulled out a beautiful pendant—a black metal chain holding a swirling stone. My hand reached out to touch it, the dormant power drawing me closer. Just before I touched it, my mother pulled it back.

My gaze snapped up to her face. Her jaw was tight; she appeared to be leashing her anger.

"This is for you to protect, Adira. You must never take it off. You will know when the time is right."

My brows furrowed in confusion as I thought about her words. Every so often, she would speak in riddles regarding my future. I stopped trying to make sense of them.

A logical question wormed its way through my mind.

"What if someone takes it off of me?" I asked.

"They won't be able to. I have a spell that will keep it on you no matter who tries to take it off. You will be the only one able to remove it." She leaned in close. "And you mustn't remove it."

I knew better than to ask why, so I tried a different question.

"How will I know when the time is right?"

"You will know," she stated without doubt.

I heaved a sigh, relenting to her crazed notions.

"Okay, put it on me."

She stared at me for a long moment, urging with her eyes to understand the importance of it.

"I won't take it off. I promise," I told her.

She nodded at my admission, securing it on my neck. It felt cold and heavy at first, but the longer it stayed against my skin, it seemed to come alive, thrumming lightly. My mother must have seen the panic on my face because she clasped my cheeks, forcing my gaze to hers.

"You may feel discomfort when you are wearing it, but you must not succumb to it. That's what it wants," she told me. Her hard gaze portraying her seriousness. I tried to draw back from her.

What did she put on me?

The panic dulls as the vision fades. I blink back the remnants of the image and focus on the beings in front of me.

The Arae nod lightly, knowing where my mind went.

"The pendant must only be removed when you reach l'antica terra, the ground first touched by our presence. This pendant has the power to trap, not defeat. When you remove the pendant, the instructions will become clear."

The middle Arae waves a hand to the side. The world tears in two, creating a portal. The clearing crackles with purple energy. I swallow against the copper taste already filling my mouth.

"Pass through here. L'antica terra awaits you, the prophecy awaits you."

My blood freezes at those words. I didn't think it would happen so soon. I thought we would have more time. I take a small step closer to the Arae, putting slight distance between Soren and me.

"The last part about the prophecy... does it mean... I mean, is it really about Soren?" I finish off weakly.

A brief crease in their brow is their only sign of confusion. "But of course, he is your true mate of heart."

I gasp at the news. "What?"

They tilt their head at my reaction. Soren steps toward me, reaching out a hand gently, like he's scared he'll spook me.

"We were blessed and marked right after we escaped from Conri, princess," he tells me, confusion marring his brow.

I frown, scouring through my memories to find it. A hole of time where our escape should have been greets me.

Understanding dawns on his face.

"This must have been one of the memories the ancient object took from you."

A painful thrum beats in my chest like it knows the truth. I pull down my shirt, seeing the mark over my heart.

Happiness bursts through me, followed quickly by horror. I reach for him, grasping his chest. The mark throbs as if knowing the life of the bond is soon to fade.

"I knew it would be you, but I was still hoping there would be a chance it wasn't," I admit in a shaky whisper.

"I know, princess. It will be okay," he tells me, pressing a soft kiss to my head. My eyes find the beings that chose me as a pawn in their plans, my ire rising up swiftly.

"It's not fair. Why must he die to complete the prophecy? I don't understand!" I shout at them.

Their eyes turn an even deeper purple. Their forms seem to stretch impossibly tall above us.

"Those who dare to question us are naught long for this world. We have been around since the beginning of time and will be around long after you are gone. Learn your place, child. This is what you were born to do."

"I'll accept help, but I won't cede my will." I curb my tone, smart enough to know when not to push a powerful ancient being.

One of them lets out a deep chuckle, the sound shaking the trees. "Freewill. Humans place such high value on it. They don't know how easily we can take it away from them."

My muscles lock, the underlying warning clear to me. Soren shifts closer to me, his own fear trickling down the bond.

"Now," they continue, their eyes flaring, "pass through the portal and finish what you were chosen to do. Dire consequences will befall this world if you fail. The Vormr is just the beginning. Fulfill the prophecy and the Vormr will be stopped. Your beast will be... tied up until you complete this. Collateral to ensure you follow through."

They flash out of existence. The warning ringing in the air between us. A second later, my feet move forward. I frown down, realizing Soren has an uncomfortable look on his face too. Eyes wide, I try to call for Lyra, but there is no response. Panic claws at my chest.

"I'm not doing this," I say, the lack of control chilling my blood.

"Neither am I," he responds through gritted teeth.

We share a look, disbelieving of the Arae's cruel coercion.

Our steps walk steadily toward the portal. I try to call upon my magic, but it's trapped. Closing my eyes, I concentrate on my reserve, noticing that it's thrashing behind a purple wall of energy. I instinctively recoil, feeling violated.

Glancing over at Soren, I notice the helplessness in his eyes.

I press my lips together, holding back a string of curses. Swirls of purple energy reach out to us as we near it. A pounding thrums in my head, matching the beat of my heart.

We step through the portal.

Chapter 52

Soren

The feeling is more intense than any other portal I've been through. The sharp sting of copper overwhelms my senses. My body feels like it's been stretched and shrunk as we whirl down the tunnel of energy. My vision twists in a spiral of color. I blink, trying to clear my sight.

Finally, we land in a heap on the soft grass.

My stomach churns, I focus on my breathing to minimize the effects.

Once the dizziness fades, I look up, taking in my surroundings. The sun is dipping low in the sky, signaling the start of dusk. Taking a deep breath, I notice the air is once again stifled.

We are back in Enelon.

I begin to recognize the forest around us, but the area feels different—heavy with destiny. The stale air seems to pulse from the ground. I peer down at it. The brown terrain looks slightly darker than the normal forest, tinted by a deep red. The cliffs drop off to the right, opening up for the sunset.

"We're only about a day's walk away from the castle," I tell Adira.

"This can't be happening." She whispers to herself, the denial clear in her tone.

The ancient ground hums in front of me, like its preparing for the blood it's going to consume. My blood. Adira stares at the same spot. Nerves trickle in, turning my hands shaky. *I'd have traded a thousand detours for one more day with her.*

She turns to look at me, her emotions locked down. She clears her throat. "We need to set a trap for Conri."

I nod to her, trying not to focus on my limited time. *Just enjoy being with her. Help her succeed in fulfilling this prophecy.*

A wave of renewed determination washes over me, stripping away my fears. I take in her serious expression, awed by her beauty even when she's repressing her emotions. *I hope she can move on after I'm gone.* My chest aches at the thought of being without her.

Hey, princess. I say in her mind, hoping this intimate form of communication will encourage her to face our truth.

She starts, having been lost in her thoughts. Then, she turns to me, giving me her attention.

Hi.

I know this is going to be hard. And I'm so sorry you have to do it.

She gapes at me. *You're sorry? I'm sorry! I have to... I have to end your life.*

The words sound choked, like she could hardly think them.

I step toward her, leaning my forehead against hers.

I know you do, princess. But it's not your fault. I don't want you to shoulder this burden. And after I'm gone... you'll be free from the control of the prophecy.

I pause for a moment, squeezing my eyes shut, wishing I could change the outcome.

Promise me that you'll try to be happy. I want you to meet someone you care about and build a life with them. Find your happiness. You deserve it.

A tear slides down her cheek.

So do you. I don't want you to leave me. I know we haven't known each other long, but you are the other half of my heart. I can't just go on without you here with me.

I wipe her tear away.

Remember? It's me and you. Until the end. Her tone is pleading as she tightly grips my shirt.

My chest cracks at those words. A thickness fills my throat, and I'm suddenly glad that the conversation is through our minds.

Me and you, princess. Until the end. I repeat back to her, kissing her softly on the lips. *That's still true. It just turned out that the end is sooner than we'd hoped.*

Adira doesn't respond, but a deep ache comes through her side of the bond. She wraps her hand behind my neck, pulling my head down to hers.

Her soft lips swipe across mine lightly. I grip her waist, deepening the kiss. She melts into me, exploring my body leisurely.

It feels like a goodbye.

My heart tightens painfully at that thought. I ignore it for now, focusing on my heartmate.

The need to be closer to her overcomes me. I back her up against a tree, pressing into her body. She moans breathlessly, moving her hips for more friction. I kiss her neck, tracing a hand down her smooth skin. She pulls off her shirt, motioning for me to do the same. I quickly shuck it off, returning my hands to her body.

I cup her perfect breasts, groaning at the feel of them. *Gods, I'm going to miss this.* She leans into my touch, the hands trailing over me becoming more frantic.

I need you.

The second-best three words a man could hear.

Lifting her up, she wraps her legs around my waist. I walk backward, not breaking the kiss. I find the patch of soft grass I noticed earlier and set her down onto it. Her hands go to my belt, but I stop her.

Not yet, princess. You first.

I trail kisses down the front of her body, stopping when I reach the hem of her pants. She lifts her hips as I pull them down. I press a kiss to the edge of her inner thigh, groaning as her sweet scent envelopes me.

My cock strains against my pants, throbbing with need.

I tear off her underwear, desperate to taste her. I thrust my tongue through her seam, her hips bucking up from the intrusion. Reaching a hand up, I press her hips down, holding her still while I plunge my tongue in and out of her. Her breathing grows quicker as I swirl my tongue around with practiced skill.

She whimpers as she climbs higher, and I almost come in my pants from the sound.

She cries out my name as she tips over the edge. I lap up her release greedily, unwilling to miss a single drop.

Kissing my way up her body, I take in her dazed expression and shoot her a cocky smirk.

She rolls her eyes playfully, but her deep gaze shows her emotions.

Reaching down, she cups me through my pants. I groan, twisting away.

"Princess, I won't last if you do that," I tell her.

She grins wickedly. *Maybe I don't want you to last. Maybe I want you to fall apart while I take you in my mouth.*

I squeeze my eyes shut as the image comes to mind. *Think of something else,* I plead with myself, trying to keep control. Once I'm certain I won't burst at the sound of her voice anymore, I lean down, capturing her mouth with mine.

As much as I'd love that, princess. I pause as the image resurfaces. *You have no idea how much. But I need to be inside you. I need that connection right now.*

Her gaze softens at my words.

I love you.

And I love you, princess. Until the end and to wherever I go after.

Mist forms in her eyes. She helps me slide my pants down. Our pace slows once more as we take each other in. I caress her face as I line up with her entrance.

You are so beautiful.

She smiles easily at that. *So are you.*

I huff like I'm annoyed. *Beautiful? Don't you mean sexy and handsome? The most attractive man you've ever laid your eyes on?*

I hear her giggle in my mind. Then, her eyes latch onto mine, taking a more serious tone.

Not only are you the most attractive man I've ever laid eyes on. I smirk at her admission. *But you were my hope, you were my future. I never dreamed of those things until I met you.*

Her eyes shutter as she uses the past tense. Hopelessness seizes me at her defeated tone. I kiss her gently, pulling her back to the present.

I know it seems impossible to fathom right now, but you can still have those things. Even when I'm gone. Live for me, princess. You gave me something sweet to live for, you gave me love. I want you to really live. Will you promise you'll try?

She breathes out shakily, the distress clear in her eyes.

I'll try.

I eye her.

I promise. I'll try, for you.

I nod, relief flowing through me, hoping that she can keep that promise.

She drags my face down to hers, kissing me fiercely. Deepening the kiss, I press into her. She gasps at the invasion. I pause as she adjusts.

Then, she starts moving her hips.

I push in and out with a steady tempo. My eyes stay locked on hers. Our heightened emotions float around us, the air charged with our fervid energy. As our releases build, the air cracks.

We fall over the edge together. A loud burst of energy sounds as we come down from our daze. Looking to the left, we see a tree in flames. A laugh escapes me at the sight, Adira joins in. She waves a hand toward it, dousing the flames. My gaze stays on the charred tree. *Maybe the world was always meant to burn when we touched.*

I pull out of her slowly, wincing at the loss. We lock eyes, the unspoken realization that our time is running out reflecting to each other. I swallow thickly, knowing that this was our goodbye. As night falls around us, I tug her against me, not wanting to be apart from her. I revel in her warmth, the silence of the night straining with words unsaid.

"We need a plan for Conri." Adira mutters, seeming resistant to the conversation.

I kiss her shoulder. "Let's think of a plan then, princess."

She sighs into me, snuggling in closer.

Her words echo in my head, mirroring my own thoughts.

What am I going to do without you?

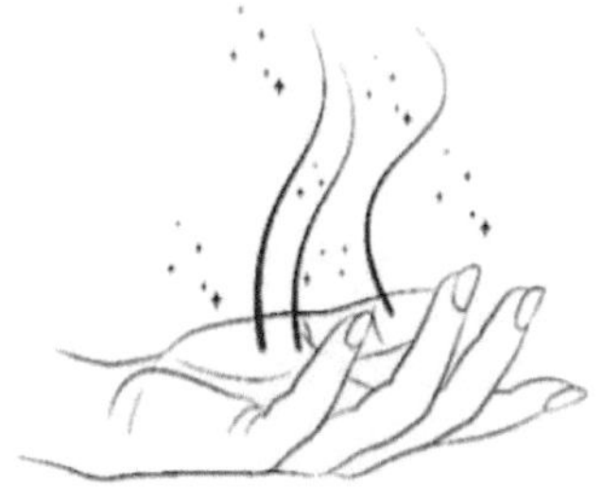

Chapter 53

Adira

I blink against the glare of the sun. Soren shifts behind me. Dread fills me even after we solidified the plan.

I breathe in deeply, trying not to dwell on my unease.

Tell yourself the plan again, Adira. Focus.

My mind recounts the agreed-on plan. First, we send a letter to Linnea, enticing Conri by telling him we know how he can regain his powers. We will tell him that we want to be pardoned from all crimes and left alone for the information. Hopefully, this will keep his suspicions at bay. Then, we will trigger the magical barrier we set, forcing him and his guards to be trapped in the clear wall as they watch me complete the prophecy.

I swallow hard, ignoring the obvious way the prophecy will be fulfilled.

When the realms are rebalanced, I will speak the words of the ancient spell to entrap Conri.

Opening my hand, I eye the pendant. My neck feels bare without it. I think back to the feeling of removing it—it felt like removing a limb. Once it was off my body, the spell came to me clearly.

I shakily draw in a breath. *It's almost all over.*

Soren stirs, drawing my attention.

Morning, princess.

A sad smile stretches over my face.

Good morning.

I twist to look at him. My heart aches with what is to come. *I won't get to wake up looking at his handsome face or see his frustratingly cocky smirk again.*

He pulls me close, probably sensing the unrelenting dread I'm projecting. My breath catches in my throat. I choke back a sob, but it bursts free. Soren's pain mirrors mine as he rubs my back gently.

"I don't know if I can do this," I admit to Soren in a shaky, quiet voice. Pulling back, he drags my gaze up to his.

"You can," he says confidently. "You are the strongest person I know."

I whimper slightly. Then, a wave of anger hits me.

"Fuck the realms. Fuck the Arae. They don't get to win. Why can't *we* win for once? We've never had any choices in our lives—can't this be our choice?" I plead with him.

He screws his eyes shut, leaning forward to rest his head on mine.

"It's not fair, princess. You deserve so much more than what has been forced upon you. But if we don't fulfill the prophecy, there won't be a world to live in. Everything will fall apart, starting with Modereo. And I know you couldn't live with yourself if you let your friends die."

The truth of his words washes over me, soothing the anger and leaving only frustration behind.

"It's just so hard," I say, my voice cracking.

"I know, princess." He leans in, giving me a light kiss.

Pulling back, his soft expression hardens. "We should set the trap. It's time."

I stand up, my legs feeling like rubber. I sigh inwardly. *My mother would see this as a weakness.* I immediately scold myself. *If loving someone is a weakness, then I will gladly suffer the consequences. The time I had with Soren was short, but if the choice was to not experience love at all... well, let's just say I would still choose this path even with the outcome.*

"I'll send the letter," I tell Soren in a tired voice.

Closing my eyes, I picture the letter. With my heightened powers, the image comes faster than it ever has. Sensing a thread of energy, I shoot it down, sending it to the castle. I spell it so that only Conri can open it.

"It's done," I tell Soren.

His eyebrows raise. "That was fast."

I shrug. "It was easier with my new powers."

He nods like this makes sense.

"Let's set the trap."

"How do I do that?" Soren asks, holding his hand out like he can see his new powers.

"Imagine your powers rushing up to the surface. Then, latch onto one of the threads of energy and picture what you want in your mind. I imagine a barrier of sparkling energy before it fades to invisible."

"Okay, let's try." He picks up a handful of dirt, holding it in his hand. I grab his other hand, immediately feeling his magic link with mine. Our connected power caresses my senses, a moan almost escaping me at the sensation.

My power rushes out quickly; I imagine a large wall surrounding the area. A steady stream of energy bursts out of me, and I sense Soren's magic doing the same. The wall is quickly built, our magic taking root in the earth and settling.

Opening my eyes, I see the same clearing, but if I concentrate, I can feel the energy of the shield, waiting to be activated.

A faint bell echoes in the distance. We both turn toward the sound, realizing it's coming from the direction of Linnea.

"He must have sounded the alarm to gather his guards." Soren pales slightly as he says this. "He will be on his way now."

I give him a weak smile.

"We better get some food then."

We head back to our packs. My mind is spinning with what I'm about to do. I try to slow my breathing, but my chest doesn't untighten. I take the food Soren is holding out for me and settle against a tree.

A strained silence falls over us as we eat, both of us preparing for what is next.

****

The sound of horses' hooves stomping against the ground pulls us from our silence. We leap up onto our feet, moving forward toward the ancient ground. The thundering sound gets impossibly loud before the guards shoot through the trees, surrounding us quickly.

A steady trot sounds to our right. A ball of unease sits heavy in my stomach. We turn toward it, knowing who it will be. A magnificent white horse with a long mane comes into view; atop it is Conri. His expression shows dull amusement, but his eyes dance feverishly.

"Adira. How nice to see you again," he says with mock pleasantness, ignoring Soren completely.

"I wish I could say the same," I spit back.

His fake pleasantries fades.

"Watch your tone with me, girl. There are more of us than there are of you," he threatens.

Soren growls at his threat.

Conri turns his sneer on Soren.

"And you. I think you disappointed me the most. You had so much potential."

Soren ignores him, angering Conri further.

"What information do you have?" he demands.

"I know how to reverse the spell your brother did on you," I tell him. His eyes narrow in suspicion, but I spot a flicker of hope flashing through them.

"Yes, that's what you said in your letter. Why on earth would I believe you?"

I reach into my pocket, pulling out the *passato riflesso*. I hold it up to him. His guards stiffen, their hands going to their weapons.

"Because I used this."

His eyes narrow as he studies it.

"Is that the *passato riflesso*?" he asks, a hint of disbelief in his tone.

"Yes. I saw the past and how Cain tricked you. I can reverse it."

He stares at me for a long moment. Before he can dwell further on his suspicions, I keep talking.

"We want you to leave us alone. Don't come after us when we are gone. If you promise this, then I will tell you how to reverse the spell."

"And what if I don't want to make a bargain? What if I just want to take what's rightfully mine?"

I open my mouth before closing it at his comment. *Is he for real? There's no way I will tell him for free.*

"If you kill me, you will regret it," I warn him.

"And why is that?"

I smirk at him, knowing the news will rattle him.

"The only way to reverse the spell is to have a child you sired willingly turn their powers over to you."

He scoffs. "I scour weakness from my bloodline. There are no loose ends."

My gut churns at the news. I breathe in deeply. "That's where you're wrong," I say lightly, offering up a half-grin.

The silence drags as I wait for him to ask, his impatience wins. "You misapprehend your station, girl. Speak, or watch your world expire."

I keep the mocking smirk on my face. "Didn't you ever wonder where your mistress ran off to? Why did she run off so suddenly?" I taunt him as I press a hand to my stomach. His eyes draw to the movement, widening slightly.

"No. Impossible."

I tilt my head at him.

"Hello, father. Isn't it ironic that you tried to kill the only person who could restore your powers?" I laugh bitterly.

His expression changes from shock to triumph. He waves a hand to someone on his left.

Before I can react, a gust of wind travels to us. When I go to take another breath, it gets stuck in my throat. Soren claws at his own throat beside me.

By the gods, they have an air wielder.

My magic screams inside me, an urgent feeling latching on. It surges through me, pressing out the unknown energy. Soren gasps as he sucks in breaths.

A quick flash of surprise crosses Conri's face.

I yank on my anger, letting the emotion strengthen my magic.

"That's enough," I say darkly.

Conri nods his head, and his guards unsheathe their weapons, drawing forward.

I hold my hands out and set off our trap. All the men in the clearing freeze in place, unable to move even an inch.

I keep my magic flowing out, assessing all the men to ensure the trap stays secure. I grit my teeth as my power strains against me. Knowing I will reach the bottom of my reserve soon, a sense of urgency fills me. My body doesn't detect the same urgency my mind is telling me. I turn slowly, knowing what is waiting for me.

Soren has moved to the center of the ancient ground.

He watches me with a sad but firm expression. I walk over to him slowly, but my body feels as though it's floating. The taste of salt reaches my lips. I lift a hand to my face, realizing I'm crying.

Once I'm a foot away from him, he presses his forehead to mine. Even the trees lean closer, listening. The wind doesn't dare move. Bringing his hands up, he wipes my tears away. "No matter how it ended, I wouldn't trade the time with you for anything. You brought me back to life. You gave my heart a reason to feel something other than vengeance and hatred. I love you, Adira Selcouth. And I will continue to love you, no matter where I end up."

His eyes don't leave mine as he speaks. They glisten with unshed tears.

"I love you, Soren. You came into my life swiftly and knocked it off-kilter, but I wouldn't have wanted it any other way. You are it for me. It's me and you. Until the end."

He smiles slightly.

"Me and you, princess. Until the end."

I lean forward, kissing him through my salty tears. Before I can talk myself out of it, I bring the dagger to his heart. Though I want to blame the Arae in this moment, this is my hand— not theirs.

I break the kiss, gripping the dagger tightly.

"I'm sorry," I sob out, pushing the dagger into his chest. He sputters, blood dripping out of his mouth. My cries echo through the trees, drowning out the muffled voices of the men. I twist the dagger, wanting to end his pain faster. He slumps to the ground, and I fall with him. My chest starts to burn. I place my hand over my mark.

I gasp at the rapid throbbing. My eyes don't leave Soren.

He takes his last breath, his blue eyes staring, unseeing, at the sky. His blood seeps into the ancient ground. The area humming as it takes his life.

I grip my chest just as a blinding pain rips through me. The feeling is ten times worse than the way my magic is still pulling at me.

It feels like my heart is being ripped from my chest.

I look down at the only man I've ever loved. Dead. By my hand.

What have I done?

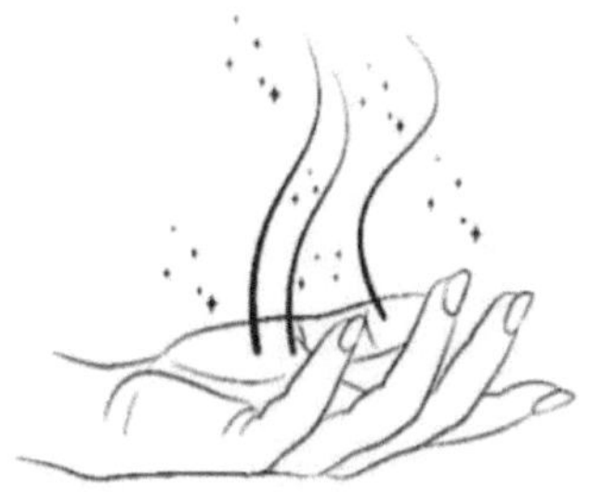

Chapter 54

Adira

Grief rolls through me. Consuming my every thought. Blocking out everything else.

A shout draws me from the depth. My mother's voice rises angrily through me. *Get up, Adira. You are not done.*

I focus on her ire, turning my emotions to match. My glazed eyes start to focus. I notice the guards have started wiggling against their invisible ties. Then, I notice the deep ache my body has as my powers continuously flow out of me. I clench my teeth together, realizing how dangerously close I am to the bottom of my reserve.

My eyes meet Conri's. He is staring at me with mild horror. I twist my head to the side, realizing the ground is shaking. The air becomes charged as the clouds swirl above us.

The sight of his face sends me into a rage. *This is his fault.*

My power reacts to my flare in emotion and bursts out, killing all of the guards. I refuse to let myself feel guilty about that. My magic seems to know that I can't kill Conri the same way and holds off. The sky flashes purple, and a large fissure appears near the edge of the cliff.

An overwhelming scent of copper fills the air, giving it a sharp sting. Even Conri appears to be concentrating on that. My vision goes white, and my body plummets, the ground beneath me seeming to have disappeared.

A minute later, my feet land back on solid ground with a jarring thud. I shake off the disorientation. The world quiets as it settles. I glance around in awe, seeing that there are no longer cliffs beside us. The bodies of the guards are gone. I hold my breath, turning my head toward the ancient ground. The spot where Soren lay is now empty. My heart cracks all over again.

Finish this. A powerful voice hisses in my ear.

I shiver at the tone but focus on the task at hand, pulling out the pendant. Conri's eyes narrow on me. I latch onto the darkness that is tugging at me, succumbing to my vicious thoughts.

I glide forward into the clearing, stopping a few feet from where he is still struggling with his binds. My magic jolts slightly, warning me it can't hold on much longer. I revel in the pain, using it to keep me focused.

"Oh, look, father dearest. The realms are rebalanced," I mock. "Too bad you won't be sticking around to see."

"You are my echo, Adira." He spews out, gesturing to the blood still tainting the ground. "You can't silence me without silencing yourself."

A flash of desperation goes through his eyes when I only smile. "Then I'll scream loud enough for both of us."

He tries to speak, but I cut off his airway, tired of hearing his bullshit. Panic shines in his eyes, I smile wickedly at the emotion. *Finally.*

I pull out the pendant, grasping it in my hand. I lift my palm toward Conri to finish this.

"*Pro entitate quae ita corrumpitur, mitte eum in somnum aeternum interrumpendum.*" My voice takes on a primitive tone as I speak the ancient words.

An old energy bursts from the pendant, shattering the foundation. The swirling black energy moves at an unnatural pace, flying out toward Conri.

A flash of true terror passes in his eyes before his essence is sucked into the device. The pendant flops to the ground. Conri's horse whinnies frantically and gallops away.

Silence descends on the clearing.

I walk over the trampled grass to grab the pendant. The necklace is once again whole, but instead of a black swirl of energy inside, it now holds a solid deep red hue, as if angry. A flash of color catches my attention.

Purple energy streaks across the sky, coming right for me.

Chapter 55

Adira

The blinding light fades, revealing the Arae. I turn from their powerful forms, my gaze finding the spot again. No more Soren. The proof of his sacrifice gone, as if it didn't matter. My heart catches in my throat.

"Where did the b-bodies go?" I choke on the word.

"The dead are part of the realm's renewal—flesh into soil, soul into eather."

I squeeze my eyes shut. *He's really gone.* I feel myself starting to crack, so I shove every emotion down before turning my attention to the Arae.

In a flat tone, I say, "Well, I did it. Are you happy?"

I toss the pendant at them. They catch it with a frown.

"Do whatever you want with that. Just keep him trapped in there."

"You have done it. The realms are rebalanced, the Vormr stopped, a monster trapped." They gesture to the necklace.

I manage a shrug, not able to muster up the excitement for this 'accomplishment.' Their purple eyes are intense as they track my movements.

I turn away from them, numbness spreading through me. Before I can take another step, they speak again.

"Wait."

It takes a second for the word to register through my fuzzy brain. Turning, I face them.

"What." I respond with a bitter tone. *Haven't they done enough?*

"Balance demands sacrifice. Sometimes, the scales tip twice." They say ominously. "'End' is only a word until meaning is placed upon it."

What the fuck?

"Okay, thanks," I mutter, waving them off. The energy shifts as they spark away. Another voice breaks through the fog.

Little one?

I almost cry in relief. She flies into view, dropping in front of me. I immediately lean into her neck.

Lyra, I've missed you.

I've missed you too. Are you alright?

The emotions rise up at the question. I choke on a sob. *No.*

I hear Lyra's sigh through our bond, like this is hurting her as much as me. After all my body is drained of its tears, I press back from her now-matted fur. Indecision floats through the bond.

I will tell you something, little one. But you must not act too rashly.

What is it?

I sense her hesitate.

When someone dies, their soul still exists.

How do you know that?

We can feel the echoes of souls in the wind.

My heart perks up at that.

What does that mean?

It means that Soren isn't really gone. You can get him back.

My eyes widen as my chest inflates with hope.

But the path back is through the shadows, and every soul pulled from it brings darkness with it, Lyra cautions.

The warning rolls off of me, the thought of being with him again overwhelming all my other senses.

I don't care how dangerous it is. I will do anything to get him back.

Author Note

Gah, I know, the ending! I brought them back together just to rip them apart. But this was something that Soren had to do to begin to forgive himself for the atrocities he let Adira go through.

Will Adira let this lie? Nah, she's a badass who doesn't care what the Arae have in store for her. She's stubborn enough to carve her own fate.

If you've made it this far, I want to say thank you for joining Adira and Soren's journey! I had so much fun writing this book and an even better time on the next one. I can't wait for you to read/suffer through it.

For more information, check out my website

sarakohan.ca

Acknowledgments

This one may seem strange, but I want to acknowledge a whole country. Italy. I moved here and have had so much more time to write which allowed me to develop this book quickly. I found inspiration everywhere, in the cultural differences and in the quiet of the rolling hills. So, I am very grateful for that.

I also want to thank Books Publishing Company who have been amazing from the start. Thank you to Sebastian & The Editorial Team. As well as Natalia, who helped me every step of the way and answered my millions of questions.

About the Author

Sara Kohan was born and raised in Canada and moved to Italy in 2024. She is an avid reader who enjoys traveling. Sara's love of reading came from her mother and aunt who always encouraged her to read. Sara worked at a public library in her town for the entirety of high school. After reading so many books, Sara finally took a chance on writing her own.